W9-BDS-720

THE TIME IN BETWEEN

David Bergen

THE TIME IN BETWEEN

A Novel

RANDOM HOUSE

NEW YORK

Published in the United States by Random House, an
imprint of The Random House Publishing Group, a
division of Random House, Inc., New York.

RANDOM HOUSE and colophon are registered trademarks of
Random House, Inc.

LIBRARY OF CONGRESS CATALOGING-IN-PUBLICATION DATA
Bergen, David.
The time in between : a novel / David Bergen.
p. cm.
ISBN 1-4000-6240-3
1. Vietnamese Conflict, 1961–1975—Veterans—Fiction.
2. Fathers and daughters—Fiction.   3. Canadians—
Vietnam—Fiction.   4. British Columbia—Fiction.
5. Divorced fathers—Fiction.   6. Missing persons—Fiction.
7. Vietnam—Fiction.   I. Title.

PR9199.3.B413T56 2005
813'.54—dc22
2004051495

www.atrandom.com

Printed in the United States of America on acid-free paper

2 4 6 8 9 7 5 3 1

FIRST U.S. EDITION

To Tran Cau and Hoang Dang

THE TIME IN BETWEEN

THE TYPHOON ARRIVED THAT NIGHT. ADA WOKE TO THE SOUND of rain driving against the windows. Above them, on the rooftop, chairs fell and banged against the washstand. The corrugated tin on the stairwell roof worked loose and flapped for an hour before it broke free and fell like a whirling blade down onto the street. Ada was standing at the window watching the palm trees bend in the wind and she saw the tin roofing fly by and land on the tennis courts in the distance. The power went out and then flickered on and finally cut out completely. Ada woke Jon, her brother, who had returned while she was sleeping, and she held his hand and said, "I'm frightened."

He sat up and said, "It's a small storm. Don't worry."

She could smell sex on him; sometimes the smell was musty and bleachy but tonight it was sweat and the slightest hint of old saliva. That smell. She stood and walked across the room. "The boats are coming in," she said. "They know something we don't. I've counted thirty already."

The wind pulled at the hotel sign and threw it onto the street below.

"Get away from the window," Jon said. "The glass could fall in."

She sat at the edge of his bed and he held her hand and they listened. The wind arrived from out of the sky and from across the ocean and it seemed that it would never end, until it slid away, a deceptive and distant howl, and then returned just as quickly, banging against the trees and buildings, and everything loose was pulled into the maelstrom. She wanted it to stop. She began to shiver and even though Jon was beside her she felt very much alone.

"Look at us. We're so stupid," she said.

"Here," Jon said, and he made her lie down and he covered her. He held his hands over her ears and put his thumbs against her eyes until the hollow core of the typhoon descended. And with that awful stillness came the everyday sounds: the clock on the bureau; something, perhaps a rat, moving about on the rooftop; the dry cough of the old man below them; the song of a woman calling again and again.

"It's gone," Ada said.

Jon said it would return. She said that the waiting frightened her more than the wind. She said she believed that their father was dead.

Jon was quiet. A siren sounded. The lights flashed across the dark sky and then disappeared.

PART ONE

THE ROOM WAS FULL OF LIGHT. FROM THE WINDOW THEY COULD see the port and the fishing boats and the oil tankers, and at night, when it was clear and calm, the lights of the squid boats far out at sea were like bright stars. In the afternoon, as the sun descended and the air cooled, they left their room and climbed the stairs to the hotel rooftop, where Jon lay on the hammock and read while Ada looked out over the city. There were the broad streets and the cement electrical poles and the palms and far off to the south the tennis courts, where a group of schoolboys in their white shirts and blue shorts played soccer, the bright smack of the ball carrying up to the roof.

The night before, she had dreamed of her father. A clear, pitch-perfect dream in which her father had been smiling from a distance and waving at her to come. "Come," he had cried out, and Ada had toddled forward and fallen on her face. She woke from the dream and heard the fan spinning slowly above her bed, and beyond, through the window, there was a flash of lightning and then thunder. She called out to Jon, said his name several times, but he slept on. She got up and went to the bathroom, and when she came back she stood by the window and watched the night. The neon sign of the hotel sent a glow back onto her face; blue and white and then blue again. She opened the window halfway and leaned out and saw two men walking arm in arm on the street below. They were singing and then talking and then singing again. The men had seemed harmless and the singing was especially musical.

Now, watching the soccer players, Ada turned to Jon and told him about the dream. "I tried to wake you. I hate dreaming about him. Either he disappears or he turns away or I end up cutting off my arms to try to get his attention."

Jon closed his book. He looked at Ada, and then after a long while he said, "I'm glad that I don't dream about him. The lieutenant yesterday, Mr. Dat, said that he couldn't be sure but he thought that we wouldn't find him. I didn't really understand everything he said. He was using this garbled combination of French and Vietnamese and English and he kept saying *va, va* and *oui, oui,* and at one point I went *va* and he smiled and said, 'You speak our language.' He has beautiful hands. His wrists are thin and the nail on his little finger is long. He said Dad's dead." Jon paused and laid the book on the table. "I asked him if he had ever met our father, or seen him around town when he lived here during that month. He looked at me and then he said, 'Not yet.' It was the oddest thing. I wasn't sure if it was a language problem or if he was playing a game. What does that mean? Not yet."

Ada leaned forward and stubbed her cigarette on the cement floor. She said, "You didn't hit on him. I hope you didn't do that."

Jon raised an eyebrow. "Did you hear what I said?"

"I heard. He has to make a living and we're not paying him anything and if we did he'd throw clues our way. That's what he was doing, giving you some hope so that you would offer him some financial reward." She waved her hand up at the sky. There was a hazy whitish ring around the sun. "The thing is, Jon, you have to be careful here. How do you know that your proclivities will be tolerated?" She closed her eyes sleepily and then opened them and smiled as if pleased by her question.

He rose and stood over her. He whispered in her ear, "I don't. And I am being careful. Very."

She loved his smell, the smooth skin of his face after he had shaved. "This trip has become a joke," she said. "For three weeks now we've searched uselessly, and here we are, back at this hotel with nothing except what we came with; a tattered photograph of him and our bags and the clothes we wear. We're running out of money."

Jon was dismissive. "Del will put more into the account. She said it wasn't a problem. She just has to ask Tomas."

Ada said, "Haven't you noticed how utterly privileged and fat we are?"

"We?" Jon said. "Fat?"

"I mean the tourists, like us. Those big groups that climb off the buses by the Empire Hotel and then stand around and sweat and wave brochures in front of their faces and call out for each other and then drink iced tea in the air-conditioned café."

Jon smiled. "Don't worry, Ada," he said. "You're not like everyone else."

She ignored him and said that she was going over to My Khe. She was hot, and tired of walking around town. There was nothing more to be done. She wanted to swim and asked if he would come with her.

He said that he didn't like swimming there. The undertow scared him.

Ada went into the bathroom and changed into her bathing suit. She put on shorts and a long-sleeved top and leather sandals; carried a bag with a book and bottled water and an apple, under her arm a small mat. She wore a straw hat with a wide brim. She studied herself in the mirror and experienced a moment of hope.

.   .   .

ON THE FERRY THAT TOOK HER TO MY KHE, A BOY SAT DOWN
beside her and asked her name. Before she could answer he said
that his name was Yen and he was fourteen, maybe, and where did
she come from? His hands were dirty, as if he had been repairing
something, a bicycle or an engine, and when he saw her studying
his hands he put them under his bare thighs and said that he was a
mechanic for the ferryman, but only when it was necessary. And
today it was necessary. He grinned and shrugged. He said that he
had plans to be a lawyer, not a mechanic, though he did know how
to fix many kinds of engines. Diesel, two stroke, fuel injected,
combustion. He lifted one hand and raised his fingers as he rolled
out the list, then put his hand back under his leg. He said that his
father was the man who ran the ferry.

"Do you have a motorcycle?" he asked.

She said she didn't.

He nodded. "Would you like one?"

"No, I wouldn't."

"And, excuse me, your name?"

"Ada."

"That is your whole name?"

"Ada Boatman."

He repeated after her, considered the vowels and the meaning,
and then ducked his chin at the ferry they were riding on. "A boat.
Like this one."

"I guess," she said.

"You are not sure?" He fished in his shorts pocket and pulled
out a package of cigarettes, lit one and exhaled at the sky, then held
the pack out to her.

She shook her head. She would normally have smoked but
thought it wrong to accept a cigarette from a child.

"Do you like hashish?" he asked. "I can get you that or I can
get you cannabis, or perhaps you like women?"

Ada said that she didn't need anything. Yen lifted his dark eyes and said that she was being modest. "Is that right?" he asked. "Modest?"

Ada said that modesty had nothing to do with it. She did not want what he was offering.

He said that everybody wanted something that they couldn't have. "Take me. I need money so that I can go to school and become a lawyer. Why are you here in Vietnam?"

Ada looked at him. His bare knees were dirty. He wore rubber flip-flops, one of which had been repaired with a red wire. She asked him if he was looking for money.

"No. I am not a beggar. I earn my money. As I said, I repair engines for my father and I procure things for tourists." He said *procure* slowly, with a slight affect, as if it were a newly acquired word.

They passed a ferry going in the other direction and on the far shore Ada saw billboards advertising beer and televisions and beyond that there were the tin roofs of shanties and warehouses.

Ada turned to Yen and said that what she wanted he could not get. It wasn't realistic.

Yen laughed. He thought that *realistic* was a good word. "I like that. I will use it. How do you say? I am realistic?"

"I meant possible," Ada said. The ferry was docking and the people around them rose and pushed toward the gates.

Yen followed her along the gangplank, through the terminal, and up the narrow lane. He skipped beside her, dodging passersby. He said, "So you are a tourist."

"Sure. Call me a tourist."

"And you are in need of a guide?"

She said she wasn't. Stopped and looked at the boy. "Listen," she said, "I want to be alone. Could you leave me alone?"

He bowed slightly. He stepped backward, said, "See you again," and disappeared into the crowd.

She continued up the lane and crossed over a main road. She walked another half hour, cursing her shoes. They were new and her heels were blistering. The sun was above her; she was sweating into the band of her hat. She was determined not to stop. If she did the people would gather round to watch her and she was tired of being watched. Just the day before she had stopped at a café near the Cham Museum and two teenage boys had sat down with her. They had wanted to be guides, or perhaps help her find something. They had practiced their English, which was minimal.

And so, now, she carried on, regretting her decision to walk instead of hire a taxi. When she finally reached the beach, she set up her mat on the sand halfway between the water and the verandahs of the restaurants. She removed her shirt and shorts, placed her shoes beside her bag, and took out her book and lay down on her stomach. Later, fatigue overcame her and she put her head into the crook of her elbow and slept.

When she woke, she was aware of a game taking place around her, of boys laughing, the spraying of sand, shouts. She sat up. A voice called out and Yen appeared. He moved about on the beach quickly, waving his arms, jabbering. The game halted and the group dispersed. Yen turned to Ada and said, "I am sorry. These boys are rude, as you can see. They have no respect for private space."

Yen was standing several yards from her. At his feet was a beach umbrella. He pointed to it and said, "For you. Sunstroke can be dangerous." Without waiting for permission he pushed the stem of the umbrella into the sand and opened it. Then he sat at the edge of the shade and waved a hand at the water. "Beautiful," he said.

Ada took her water bottle from her bag and drank while Yen happily looked at her legs and stomach and breasts. He lit a cigarette and offered her one. This time she accepted.

"Good for you," he said.

They smoked and looked out over the water. Yen motioned to her book. "I do not know that book," he said. "*The Great Gatsby.* Is that how you say it?"

Ada nodded. She said that it was not an easy book. It looked easy, but it wasn't.

"Are you a teacher?" he asked.

Ada shook her head. "Oh, no."

"What then?"

"A chef," she said, and then added, "Sort of."

"What is that, sort of?"

"I was in school."

Yen looked pleased. "Do you swim?" he asked.

"Yes."

"The front crawl?"

"Yes."

"And the butterfly?"

Ada shook her head.

"I have seen the Olympics. All the beautiful sports of the Olympics. Of course there are very few Vietnamese athletes at the Olympics. We have never won a medal. Why is that? Because we are poor. We do not have time to train for figure skating or jumping or throwing the spear. We maybe have a good athlete in shooting or Tae Kwon Do, but, no winners. Still, I love to watch the Olympics. Do you, Miss Ada?"

Ada was aware of Yen's feet and his small ankles. His shins were bruised and pocked by what looked like old insect bites. He hugged his knees as he talked. His hair was cut short and this made his dark eyes larger, two pools that appeared to alternate between longing and impudence. But he seemed innocent enough. She asked him if he was thirsty or hungry.

He said he wasn't.

She offered him the apple from her bag. He took it and wiped it against his shorts. Put it in his pocket.

She sat up and pulled her hair back into a ponytail and told Yen she was going for a swim. He said that he would watch her things, that anything of hers would be safe in his hands.

She walked down to the water and waded out up to her waist. She dove in and came up for air and dove under again. She swam out past the breakers, feeling the occasional tug of the undertow. She swam for a while, looking every now and then toward the shore, where she could see the small shape of Yen and the canopy of the umbrella. When she came out of the water, he stood and waited for her to lie down on her mat, and then he resumed his position at the edge of the shade.

He told her that everything was safe.

"Good," she said. "I don't see why it wouldn't be."

"Oh, Miss Ada, you don't understand. There are thieves everywhere. You can trust no one, especially here on the beach. Why are you here?"

She wrung out her hair. "What do you mean?"

"You and your brother walk around town talking to shopkeepers and taxi drivers. There is something you are looking for."

She eyed him and asked if he went to school.

"Sometimes. When I am not busy with my customers." He jabbed his cigarette into the sand. His smile was crooked, and this made him look older than he was.

Ada asked where he had learned his English.

"Why, is it bad?"

"No. It's very good."

He said that there were things he could improve on. "I know about contractions," he said. "It is very difficult to remember to squeeze the words together. Isn't it?" His tongue tripped slightly. "I am very lucky," he said. "I have people like you to teach me."

Ada was lying on her back. She said, "I don't need a translator. I have one."

"Oh, yes, I have seen the one you have hired. Dinh. He is very

THE TIME IN BETWEEN

well educated but he doesn't understand people." Yen patted his stomach. "Here," he said. "He doesn't understand things right here." He laced his fingers and announced that Dinh was well on his way to becoming a dentist and what did she need, someone to fix her teeth or someone to show her the path?

Ada ignored this and closed her eyes.

Yen said, "I can see that you are sleeping and so I will leave you. I will go up to the verandah behind us and I will watch over you. When you are ready to leave, just whistle."

Ada opened her eyes. She said that she didn't need his help. He might as well go away. And besides, she didn't know how to whistle.

He stood. She saw his dark face above her.

"Good-bye, Miss Ada."

She closed her eyes again and heard the call of a child down the beach and the movement of the water against the shore. When she sat up, the boy was gone. She swam once more, and when she was ready to leave, she packed her things and put on her shorts and top and walked up to the road behind the restaurants. She looked for a taxi or a cyclo but there was nothing, just the sun and the dirt road and a few houses lining the road. She asked at a restaurant about taxis, but the woman in charge shook her head and shrugged.

Ada looked around for Yen, but he had disappeared. His umbrella was still in the sand, where he had put it. She imagined he would be back and she thought she could wait and he would find her a taxi, but this would be hypocritical. So, she retraced the path that had taken her to the beach. It was easier going home. The sun was lower and the path descended slightly.

On the ferry, an old woman held out a plastic bowl and Ada gave her some change. Then she sat back and watched the harbor. She loved the light at this time of day, just before five, an hour till darkness. It carried her away from herself, from her reason for

being here, and she welcomed the lightness of the moment, however brief. The sky was dusty and the ships in the distance were a
soft gray.

WHEN ADA AND JON HAD FIRST ARRIVED IN DANANG BY TRAIN
from Hanoi, they took a suite at the Binh Duong Hotel and then
spent the next two weeks walking the streets, entering shops and
handing out pictures of their father. Written on the backs of the
pictures, in Vietnamese and English, was "This is Charles. Have
you seen him?" They enlisted a university boy named Dinh, the
son of the hotel owner, to translate for them.

Everyone had seen Charles. They had seen him walking, or
riding a motorcycle. One woman, a young hairdresser wearing
tight jeans, thought she had had him as a customer, though she
couldn't say for sure. Maybe not, she said. And she smiled. A hotel
sentry had seen him with a prostitute. At first Dinh appeared to
have trouble telling them this. He said that Charles was with a
woman of ill repute. A woman of the night. He looked at the
ground. Stared off into the distance and then sighed. "A prostitute," he said.

"I doubt it," Ada said. "He had his demons but that wasn't
one."

"That is what the man saw," Dinh said. "Though he can't be
sure."

"Of course he can't. Nobody is ever sure in this country," Jon
said.

Dinh nodded slowly. He said something to the sentry and the
sentry gazed off into the distance, as if pondering a deep and impossible question, and then he spoke for a long time and when he
was finished he looked at Ada and smiled.

Dinh said, "He thinks now that it probably wasn't Charles.
That it may have been someone who looked like Charles. He

said there was a man here, a German, who had the same kind of eyes as Charles. It was probably the German man who spent three hours in the room with the girl of ill repute. That is what he believes."

Ada pushed past the sentry and went into the restaurant and sat down and watched from the window. Jon was talking and Dinh was wiping sweat from his forehead with a blue handkerchief. Finally Jon walked away and joined Ada in the restaurant.

"It's so calm in here," Ada said. She motioned at the lobby and the marble columns and the beautifully dressed waitresses and she said, "I was imagining Dad coming in here and sitting down at a table with a woman he didn't know. What would he talk about? What language would they speak?" Jon listened to her but did not say anything.

A few days later, near the harbor, a cyclo driver said he had taken Charles over the bridge and down along the sandy road to Maryann's, a restaurant on China Beach. The driver said he had waited there and then driven him back. Charles hadn't talked to anyone. He hadn't been with anyone. Ask Maryann, the man said.

So Jon and Ada went to Maryann's. They passed down through the furniture market, beyond a factory that produced mattresses, and over the bridge to the island, where a few empty hotels sat stranded and forlorn. They followed the beach road to the shantylike restaurants that served beer and *pho* to lovers who huddled out of the wind and watched the waves break against the shore.

It was a wet day. The rain drove against their foreheads and faces as they walked along the beach toward the entrance to Maryann's. They sat inside, out of the rain, and ordered two beers. Ada used Jon's jacket to wipe her hair and face. Her shirt, thin and white, clung to her body and her skin showed through. Jon wiped a few drops of water from her forearm. They shared a cigarette and then they pulled out their father's photo and showed it to the young girl who was serving them. She turned the photo in her hands and studied it, made a face, and then looked at them and smiled. "Very handsome," she said.

"Have you seen him?" Jon asked. "That is our father. His name is Charles and he was in Danang last month. A cyclo driver said he came here, to Maryann's. To this restaurant. Do you remember him?"

The girl walked over to a stairway and yelled something, twice, and waited.

"Brilliant," Jon said. "She understood every word."

An older woman appeared, holding the railing of the stairs, stepping carefully down onto the cement floor. She took the photo from the girl and looked at it. The girl spoke quickly and quietly, and then the woman came over to Ada and Jon. She said, "I am Maryann."

Ada introduced herself and Jon and then asked Maryann if she spoke English and when she nodded Ada said, "Did you ever see the man in the photo? He's our father. We were told that he came here, maybe a month ago or so."

"I saw him. He was here three or four times. He sat over there on the deck and drank and ate and then he went away."

"Did you talk to him?"

"A little. He said that he had come to this same restaurant thirty years ago as a soldier." She shrugged. "This is probably true. I was a young girl then. Many Americans have come back and told me the same thing. That is good. I need the business."

"When was the last time you saw him?" Jon asked.

Maryann said that it was probably at least three weeks ago, maybe more. On a windy day. "Like today," she said, and she hugged herself and offered a mock shiver.

The young girl brought over a plate of fried fish and raw carrots. She placed it on the table. They ate the fish and watched the rain fall. Ada began to speak and then she stopped, aware that her words would mean nothing at this point, because they were words that had already been said, and so they each drank another beer and rode back on the cyclo they had come out on.

THAT EVENING SHE WALKED ALONE TO THE EMPIRE HOTEL AND drank coffee in the dining room and ordered a strudel and ate it slowly, looking out at the street. When she was finished she stepped outside. Down the road, closer to Bach Dang Street, two women stood side by side. Their faces were powdered white and they waved at passing cyclists and pedestrians. Ada approached them. They were young, maybe twenty, perhaps less. One had a round face with a smile that revealed bad teeth. Her breasts were small and she wore blue stockings. She looked at Ada and said, "Want to fock?"

Ada shook her head.

The girls giggled and the one with bad teeth touched Ada's arm and ran her hand up and down the silkiness of her skin. "Beautiful," she said, and then she chirruped, "Twenty dollars. For you."

Ada turned away and walked back up toward her hotel. The boy Yen appeared and, walking beside her, asked if she truly wanted to buy one of the women back there.

Ada said, "You're impossible. I don't want you following me."

Yen nodded. "I see," he said. "So, you don't like me?"

"That's got nothing to do with it."

"The girl you were talking to? She has bad teeth. I know a girl who has beautiful teeth. She is lovely to kiss."

"I don't want a girl."

"But, you were talking to one back there. Were you asking her the time?"

Ada shook her head. She stopped walking and faced Yen.

"Good-bye," she said. Yen grinned and said good-bye. Ada crossed over to the harbor side of the street and sat down on a bench and reached into her purse for a cigarette. The air was warm; a few mosquitoes circled her head. She brushed at them and looked out over the water, aware of the smell of diesel fuel and the sound of the waves lapping at the retainer wall.

She heard footsteps and turned. A man stood a fair distance away from her. He bowed slightly and said, "Don't worry, you are not in danger. I have been watching you and you are safe. Though you are foolish to be sitting out here all alone in the middle of the night. You are a woman and beautiful and you are a foreigner and you probably have lots of money. It is not safe for you to be sitting by yourself near the harbor on a dark night."

He took a step forward. The dim streetlight revealed his face. He was short and older, probably fifty, though Ada couldn't be sure. He wore suit pants and a white shirt buttoned all the way up, and glasses that were black-rimmed and thick. He seemed harmless, though it might have been the glasses that projected safety. He spoke English perfectly; the only flaw was in the perfection.

"I'm Canadian," Ada said.

"Of course you are. This is even better. But still, the average criminal on Bach Dang Street is not going to stop and ask the nationality of his victim. And even if he did I do not think he would be partial to certain groups. Do you?" As he spoke he crept forward. He was now standing in front of her and she saw his clean leather shoes and his hands, which were cupped as if he were about to dip them into water.

Ada stood. She was looking down at the man, who shuffled his feet and stepped backward to give her more space.

"Vo Van Thanh," he said. "Or just Thanh."

Ada looked around and was conscious of their isolation.

"Don't worry," he said. "I will walk you back to your hotel. Is that okay?"

She allowed this, and as they walked Thanh kept a good space between the two of them and he spoke to her about the places they passed: the photo shop that sold yeast imported from Thailand; the pool hall that fronted for cockfights and boxing matches—he said that his son, who was an excellent lightweight, fought there sometimes, and as he said this he raised his own fists and feinted left and right and his leather shoes flashed; and the library in which there were numerous appalling novels about the glory of the Vietnamese state. As they approached the Binh Duong Hotel, he said that the owner of the hotel, Mr. Duong, had married a woman who was too beautiful for him. She had a fondness for men from other countries, typically workers from Czechoslovakia and Russia. "Miss Binh likes Germans as well and the occasional American. Perhaps you should warn your brother."

Ada wondered how Thanh knew about Jon. She said, "My brother would not be interested."

Thanh did not respond, though he did cup his hands once again and clear his throat. At the entrance to the hotel they paused and Ada turned to thank Thanh.

He said, "I knew your father, Charles Boatman."

Ada lifted a hand as if to fend off a bright light and she asked, "Oh? How?"

"I was his guide. His translator. For the month that he was here. And then he was gone and you arrived and now we are standing in front of the same hotel where he stayed. What do you call this? Symmetry? Serendipity?" He said that there had been a sadness that emanated from Charles Boatman, and no amount of talk or food or even the love of a woman could remove that sadness. "He disappeared one day. I came to pick him up and he was gone. Miss Binh did not see him. The bellhop did not see him. No one saw him. That was a month ago."

"What do you mean, love?" Ada asked.

"Oh." Thanh took off his glasses and cleaned them on his shirttail. He put them back on and said, "There was someone." His hands moved about as if he were willing them to pluck the words from the air.

"Who was the woman?"

"It is not for me to say. I observed. He did not tell me."

Ada wondered what was true and what was not in this man's story.

He said, "I will come back. Tomorrow. Please, do not worry. I do not want to be a bearer of unhappiness. I am simply a translator. Do you understand?"

His hair was dark and combed to the side, and Ada realized that he was a careful man, both in his dress and in his speech. She said good-bye, and when she reached her fifth-floor room she was breathless and she stood for a moment in the darkness. She knew that Jon was not there but still she said his name, softly. She said it again, and when she received no answer she went over to the window. There was a lightning storm far out at sea. The flashes were dim and brief except once when the lightning went on for several seconds and lit up both the sky and the water. Ada saw what she imagined was a large ship but might also have been a gargantuan raft or a house floating out to sea.

She thought about time, about the future and the past. She thought about the mountain back in British Columbia where she had been raised, and how one year around Christmas her father had shot a deer that wandered onto their yard. Del, her younger sister, had wept and beat at her father with her small fists. Ada had been most amazed at the flatness of her father's face as he held his younger daughter until she was done flailing.

And now her father was gone, and Del was living with a sculptor, an older man who had captured her and pinned her, just as Del claimed would not happen, like a butterfly to a corkboard. And she, Ada, who for so long had floated about, brushing up against people with whom she had little connection, had left her small apartment in Vancouver and was standing in a hotel room looking out at a perplexing and alien place where the language she heard was more beautiful because she did not understand it.

CHARLES BOATMAN GREW UP IN MONROE, WASHINGTON, AND IN
1968 at the age of eighteen he was drafted into the U.S. Army. He
was not pleased to be drafted. He had seen the *Time* magazine photograph where a Marine pilot was killed in a CH-34 and the crew-
man was crying in the background. The photograph of the dead
soldier frightened him and the Marine's tears surprised him. He
was also about to get married to Sara Fonce, his pregnant girl-
friend. They had talked about running up to Canada but she said
she would wait for him. And so, after his training and during his
thirty-day home leave, Charles and Sara married and moved into
his parents' basement and then, with the same resignation that
would carry him through his next thirty years, Charles left for
Vietnam. He was situated in Danang and was in the country when
Lieutenant Calley and his battalion shot dead five hundred villagers in My Lai. He learned of it only months later, when he was
back in the United States.

When he returned, Charles told people that he had killed only
one man during his tour in Vietnam and that the man was an
enemy soldier. His battalion was usually holed up in the hills that

ringed the harbor of Danang. However, one day, near the end of his tour, Charles was walking point on a sortie near Marble Mountain when he came face-to-face with a North Vietnamese soldier and he fired into the soldier's chest. This was the story he told.

Back at home he dreamed about severed limbs and fire and the intestines of Jody Booth, a friend who had died beside him in a field outside Danang. He dreamed about pigs being strung from a rope and gutted alive and he dreamed about a young boy who looked up at him as if to ask, "Why?" He woke from these dreams and sat in his room, smoking and staring into the darkness. Sometimes Sara held him and cradled his head and said, "Charlie, what are we gonna do?" but mostly he wanted to be left alone.

Their baby, Ada, was two years old when Sara became pregnant again. Sara worked as a bartender in the evenings and he worked days as a logger, though being in the trees made him panicky, and more than once a co-worker found him huddled and shaking under a jack pine. They were still living in his parents' basement and Sara said she was tired of the family shit, of not having money, of Charles not getting serious about work and obsessing about the war. "Let it go, Charlie," she said more than once. "There's a whole bunch of mouths to feed here." She was a small woman whom, when he returned from Vietnam, he did not at first recognize. She was holding a baby in one arm, and though she smelled the same when he pushed his nose against her neck, she seemed harder to approach, as if she were afraid of him. For a while after his return she tried to get him to talk, but either he was unwilling or he waved his hand and said, "I don't know where to begin."

He loved her being pregnant. He had missed her fullness with the first baby, so now he was always touching her, holding his ear against her belly and then sliding down so that she could clamp his head between her thighs while he whispered secrets to the twins.

While Charles was overseas, Sara had taken on a lover, a bank manager who adored her but who had no interest in ruining his own marriage. The affair continued when Charles returned, and though Sara felt the occasional shiver of guilt, she rationalized that the pleasure of seeing a man who wore a suit and bought her things and told her what beautiful legs and breasts she had made it all right.

Charles knew nothing, until the day the twins turned five and Ada, who was eight, asked him if Robert was coming to the party. That night Sara came home late and found Charles sitting at the kitchen table, surrounded by dirty plates and balloons and streamers. He was drinking rye straight out of a bottle and his voice shook when he said her name. She knew that he knew. She said, "Go ahead, hit me."

"I'm not going to hit you. You know I can't do that."

Charles lifted his head and looked at his wife. Her hair was dirty; one side fell over a breast and covered half her face. He stood and went into the bedroom and shut the door. The children, who slept in the same room with them, were laid out like little packages. Charles slid the children up beside each other and lay down on the outside of the bed. He heard Sara in the kitchen, running the water, then she was in the bathroom, taking a bath. He fell asleep and woke briefly as Sara crept into the room for clean underwear and jeans and a shirt. He opened his eyes. She was naked, standing by the dresser. He saw the backs of her arms, and her ass, the full hard shape of her, and the outline between her legs as she bent toward the drawer. She put on panties and turned and slid into her jeans. Top on, no bra. She looked back at the bed, and in the half-light Charles closed his eyes. She called his name quietly, then she said, "Charlie, I'm sorry." She waited, but he didn't answer. He opened his eyes again only after she had left and closed the door. He heard her go, the click of the lock, her footsteps, the revving of the car engine, and then the crunch of the gravel as she backed out onto the street.

.   .   .

CHARLES LEFT SARA AND THE CHILDREN AND MONROE AND THE
United States. He moved across the border close to Abbotsford,
British Columbia. Rented two acres on Sumas Mountain and
bought an old caboose that he towed up the winding road. He ren-
ovated the caboose and insulated it. Installed a woodstove and
built a stack-log shed for his machine shop and raised goats and
chickens and milked one cow. In the evenings, he spread his correspondence books over the kitchen table and studied for his ac-
counting exam. He planned to make himself into something other
than a man who lived on a mountain and operated a drill press and
made machine parts for people much wealthier than he was.

He thought about his children a lot. He had asked Sara, just before he left, if the twins, Jon and Del, were his, and she had said,
"Of course," and when he had asked, "How do you know?" she
had looked at him and said, "I know." He wrote to his mother,
adding money to the envelope, and he asked her to buy the children birthday gifts. He had plans, he said, to move the children up
onto the mountain. The one time he mentioned this to Sara, in a
letter sent through his mother, her response was swift and angry.
He would never get the children, she wrote. When his mother
called him six months later to say that Sara had died, been hit riding a motorcycle close to the bar where she worked, and that the
children would be coming to live with him, Charles suffered panic
that brought him back to the hills surrounding the harbor of
Danang. When the children arrived, ferried up the mountain in his
mother's Ford station wagon, he squatted and held them and said
their names softly, "Ada. Jon. Del." Ada, who was almost nine,
looked him in the eye and said, "Sara's dead."

That evening he walked them across his land and pointed to the
tallest tree and said that a fort could be built up there. His mother
called him ridiculous and dangerous. Later, he showed Ada how to
split wood and they sat by the fire while the rain fell outside and

Charles wondered how he would manage. His mother stayed a week and then returned to Monroe, leaving the cabinets stocked with food, the clothes clean, and with the admonishment to teach his children well. The second morning after his mother left, Ada woke him and said they were hungry. "You have to feed us," she said. "We like porridge or pancakes. Jon actually likes blueberry pancakes." She said *actually* as if it were the most important word in the sentence. She was dressed in jeans and a T-shirt that was too big. Her arms were thin. He had noticed the night before that she chewed on the ends of her hair. She knew more about caring for the twins than he did, and so it happened that she was given that responsibility. On an afternoon when he came in from his workshop and found her reading to them on the couch, he saw the light falling behind Ada's head and he remembered Sara.

One night Charles sat his children down and told them that their mother was a beautiful woman, there was no one more beautiful, but she had never understood that beauty was like a pail of water. You were given so much at the beginning of your life, and if you wasted it, there was no retrieving what had been spilled. "Your mother spilled her beauty all over the goddamn land, and then she spent the rest of her life scrabbling through the sand and mud, trying to reclaim it. And she couldn't." He looked at Ada, and then at Jon, and then Del, and he said, "Don't let that happen to you, my loves."

Years later, Ada would remember those words of caution. At the age of seventeen, when Andre Toupin, the neighbor boy, tried to touch her breasts, she told him that he could only look. She stood before him naked from the waist up and watched his face soften and his eyes water, and when he reached out with his left hand she pushed it away and said, "No." He seemed astounded, as if he had been offered a view into a secret and holy place. He was not smart, but he was the only boy other than Jon who was the girls' age on the mountain, and so he was allowed visual and verbal access to Ada's body. He taught her vulgarities in French. He labeled her body parts with their French names and she repeated them after him, pointing and repeating until the pronunciation was exact, though the perfection was lost on Andre. She did not want him wasting her beauty.

Andre's mother became their father's lover. She was raising two children alone and she operated a salon out of her kitchen. Her own hair was always clean and coiffed and she was constantly changing its color and shape. The first time she cut Charles's hair he came home and said, "Claire Toupin smells awfully pretty but she sure has an empty head."

They were sitting at the table eating soup. Charles spread butter on a slice of bread. His hands were big and square and full of tiny scars from the machining. He touched his hair. "She wanted to know if I wanted some color. Hah. What, so the goats don't recognize me? To scare my children?"

The children told him that he might look good with bleached hair. Jon said that colored hair was sexy.

"What do you know about sexy?" Charles asked.

Jon grinned.

"Oh, Jesus." Charles's hand reached for more bread. "What's the boy, Andre, like?"

"Same as Madame Toupin," Ada said. She knocked her skull with a knuckle.

No one spoke for the longest time. Then their father said, "She wants us to come for Saturday supper." There was another long pause. Then he said, "Don't know what we'll talk about."

THEY TALKED ABOUT CLAIRE. SHE HAD GROWN UP IN VANCOUVER and left the city with her husband, who wanted to live simply, and then, after three months, he went back and she stayed. And they talked about plumbing, septic field versus tank. And the rabbit they were eating, which Andre had snared and skinned. Claire said she had cooked it in red wine and basil. Lots of basil. There was another neighbor at the dinner, Tomas Manik, who lived further up the mountain by himself in a large house that he had designed and built. It was all concrete and steel, and the rebar stuck out of the walls and the metal conduit for the wiring was the prettiest part in the house, except perhaps for the lampshades, which were inverted chicken brooders. Tomas was an artist and sculptor who sold his work in other countries, particularly his home country of Czechoslovakia, but he lived and worked in Canada, where he was little known as an artist. He was rumored to have family money. Tomas sometimes hired Charles to machine metal for his sculptures, and he'd been in the Boatman kitchen before, drinking coffee and sizing things up. When Tomas looked at Del, he stared at her breasts and her belly and then his eyes went up to her face. Even when he knew that she knew what he was doing, he still kept staring.

At the dinner table, Claire was flirting with both Tomas and Charles, and Andre was eyeing Ada while Jon was counting to one hundred in French with Andre's little sister. They were at ninety-eight and Jon's mouth was twisting around the *quatre-vingt* when Tomas turned to Del and asked, "Do you shoot?"

"Shoot?"

He held up his broad arms and closed one eye. Thick brows, wide jaw. "Bang," he said.

"Hunt?" she asked. "You mean, Do I hunt?"

"Yes, yes." He smiled and drank from his glass of wine, and then leaned toward Del and whispered, "I love the equipment of hunting. The dressing up, the rattle of bullets in the vest, the smell of the gun, the cold morning, the giant knife at the hip. A gun is like a hard-on." He paused and lifted his nose as if sniffing for danger. His jaw was wider than Del had first noticed. His neck was thick. She knew that he liked her. He had pronounced *equipment* wrong, emphasizing the first syllable, but she did not correct him. His hands were rough and his fingernails dirty; there was a residue under his nails. He smelled clean, however. She did not acknowledge the sexual obscenity.

Del said that her father took them hunting every fall. They hunted bear. They took a truck up into the interior and spent the day, sometimes two, huddling out of sight in trees, and when they had had their fill, they returned home. "So, yes," she said, "I hunt."

"You don't go to school?"

"Not anymore."

"How do you learn?"

Del rolled her eyes. Tapped her head. "It's all here," she said, "I just have to find it."

He laughed. It was a big laugh and it came from somewhere inside his wide chest, and when he stopped he said, "So, you're smart."

Del shrugged. She did think that she was smart, certainly smarter than Andre Toupin, who had spent the last ten years in school and had nothing to show for it, except a couple of metal studs in his nose and ears and a head full of sociological gibberish. This was their father's opinion and the children agreed. Andre was not even smart enough to understand that his own mother would soon be sleeping with their father. The Boatman children foresaw that immediately; they discussed it, and though they did not think the love would last, they accepted it. Perhaps they hoped that Madame Toupin would make their father happy. He was not particularly happy, and there was always the possibility that a good-hearted woman, even an empty-headed one, could pull him out of his despondency.

CHARLES FELT THAT IT WAS HIS RESPONSIBILITY TO EDUCATE HIS children. "You're not blank slates that need to be written all over," he'd say. "Imagine yourselves as big containers full of jumbled up letters and you have to reach in and set those letters right so that they make some sense. That's all."

"The world is your school," he said. "Nothing is banal and nothing is boring." He grinned. "Except for TV." And so, en masse, they went out into the world. They scavenged garbage dumps, visited a glass-blowing factory, and collected butterflies. One bleak rainy afternoon in January, on Ada's birthday, they stopped by a crematorium in Abbotsford where Charles told them that artists throughout the centuries, lacking models, had used cadavers.

Jon didn't understand the word *cadaver*.

"A dead body, stupid," Del said.

They went home that day and Charles killed Rosie, the black and orange pullet, dipped her in boiling water and plucked her, and then he sat the children down at the kitchen table and had them eviscerate and then dissect Rosie.

Del sat quietly.

Ada pulled out three yolks.

"Here," Charles said, holding out a mug. "We'll use those for rice pudding."

He studied Del. Said, "Well, we were going to eat her anyway. She's just furthering our education."

"But *she* is Rosie," Del said.

Charles had to allow that Del had a point. He said that this was the unfortunate consequence of naming animals, especially animals that would eventually provide you with food. "Take Ollie. What are we gonna do when her time comes? Un-name her? Even if you try you can't forget that the black goat out there with the long teats and the sad eyes is actually Ollie, the same Ollie who likes to eat my oregano plants and tomatoes. Uh-uh. The thing is, even if Ollie didn't have a name, you'd love her. And then you'd eat her."

Del announced that she was vegetarian. She'd been thinking about it for a while.

"Nonsense," Charles said. "You'll starve."

"Let her, Dad," Ada said.

"Of course, of course, she'll do whatever she wants. Go ahead, try it. And some months from now, when you're a rack of bones and I'm barbecuing moose and you're salivating, you'd better have a good speech prepared." He said that he wanted to celebrate everybody's birthday on the same day. "Next Friday. I figure we'd invite the Toupins, pull out a keg or two, maybe even get that Communist artist down here. I wonder if he paints cadavers."

"Dad." Del was shaking her head. The children were pleased that their father was happy, though from experience they knew it wouldn't last.

Still, it lasted over the following week and through the party that Charles planned for his children. Ada was eighteen. They would play Alice Cooper. Jon and Del would turn sixteen. Elvis for them.

The day of the party it snowed and by evening there was a slushy soup covering the yard. Charles packed down a rink and gathered old hockey sticks and brooms and by dusk the group was involved in a sloppy game of broomball. Tomas, who had never played before, did more shouting than running. He followed Del and told her that her red cheeks were like two apples. Claire Toupin wore a blue tam and swung her broom dangerously, like a baseball bat. Once, she caught Charles on the hand and then, nurselike, removed his glove and kneaded his knuckles. Charles wondered what she looked like naked.

Later, they sat around the bonfire Charles had built at the edge of the rink. Claire taught them a few French songs that they sang badly. At midnight they went inside and ate chili and cake. When Andre and his sister fell asleep by the stove, Claire said, "I'll take them home," and Charles said, in a moment of goodwill, "No, stay for the night. Everybody." He indicated where people could sleep and searched for extra blankets and pillows. Much later, after sharing a bottle of Johnnie Walker with the other adults, he found himself in his room, holding Claire and thinking that we must be careful what we wish for. During the night he woke, Claire's head pressed against his chest, and for a moment he was confused and he did not know whose body he was holding. He stifled his panic and smelled Claire's hair. Recalled how easily he had slid into her. He heard the crack of the wood in the stove and thought, Ada, good girl. Then he slept.

In the main room Ada dozed with her head in Jon's lap. Later, she got up and covered Andre and his sister with a quilt, and then she sat and listened to the rain fall and watched the fire. She knew that Del was with Tomas, and in the morning, before their father got up, she knocked on the door and called Del's name until she answered. Ada built a fire and made coffee, and when Del appeared, Ada handed her a cup. They sat by the stove and for a long time they did not speak. Finally, Ada said, "Dad's with Mrs. Toupin."

"I figured," Del said.

"You okay?" Ada asked.

Del looked at her hands and said, "It's still me, Del Boatman."

The rain had washed away the rink; the sticks and the brooms lay in the mud and puddles. The fire pit had filled with water; charred remains floated on the surface. When Charles came into the kitchen he went to Ada, who was standing by the sink, looking out over the yard. He hugged her from behind.

"Hey," Ada said.

CHARLES BOATMAN SOMETIMES TALKED TO HIS CHILDREN ABOUT the war. He told them about the heat and the clicking of a bamboo stand in the wind. He told them that he rarely saw the enemy. Once he told them he'd killed a man; a man in black on the trail near Marble Mountain, whom he shot in the chest. "It didn't please me," he said. "It still doesn't please me." Then he became quiet.

He said, "Most of the time there was emptiness, a great field of nothing. Nothing but ghosts."

It was when he herded Jon and Del and Ada down into the bunker he had built that their father talked about the war. The bunker was stocked with canned goods and a .303 and ammunition and gas masks and waterproof matches and half a cord of wood. This would happen several times a year, usually on the warmest nights of the summer, when sleep was difficult and the air in the caboose was close and rank. They would sit in the cool darkness of the bunker and their father would shush them and listen for noises.

"They're coming," he'd whisper, and one time when Del spoke, he clamped his hand over her mouth and put his lips to her ear and whispered, "Don't."

After, when all was clear, they remained in the dark and he told them stories. He was frank in his telling and he offered them intimate details and because they were frightened they listened without protest. He said once that he had fallen in love with a woman in Vietnam. Her name was Yvonne. He said, "I was eighteen years old, fighting in a country I didn't understand, and Yvonne offered me a comfort I had never had before. There was something inside me that badly wanted to love her. When I left Vietnam, I never saw her again. I don't know what happened to her."

He lifted a hand as if to tell them more, but then he fell silent, rubbing his hands together in the dim light of the emergency lamp. By the age of seventeen Del refused to go into the bunker with her father. Jon still went. He was less stubborn than Del and he hoped that his going would please his father. Ada went because she believed that each successive story was like a piece of thread, and she was collecting those pieces.

WHENEVER THE NIGHTMARES WOKE HIM, CHARLES COULD NOT get back to sleep, and to push away the images he played music, sometimes classical, sometimes opera that took him to unfamiliar places. The children would still be sleeping, and so he played the stereo softly. And he drank. Not a lot, but the amount accumulated so that by the morning he would be caught in a soft haze and everything around him had slowed down. He would pass the night in front of the fire, and in the flames he would see images of both fantastic beauty and dire malevolence. He saw Sara from behind, her head turned back to him as if to say good-bye. He saw a mouth opening in a scream and insects erupting from the dark maw. He saw stumps for legs and a boy's eyes. He saw the Vietnamese girl he had loved. He couldn't see her face, because he couldn't remember it. In fact, once he replaced her face with that of some woman he'd seen in town, and this worked fine. He saw Sara lying down, naked. He saw Ada as a baby, the olive skin and the chubby hands, her fat lips closing around Sara's engorged breast.

Back then, when Ada was young, everything had been possible, and now sometimes it seemed that she was his only connection to that time. She was the one he loved most easily. He worried about her; she was too aware. She watched him, and by doing this she gauged the tone of her own life. He was afraid she would end up desperate like him.

There had been a time when the kids were younger and he was still seeking help that he would drive down the mountain in his pickup and go to a psychiatrist. The cost was covered by health insurance for a certain number of visits and when the maximum was reached, he stopped going. The woman had not been useful. Only once, when Charles had described how a friend had been killed, did she tilt her head and ask how he felt.

He didn't know how he felt. That was why he was seeing her. He told her this. She smiled at this comment, as if he had said something humorous. She was older than he was and possibly attractive, but in a rich, austere way. Charles kept waiting for something to happen, for his heart to open up, for tears to come, for the stone that sat somewhere between his shoulders to fall away. At one point he even used those words, and as he said them, "I want this stone to fall away," he was aware of how simple he sounded. Even so, nothing happened.

He said, "This is useless. All you give me are empty words."

"All you can hear, Charles, are empty words. The words themselves aren't empty." She said that he was obviously in pain and she didn't know if that pain could be alleviated in a few sessions with a psychiatrist.

One day, he said, "There were worse things. Killings that were reported in major newspapers. Pictures of North Vietnamese prisoners being dropped from helicopters. Beheadings. Executions. Some by American soldiers. And I, who shot one person in a moment of fear, wake up terrified in the middle of the night. Why?"

She looked at him. She was holding a pencil and the pencil was in her right hand and the point was aimed at her temple. "I don't know," she said. "Perhaps there is goodness in you."

"What about those other men who did the killing? Do you think they're suffering today? That there isn't goodness in them?"

"There might be."

There were never any definite answers: this is what you have to do, Charles, this is how to take away the pain, I can help you. When he had finished his appointments with the doctor, he did what she had suggested. He contacted one of his fellow soldiers, Harry Widner. Harry lived in Redlands, California. They talked by phone and even planned to meet in Oregon for a weekend, to catch up, but when Charles called Harry several months later, Harry was evasive. He said he'd just gotten a job and wouldn't have the time. Nothing to be done.

Charles heard Harry's voice slipping away and he asked, "Do you think about what happened, Harry?"

"I don't go there, Charlie. It's not healthy."

"Doesn't it just arrive, uninvited? I try to send it away but it comes back and there're all these thoughts that fuck me up."

"You have to forget it, Charlie." His voice was dull. He lacked imagination, Charles thought. Even when they had been together during the war, it had seemed that Harry wasn't too perceptive. Harry had been the radio operator, the one to phone in the air strike. "Gonna wipe out this nightmare," Harry had said. Then he lit a cigarette. A brilliant day. The blue sky all around. And in the village, a dog that had survived lifted its head and howled at the sun.

THERE WAS THE SUN AND THEN SHADOW AND IN THE SHADOW A shape and the shape became a man and the man fell and on the ground, in the place of the man, there appeared a young boy with a hole in his neck.

The darkness and then the light and the boy's face came into the light. His feet were bare, his legs were bare, his chest, thin and taut, was bare. Just shorts with front pockets and the pockets bulged slightly and Charles thought later, if he wanted to believe something, he could convince himself that the pockets held grenades. More likely it was rocks, or some plaything.

When Charles was eleven he got a pellet gun from his dad. Went out into the wide backyard and shot at birds and dragonflies and smashed the window out of the neighbor's shed; a shot from a great distance that took out one pane of four, the exact one he'd been aiming at.

The fact was he had seen a man and the man had been reaching for something and so he shot him. The sun, playing hide-and-seek with the clouds, had jumped out too late and revealed the boy for what he was, a boy. But Charles had already killed him. And then, as if to underscore the necessity, Charles shot a pig that was running down the path and he shot a dog. A mongrel. An ugly little thing with a crippled back leg. No hair on the back, as if it were a large rat that deserved to die.

This little boy didn't have a gun. He didn't even have shoes.

He was lying there, one leg tucked backward, his head turned slightly as if to look over his shoulder. Later, Charles considered going back to look at the boy, maybe it wasn't even a boy, but he never did.

It had been early morning. It was Charles Boatman's fifth mission with his patrol. Six men dropped into an isolated area, scouting for North Vietnamese coming down the trail, headed south. They dug in at the edge of a valley that was green and empty. In the distance there were wisps of smoke that Corporal Abel thought might be signs of cooking fires rising from a village. After the drop, when the helicopters were gone and the silence of the countryside had settled in, they waited. For four days they watched the trail and counted the soldiers. One morning, fifty-six North Vietnamese slipped by, quiet and orderly, carrying AK-47s. Harry called in the numbers.

Charles was bunkered with Harry. They whispered through the night. Harry told Charles about the girl he'd loved and left. He wrote her every day. She was religious. She loved God and she wanted Harry to love God as well and he said that he was capable of doing that. Harry said that God was in charge. Even here, in this madness, it was a comfort to know that someone else was in control. Charles listened to Harry and thought he was a fool, but he didn't say that. He just kept quiet and read his book, a Graham Greene novel, something Jimmy Poe, a former bunkmate, had recommended. Jimmy read a lot.

All of them had books. There was a lot of waiting and the waiting was interminable and so they read while they waited. They read and when they were done they traded books. They watched the trail and ate peaches and beans out of tins and they slept and then they waited again.

They were supposed to be picked up at dawn on the sixth day. However, the helicopters were called to evacuate injured from a firefight north of their pickup and so they waited some more and then they got a call to march south, toward the area where they had seen the wisps of smoke. It was a terrifying walk. The group was skittish and by the time they reached the village they were expecting to take fire. They saw some movement. A woman cooking over a fire. A dog. A child running between the shacks.

Charles was walking point. The night before he'd written a letter to Sara. "I'm dug in and I'm looking up at the stars," he wrote. "Harry, my partner, is sleeping like a baby. He's a happy man who believes in Jesus and life after death. He would like me to believe this as well, but I've got more important things to believe in and dream about. Like this girl I know called Sara." He didn't tell her about anything that was true. He told her that all was fine. That he would be home in a couple of months and that he dreamed about her every night.

Walking point was like inviting death. You were all alone and you were the first person the enemy would see and of course you would get killed walking point. Charles wasn't killed. They arrived at the village and started a search. They set the huts on fire and there were children crying. Everything was going fine until someone started shooting. Charles had been in the doorway of a hut when the shooting started. He'd ducked and in the shadows he saw a shape and the shape moved and he raised his gun and at that point he saw it was a young boy and the boy appeared to be asking him a question but Charles shot and killed him.

Then Charles shot the pig. And he shot the dog. He didn't shoot any more people. His body moved slowly. Harry came up to him and started talking but Charles couldn't hear him, just saw his mouth moving. Harry saw the dead boy and pulled Charles away. After, he sat at the edge of the village. There was blood on his arms and boots. He didn't know where the blood had come from. He thought it might be the pig's blood and he wiped at it. The other men sat down beside him. There were only six of them and they had killed only eight people and some animals, but it was enough. Jimmy was off by himself, his head between his knees. Harry was high. He'd smoked a joint just that morning and Alex B.

had joined him and so Alex was high as well. He was bragging about his aim.

Corporal Abel called for order, and Charles threw up.

ABEL KILLED HIMSELF AFTER RETURNING TO THE STATES. BUT before doing that he got married and had children and found himself a good job at a lumber mill outside of Portland. And then, seventeen years after the war, he went over to his parents' house and late one night he sat in his father's car and ran a vacuum hose up through the window and gassed himself. Alex B. started a drywall business and got rich. Charles Boatman moved up to Canada, pulled the caboose up onto the mountain, and sequestered himself, until his children came along and forced him back into the world. And with their arrival and the added responsibility, he put his correspondence books away and gave up the notion of being an accountant.

There wasn't a lot of history up on Sumas Mountain, nor was there a lot of curiosity about where Charles Boatman came from or what his story was. That was good, for the most part. Sometimes, though, Charles wanted a listening ear, a neighbor who knew the stories, or at least had seen them on TV, and cared about them. When he began to spend time with Claire Toupin, he at first loved her innocence, her manner of asking a question and lifting her chin as if this were the most important question in the world, one that had never been asked before.

She was a small woman, and if she seemed easy and malleable it was only an impression she liked to give. She wasn't that simple. The first time Charles slept with her, on the night of the party, he was surprised by her forthrightness, by her directions, and by her knowledge. After, they lay side by side, arms touching, and he said that he hadn't loved anyone for a long time.

"I knew that," she said.

"I mean, I love my children."

"Of course." She kissed him, on the mouth and then on his chest. This might be the answer to madness.

But still the dreams came, and on the nights that Charles stayed over at Claire's, leaving his teenage children alone, he sometimes woke and sat at the edge of the bed and stared out the small window of the bedroom, breathing quickly. When Claire woke, she held him. She asked him what it was and he said, "Nightmares." Her hand running his spine, on his shoulder, fingering his neck. She pulled him back onto the bed and asked, "What was it?" and he lied and said, "It was Ada, she was drowning and I couldn't get to her," or "It was Jon, he was falling."

Claire's hair in his hands. Her head, the bluntness of her crown. As if by determining the shape of her, he could bear out his own existence. Finally, unable to sleep, he said he was worried about the kids and he dressed and kissed her good night and walked back down the mountain to his own house.

One night he passed by Tomas Manik's place and he saw the lights on and a figure walking down the driveway to the main road and he recognized Del's gait, the slight sideways bob of her head as she walked. He waited for her and when she saw him she stopped and looked back at the house and then, as if resigning herself to some sort of inquisition, joined him.

"What?" Charles asked. "You sleepwalking?"

Del said that she probably was.

"That's the artist's house," Charles said.

"That's right."

"And you're visiting?"

"I guess."

"By yourself?"

"I guess."

"That's a lot of guessing. You a friend of Mr. Manik?" He pronounced the name wrong, with a long *eee* on the last syllable, as if the man were not to be taken seriously.

"Yes."

"How good a friend?"

"Pretty good."

Charles didn't speak. They walked together in silence until they reached the house and then Charles said good night. Del looked at him and she went to her room.

He lay in bed that night and waited for sleep, but when it didn't come he got up and made coffee and sat at the kitchen table. In the morning Ada found him sleeping at the table. He woke and picked up his coffee cup and said, "Look at me, sleeping everywhere but where I'm supposed to."

Ada made fresh coffee, and while she did this he watched her. He said, "What do you think of Tomas Manik?"

Ada looked up and then away. She shrugged. "He's all right."

"You know about your sister?"

Ada said she did.

"And Jon, he knows?"

Ada nodded.

"So, I'm the only one in the dark here. Is that it?"

"Del was worried. She figured you might strangle Tomas."

"That's the goddamn truth."

Ada said that there wasn't anything they could do. Del had made up her mind. She faced Charles and said that he shouldn't do anything stupid. "Tomas pays you for your work. You need him."

Charles was astounded by his daughter's matter-of-factness. He said, "It's like I'm selling her then."

"That's ridiculous. This has nothing to do with you, Dad."

"Sure as hell does." He stood and pulled on his boots. Went outside and got into the pickup and looked out the windshield at the gray sky. Ada was watching from the kitchen window. He could see her profile and the fall of her hair. He started the engine, backed out of the drive onto the gravel road, and climbed toward Tomas Manik's house.

There was no one at the house, so Charles slid down the

muddy path toward the workshop. He didn't knock, just walked in. Tomas was working and listening to jazz. The sound system he had was big, and a high whining clarinet filled the space. Charles stood in the entrance and watched Tomas work. He was welding, his back to Charles, and there was the flare of the welder and a brightness against the far wall. Tomas pushed his goggles up and turned and saw Charles. He put his tools down and walked over to the stereo and switched it off. He said, "Charles."

Charles stepped forward. He was breathless and he rummaged about for the words that would penetrate Tomas's smooth ease. He wondered where in this shop Del and the man would have had sex. Perhaps they went into the house.

"I'm here about Del. She's been coming here, to see you."

Tomas sat on a stool. He lit a cigarette and motioned at a free chair but Charles shook his head. Tomas said that it was true, Del did come to visit. However, he said, every time Del walked the mile and a half to his shop, she was choosing to do so and there was nothing he could say or do to stop her.

"You're fucking a minor," Charles said.

Tomas raised his eyebrows. "She said that? Or you?"

Charles stepped back. "I could kill you," he said.

Tomas shook his head. "You won't do that. Not because you're incapable. I can see what kind of man you are. I have known men like you, and normally they frighten me, but you, Charles Boatman, won't do such a thing. You love your daughter too much."

Charles looked around at the sculptures and the drawings and paintings. He said, "I bet you figure you're a pretty good artist. That this is real art. Big art." He swung his arm out at the space and said, "I figure you love this work." Then he said that it was dangerous to love something too much. Especially something inanimate. He walked over to a sculpture of stainless steel. It was a man, ten feet tall. Testicles of ball bearings and a penis of solid steel, turned slightly, with a circumcised tip of hammered copper.

Charles had milled the metal for the piece and delivered it three weeks earlier. He touched the ball bearings and said, "I could castrate this fellow for you."

He looked over at Tomas, who was no longer smiling.

Charles patted the hollow thigh of the sculpture. "If you hurt her, I'll kill you," he said. Then he turned and walked to the door and stepped outside and walked back up to his truck. Sat in it and thought about Tomas and thought about Del. His hands were shaking. He started the truck and drove home and found Ada at the kitchen table. She'd done the dishes and made herself toast and eggs. She asked if he wanted some, and then, not waiting for an answer, she got up and turned on the element. Fried him eggs and laid them out on a plate with buttered toast.

Charles ate and watched Ada watching him. Finally, he said, "You wouldn't do anything like that, would you? Run off with a man twice your age?"

"She hasn't run off, Dad."

"She will. I can see it." He drank his coffee, put the mug down, and said, "I want to burn the man's shop down. But like you said, that would be like torching my own income, seeing as I supply him with all his metal. And so, here I sit, believing that money is more important than my younger daughter."

"It's not."

"No?" Charles loved Ada's confidence, the fact that she didn't trust the obvious. Whereas Del was enthusiastic and gullible, Ada was skeptical. She would suffer for it. He didn't tell her that, but he could see that hers would not be a naïve existence. He said, "The man's too damn smug." Then he sighed and asked Ada about Claire Toupin. What did she think of her?

Ada made a face. Said that it was unfair to ask, because obviously *he* liked her and it didn't matter what Ada thought.

"Oh, it matters. It might not change anything, but it matters."

"She's plastic," Ada said.

Charles lifted an eyebrow and said, "Well."

"At least she looks that way. And even when she talks, every-thing's so exciting. She's too happy. She doesn't seem very"—Ada moved a hand, looking for the word—"very aware."

"She's good for me."

"I know."

"I could use some happiness."

"I'm glad for you, Dad. Really." She stood and kissed his fore-head. She had just showered and he smelled the shampoo and her hair was still damp. Its length fell forward and brushed his cheek and he recalled Claire's hair falling against his chest. He wanted to hang on to this brief moment.

CHARLES DID NOTHING ABOUT TOMAS AND DEL. HE THOUGHT about it. One night, he left the house around 3 A.M. and he walked up the hill, carrying a jerry can of gas. He went directly toward Tomas's workshop and he stood and imagined what havoc would transpire as the building went up in bright flames. There would be the fire trucks arriving too late from the valley, and the police would come and questions would be asked and of course every-thing would point back to Charles Boatman and, in the end, Charles couldn't imagine leaving his children alone. He would be put in prison and Ada would have to take over the house and the responsibilities, and so, he couldn't act. It wasn't cowardice. He was a practical man.

He was aware of Del's movements back and forth between the two places, but he did nothing, and it grieved him that Tomas had been right. And then, one day, Del moved in with the artist. She pulled up in Tomas's pickup, loaded her things, and drove back up the mountain. Charles watched her, and just before she left, he said, "At least he could come down here and talk."

"He's scared of you, Dad," Del said.

Charles thought about this and it didn't surprise him. What surprised him was Del's acceptance of this fact, as if she knew that her father was capable of some sort of madness. It was as if she had thrown up a mirror before him and he hadn't recognized himself.

Still, after a month or so, Del brought Tomas down to the caboose for a visit. She'd made a cake and sat beside Tomas and urged him to eat. She clung to his arm and kissed his big head and put her hands against his neck and the side of his face. He was brash and full of bluster and talked about his projects and the money he was making, but he never looked Charles in the eye.

Later, Charles asked Ada, "What did he think I was going to do?"

"You're unpredictable, Dad."

"Ach, that's bullshit. Anyways, Del sure seems fired up for him."

And then, within the month, Ada moved to Vancouver. She was studying culinary arts at a local college. And then Jon moved out as well. He found a place in Abbotsford where he planned to finish high school. Only later did Charles learn that Jon had moved in with an older man, a high school history teacher, but by the time Charles heard about this, his own demons had come back and he didn't have the wherewithal to confront Jon.

The silence defeated him. At first he had been pleased to think of living on his own again. Claire could visit without interruptions, there would be less food to buy, less cleaning, fewer troubles, not as much money needed, though it became quite clear that Ada needed her tuition fees and rent money; she had a part-time job but she was hard-pressed to pay for the apartment. So, Charles helped her out. Del and Jon seemed to need nothing, which was disconcerting.

In the mornings, as the rain drove against the windows, he considered his day and discovered that hope had previously been based on busyness. With the exodus of his children, he felt ancient and unmoored. Too much time to think. He still worked in his machine shop, and Claire slipped over some late afternoons for a quick moment in bed, but even these moments were elusive and ultimately left him more despondent than he had been before. In the end, life with Claire did not last. The expectation the children had visited upon this affair dissipated. "I am incapable of love," Charles told Claire, and she, though she wanted to, lacked the wherewithal to convince him otherwise.

Over the years that followed, light and shade fell across his memories. A whole history arrives with absolute clarity and then disappears like the sun that comes so rarely into the valley— expectation, and then disappointment. There gradually emerges a series of images, built up over time. A ferry arrives from a distant shore. A boy in shorts makes fast the ropes. A blind man sings a song that is off-key but hints at a ballad that is familiar and haunting, some tune about love and death and mourning. The boy in shorts opens his mouth as if to speak and then becomes a body on a bier that is being carried by the blind man and Charles. A sign appears indicating a name—the Han River. Charles did not tell anybody about these images.

LIEUTENANT DAT WAS A SMALL MAN WHO WORKED FOR ROOM 19, a division of the Danang police force that concerned itself with foreigners and religion. Dat was the policeman to whom Ada and Jon had been directed when they first arrived in Danang and he was the man to whom they kept returning. They would meet him in his office and ask if there was any news of their father. Dat would shake his head mournfully and then ask if they needed anything, a guide perhaps, or an evening out on the town.

Jon asked about their father's valuables. Could they have them? Dat, who had none of Mr. Thanh's tact or efficacy in English or even kindness, shook his head and said they were being held.

"Why are they being held?" Ada asked. Dat motioned at her legs and said that Ada had no idea how men in Vietnam would view so much bare flesh. She wore shorts and her legs were long. He said that she should wear dresses, or pantaloons.

She said, "Pantaloons?"

She asked at least to see a list of their father's valuables, and Dat shook his head and said, "No."

"Were you aware of him?" Ada asked. "Did you see him around town?"

Dat smiled. "There are many tourists that pass through. I cannot be aware of every one."

"But you were aware of him missing. That's why you took his things."

"The hotel contacted me about a foreigner who had not returned to his room for a week. I made some inquiries, determined that this man, your father, was missing, and so I took his personal belongings. They are part of the investigation. Until we know what happened, we must keep his belongings. Do you understand?"

Ada said no, she didn't understand. She closed her eyes and bit her lip. She hated this man with his officious and oily demeanor, who seemed more interested in telling her how to dress than in looking for a missing foreigner. On this day she had come alone to see Dat because Jon was tired of the nonsense that went on at Room 19. "It's not even a real room," he said. "And this Dat isn't a real policeman. He just smiles at us. I refuse to be humiliated."

And so Ada sat on a wooden chair before a wooden desk that held a single object, a letter opener with a black handle. Dat leaned back and studied her. He asked where her brother was, wasn't he concerned for her safety?

"Was there a letter?" Ada said. "Written to us, or to someone else?"

"No letter." Dat offered his empty palms.

"And so you're still looking for my father? You're going out and asking people and sending out information and talking to other policemen from other cities?"

"Of course, Miss Ada. Every day." He lifted a hand as if asking for silence and then said, "He had a lover."

"What do you mean? A Vietnamese woman?"

"American."

Ada laughed. "I don't think so."

"It does not matter what you think. It matters what is, in fact, true."

"Who is this woman?"

"I cannot say."

"Because you don't know."

"You are sometimes rude, Miss Ada. You think that you are always right, or that I am perhaps stupid, or that I am a smaller person because I am not as rich as you. This is false. You must not assume to know me."

"I'm sorry. I don't mean to be rude. I'm worried. I'm tired. I am given no information. I just want to know what happened to my father."

"Of course. And when we are sure about this American, we will talk to her. And then we will talk to you. These things take time. I am all alone and I have other things in my plate." He smiled, pleased by the words he had chosen. He lit a cigarette and turned to look out the window. Ada saw that she was being dismissed.

THAT EVENING, ADA WENT OUT ALONE AND WALKED THE STREETS and then stopped for a drink at a garden café. There was a blind man sitting in a corner with a dog at his feet. The man looked to be her father's age. He was American and he was an ex-soldier: she knew this because the man was wearing his old fatigues. He sat alone and felt for his food with his hands and occasionally bent to offer the dog a morsel. He moved his head back and forth and at one point he called out, "Young girl," and when the waitress arrived he said he wanted another beer and more fish.

The waitress slipped away and asked Ada if she wanted another drink. Ada said no, she was fine, and as she spoke the soldier looked up and stared at the spot where Ada sat.

He called out, "American?"

She looked around the empty café. A blond girl in a bikini smiled at her from a Danish beer poster.

"No," she said, "Canadian."

The soldier considered this and asked, "Are you alone?"

"I'm waiting for my brother," Ada said.

A large hand rose and fell. "Join me till then."

Ada did not want to face the man. She did not want to sit across from his stripes and his medals and have him tell her war stories, about how generals led from the rear, and how he came to be blind, and the drama of his life. Finally, he would tell her why he was here and what he was looking for and how he had not yet found it.

The man lifted his head in anticipation.

"I'm sorry," Ada said. "I'm actually meeting my brother in a few minutes. At a different place." She stood, put money on the table, and picked up her bag.

The soldier stuck out his hand. "George Giguerre."

Ada looked at his hand and then walked over and shook it. "Hello," she said.

George said he was here alone. "Except for Julie." He pointed at his dog, whose head was down, jaw pressed against the floor.

"Pretty dog," Ada said.

"That's what I'm told. Tourist?"

"Yes. Yes."

"Thought so. You're about twenty-two."

"Twenty-eight."

A nod and an angling of the head. The thick hand came back out. "Nice to meet you."

Ada shook his hand again and pulled away. She stood outside the café, her hands in fists, breathing quickly. The blind man's desperation and his uniform and his soft hand, all of this had dismayed her. She imagined her own father sitting in a bar in some other place, perhaps Hanoi or Ho Chi Minh City, nostalgically telling strangers about his history. She lit a cigarette.

THE TIME IN BETWEEN 55

The boy, Yen, appeared at her side and said, "I have a bird for you." He held up a small bamboo cage. "From me to you."

Ada stepped back. "I don't want a bird."

"Yes, you do. It's good fortune. And besides, the bird is an orphan and needs an owner. Please. It would make me very happy."

Ada put out her cigarette and began to walk away, following the path along the river.

Yen caught up to her and said, "Just yesterday I saw you at Christy's. With your brother, playing pool. I said to myself, Yen, Ada is unhappy. What would make her happy? And I thought of a bird. So, I bought him for you and he lives with me at Mr. Minh's but Minh doesn't like birds so you must take him. I give him to you, with levity."

"Who is this Mr. Minh?"

"My uncle. He works at the Chess Hotel. He is an underchef and I know you are interested because you are a chef as well. So was Bac Ho, Ho Chi Minh. It's perfect, you see. Uncle Ho, Uncle Minh, and Miss Ada. All of you making food. That makes me feel full of fortune. I do not think, Miss Ada, that this was chance. It was planned long ago, our meeting."

Ada kept walking. She did not argue with Yen.

He said that he wanted her to meet Minh.

She said, "No, I'm tired."

"He thinks maybe that he met your father. Or saw him."

Ada stopped walking. "What do you mean? Where?"

"He is not sure. He thinks maybe he saw your father one day in the restaurant. I had a photograph of your father that I procured from a shop owner, one of the shop owners you talked to, and I showed that photograph to my uncle. He recognized something, perhaps the shirt, or the hair. Of course, he might be wrong. This happens."

Ada, alarmed, said that Yen had no business following her or taking her father's photograph to show to some uncle of his. She said that she would like that photo back. She began to turn away but Yen shook his head vigorously and said that he meant no harm. No harm at all. "Surely you must want to see what Uncle Minh has to say."

He beckoned and set off at a quick walk. She followed at a distance. He did not speak as he guided her, birdcage swinging from his hand, through the streets to the rear entrance of the Chess Hotel.

"Come," he said, "I will introduce you to Minh." He set the birdcage down by the door. They went down a hallway, past a bathroom with a squat toilet and beyond that a storage area with dry goods and pots and pans. The kitchen was small: a five-foot grill and three gas elements, a fridge and freezer. Yen called Minh's name. A man appeared; he was not more than twenty-five, maybe younger. He was shirtless, and Ada was aware of his smooth chest and dark nipples. She looked away and then at his face. He shook her hand, said her name, and drew out the last vowel into an expression of surprise.

"He wants to make you onion soup," Yen said.

Ada said she wasn't hungry. "When did he see my father?"

Yen spoke to Minh, who folded his arms and said something back, then smiled at Ada.

"How about salad?"

"No, no, thank you."

Minh left and returned with a glazed pastry that had half a peach at its center. He put it in a box and handed it to Ada.

She said, "My father, you saw my father."

Yen said, "Minh didn't make it. Soon, one day, he will know how to make peach pastry. But, not yet." His voice got softer and he went up on tiptoes and said, "He saw your father, or a man that looked like your father, one afternoon in the restaurant of the Chess Hotel. He was eating peach pastry, just like the one you hold in your hands, with a beautiful woman. This is what Minh knows. And I know the rest."

He paused, licked his lips, looked up into Ada's face, and said,

"She is American. She is Elaine Gouds and she lives here in Danang with her husband, Jack, and they have two children. This is what I know."

"Can I meet her? This woman?"

Yen shrugged. He said that he did not have that kind of power. He was not a magician.

"You know where she lives, don't you?"

Yen said he did.

"Take me there."

Yen waved a hand. "Not tonight, Miss Ada. It is too late. Tomorrow."

Ada walked outside and stood in a light drizzle. An umbrella snapped open and appeared above her head.

"Please," she said.

"That man you met in the café," Yen said. "George. I knew him. For two days I was his guide, fed his dog fresh bones, took him to Hoi An, made sure he was safe. And then one day he called me a name and hit me with his cane. See?" Yen raised his arm and showed Ada the welt just above his elbow.

"Oh," Ada said. "What did you do?"

"Nothing. Well, I might have tried to take his dog. But just for a walk. It is a large dog with very shiny fur. Of course, you have met the dog."

"Did he pay you, this George?"

"A little."

"I guess I should pay you," Ada said.

"Oh, no. Never." His black eyes, hard and bright.

"Tomorrow," she reminded him. "You will show me that woman's house."

"Absolutely," he said. "I will meet you outside, right here, at two o'clock." And he stepped sideways and then turned and disappeared into the darkness. Ada raised a hand to call out that she had his umbrella, but he was gone.

· · ·

AT NIGHT, SHE WOKE AND REALIZED THAT THE RAIN HAD STOPPED. She went to the bathroom and then stood by the window and watched the harbor and listened to the sounds of the city. Jon had not yet come home. She saw her reflection in the dark glass of the side window. She was too thin: her legs, her arms, even her face had diminished. She leaned out the window and saw, on the street below, a motorcycle pass, its taillight glowing red and then disappearing around a corner. The sign on the photography shop blinked on and off, and in the doorway of the shop she saw, intermittently, the shape of something; perhaps a small animal curled into itself, or maybe a person, its back to the street. She stood for a long time, smoking and watching, and then she closed the window.

She was still awake and sitting in the darkness when Jon came in. He reached for the light and she said, "No, leave it off."

She lifted her nose. He smelled of cigarette smoke and something—or someone—else. He was breathing heavily from the climb up the stairs. "Where were you?" she asked.

He said that he had been out at a small bar where young people danced to music from the seventies and sang karaoke. "It was strange." He paused and then asked, as if to deflect further questions, "Are you okay? Did something happen?"

She shrugged her shoulders, even though she knew that he could not see the gesture. She said that she had been thinking about home and about Del. She had tried to call but no one answered. Of course, it was noon or later there, and why should Del or Tomas be waiting for a phone call from her. She said that she missed the mountain and the smell of the mountain and she missed the mornings when they were young and would find their father sitting by the stove drinking coffee. "I miss him," she said.

Jon came to her and stood behind her and wrapped his arms around her chest and pressed his cheek against her head. "Don't," he said. "You're making yourself crazy."

"And I worry about you. This city isn't safe in the dark."

"I'm here. I'm safe."

She felt the heat of his breath against her head, his forearms against her breasts. "What will we do?" she asked. "Do we keep looking? Give up? Go home?"

He released her and stood by the window and when he spoke his voice was quiet and floated upward. "We can't give up yet."

"But I'm the only one looking. Jon, back home, when we hadn't heard from Dad and we thought something was wrong, and we met with Del and Tomas, you said you wanted to come with me. We agreed to come here together to look for Dad. The problem is, you just don't want to face the fact that Dad is missing and maybe dead." She paused and then said, "I'm so tired."

Jon did not answer. In the darkness, she said, "Do you think he wanted to disappear? People do sometimes. Maybe that's what he wanted."

Jon sat on the edge of the window. He was facing Ada now and he leaned forward. "He wasn't happy in the last year. You know he wasn't happy."

Ada shook her head. "But coming here seemed to be something he wanted to do. I still remember his phone call. He announced that he was going to take a trip to Vietnam, as a tourist. He sounded so hopeful, which was odd for him."

"He was always able to dupe you. Or himself, as if everything was fine when he was with you."

"I'm not naïve," Ada said.

"He liked you best," Jon said.

Ada began to protest but Jon interrupted. "He adored you."

"Adores," Ada said. "He's still out there somewhere, adoring me."

"Of course he is."

"Did he tell you something different? Before he left? Did he say, 'Jon, I'm planning on going to Vietnam to disappear'?"

"He told me very little. He phoned right around the time Anthony had decided to leave, though I never mentioned it. Maybe I thought it would please him too much. Anyway, at the end of the phone call, he said he was going to Danang. Just for a while. He did call me several weeks later, when he was already here, but I'd been sleeping and the conversation was kind of slow. He seemed to be elsewhere, though he was affectionate. He said he loved me." Jon stopped talking. Looked down at the street. Finally, he said, "And, here we are."

He lit a cigarette and offered Ada one. A light flashed in the harbor. A ship's horn sounded. Ada said, "Dad asked me one day if you didn't ever like girls. I said that you liked girls, that wasn't it, you just weren't physically attracted to them." She paused.

The darkness was a fine thing. She could not see Jon's face, and this made intimacy more possible. She asked, with more cynicism in her voice than she intended, "So, is it fun? Is it fun with strangers?"

Jon gave a little laugh.

Ada said, "I knew a boy in college, several years ago, who wouldn't let me close my eyes. He wanted to be a filmmaker and thought that everything should be observed. It was bizarre. Once, we modeled for each other, we weren't wearing clothes, and we looked at each other through binoculars." She laughed quietly, then stopped and said, "Oh, why did I tell you that!"

"That's okay. I won't tell anyone."

She stood and without turning on the light she found two glasses and the half-full bottle of whiskey and she brought it back to her chair and poured out equal amounts. They touched glasses and drank.

She spoke quietly. "What you said, about Dad liking me best, does that make you angry?"

"I'm not angry." He paused and then said that he was lucky in a way. "His love for you is like a weight that you have to carry."

Ada denied this. She said, "If Dad's dead, I just want to know. I just want someone to climb those stairs and knock on the door and tell me that he's dead." She lifted her hands and let them fall.

Jon took her hand and held it. He said it was late, they should sleep. He said that in three hours the sun would come up and then, maybe, everything would seem clearer. He went to the washroom and came back with a small pill and a bottle of water. "Take it," he said. "It'll help you sleep."

"I've been drinking," she said.

"Take it." He placed the pill on her tongue and made her drink. Then he guided her to her bed, helped her undress, and pulled the sheet up. She watched him move about the room. He folded her jeans and top and went to the washroom, and when he returned he sat by the window and finished his drink. Her eyes closed and then opened and she saw him sitting at the desk, huddling under a pool of light. He was reading. She wanted to call for him but her tongue was thick and only a soft noise slipped out and then she slept.

WHEN SHE WOKE IT WAS AFTERNOON. SHADOWS ON THE FAR WALL, the sound of horns and motorcycles in the street below, the maid talking in the stairwell. She found Jon on the rooftop, tanning in his boxers. His legs and arms were thin, his chest narrow. He saw her and said, "Hi."

"I hate sleeping late," she said.

"Some boy's been asking for you. He was down in the lobby this morning all dressed up and holding a birdcage. We talked for a bit. He told me he saw you last night and that you've talked before. His English is quite amazing, though sometimes he mixes things up. How old is he?"

"Too young for everybody, including you." Ada pinned her hair up. Said she was going to find an American woman who knew their father. "Will you come?" she asked.

He said if she really wanted him.

"Come. Please."

They found Yen squatting outside the hotel entrance. He pushed his hand at Jon's and said, "Pleased to meet you." The three of them walked down Bach Dang Street and then left to the Han Market and on down close to the Cham Museum, where Yen pointed out the school that he was supposed to be attending. "I will be in the eighth level," he said. He was still holding the birdcage. It swung at his side. He corrected himself. "I would be. Is that better?" He looked up at Ada.

"Yes, it's better."

Yen held up his small wrist and adjusted a watch that looked very expensive and new. He called out the time and then grinned and said, "A gift from a woman named Irene, who is German."

Ada shook her head.

"You do not believe me. Fine."

"It's none of my business," Ada said.

"What is the truth is this: Irene is my lover."

"What are you talking about?" Ada looked at Yen and then Jon, who seemed amused.

"Irene is staying at the Empire Hotel. I go to her and she loves me and then she pays me. See?" He held up his wrist again and showed them.

Ada said that this was something she did not need to know. Then she shook her head and said that Yen should be careful. He did not understand the worth of the watch.

Yen said that Ada didn't have to worry. He wouldn't steal from her. Ever. She was different. He said that she was much more beautiful than Irene. His gaze moved from her face to her chest and then back to her face. He hopped slightly and slipped the watch from his wrist into his pocket. Ada put her hand through Jon's arm and drew him close. They turned down a narrow street, and Yen halted before a white stucco house of three stories. "Here," he said, and knocked on the door.

From above them, on the balcony of the house, someone laughed. A child's blond head peeked over the railing and called out, "Hello. Who are you?" A woman with dark hair appeared beside him.

Ada said her own name and the name of her brother. She said that they wanted to speak to Elaine Gouds.

The woman disappeared. When she returned she leaned out over the railing so that Ada could see her shoulders and chest. She said, "Hold on, Ai Ty is coming."

Ada and Jon were let into the house by an older woman, who when she saw Yen, spoke to him with a hard tone.

Yen told Ada that he would wait across the street. "Not to worry," he said. "I will be safe."

Ada did not argue. The older woman sullenly led them up two flights of stairs and into a musty-smelling room that held a TV and a small daybed. The floor was scattered with children's toys.

The woman who had called down to them was still standing out on the balcony. She turned and met them as they stepped outside. "I am Elaine Gouds," she said. She did not shake their hands. She did not ask them to sit. She was angular, with a hard face, and her eyes lifted as she watched them, and this gave the impression of both doubt and hope, or weariness.

Ada said, "We're looking for our father, Charles Boatman." She stopped and breathed out quickly and said, "For three weeks now, we've been looking." She turned to Jon, who was standing near the entrance as if waiting to leave.

Ada faced Elaine again and said, "Did you know him?"

Elaine lifted her hand to her narrow neck. "I saw Charles a few times. Like everything here in this country, our meeting was pure chance. We first met at Christy's, an American bar on the harbor front. We played Scrabble once and another time he sat on this balcony and we drank wine. I haven't seen him for over a month. Neither has my husband, Jack. I am telling you everything that I told Lieutenant Dat."

"Lieutenant Dat was here talking to you?" Ada asked.

"Yes." Elaine's arms were folded across her chest. Her eyes looked tired and did not settle on either Jon's or Ada's face. She wore tight dark jeans that revealed her thinness. She was slightly bent at the shoulders and neck, and this made her appear worn down. She took a step forward, as if to say something else, but then she turned away and said, "Jack's home. Perhaps he can tell you something."

There was a shout from the entrance below and then the sound of stairs being taken two at a time, and a man with a narrow nose, who looked much too young to be married to Elaine Gouds, stepped out onto the balcony.

"Visitors," he cried, and he held out a hand to Ada and said, "Jack Gouds." He tilted his head at Ada and said, "You are?" She shook his hand and told him her name and he repeated it. Then he turned to Jon and said, "We've met. At the post office just the other day. I was mailing a letter and you asked how much stamps were to North America. Jon without the *h*. Nice to see you again."

Ada looked over at Jon, who with the greeting took a step forward into the room.

Jack turned to Elaine. "Why aren't we drinking?" He said to Ada, "Beer, orange juice, wine, water?" He clapped his hands and called for Ai Ty.

"Don't, Jack," Elaine said. "She's with Sammy and Jane."

"Okay, then. Okay. I'll get us something." He came back minutes later with a tray of glasses and open beer and a bottle of wine. He passed the glasses around and handed the beer bottles to Jon and Ada. He poured Elaine a glass of wine and said, "My wife is too refined for beer." He placed his hand on her shoulder.

"Offer our visitors a seat, Jack."

Jack brought several wicker chairs and placed them around the small table. Elaine lifted her glass of wine, studied it, and then she drank. She looked at Jack and said, "You didn't tell me you'd met a new foreigner in town." She turned to Ada. "One becomes very aware of any influx of strangers, especially if they're interesting and more than tourists." To Jack, she said, "Ada and Jon are looking for their father, *Charles* Boatman."

Jack turned to Jon and said, "I didn't know that. I'm sorry."

Jon said that Jack had no reason to know. Why would he have told him?

"*I* would have," Ada said. "We've been all over town and nobody knows anything or if they do they aren't talking. Just yesterday I heard that you knew our father. A little, anyway." She looked at Elaine, who was looking down at her wineglass.

"More than a little," Jack said. "Charles became a friend. Wouldn't you say, Elaine?"

Elaine raised her head and smiled briefly. She nodded. "Yes. A friend." Her eyes moved from Jack to Jon, who was sitting forward with his elbows on his knees, an index finger tracing the moisture on his beer glass. She watched Jon carefully and then said that his father had been right about something. "When you find him you must tell him that."

Jack placed his glass carefully on the table and said, "The few times we got together—and though they were few, they were good times—those times I saw that Charles was often elsewhere. Wouldn't you say, Elaine? Not that he was unhappy."

"Oh, he *was* unhappy," Elaine said. She stood, said, "I'm sorry," and left the balcony.

When she was gone Jack explained that this had nothing to do with them. Elaine was suffering a slight depression here in Vietnam. "She finds the climate difficult. And the people. And the language. And raising children here." He laughed ruefully. "She misses home." He shook his head. "But your father. I'm sure he's gone away, south perhaps, and he'll return. This country does strange things to people. But me, I love this place."

The wind had begun to blow and a light rain fell onto the street below them. Jack said that this was typhoon season and he'd heard that Danang might be hit by a storm. "Just stay inside and away from windows and you'll be safe. Another drink?"

Jon shifted and began to speak but Ada cut him off and said, "No, we have to get back."

"Really? Jon?" Jack asked.

Jon shrugged and stood along with Ada. Jack reached out to touch Jon's elbow. He said that sometimes he went up into the villages south of Danang, or he made trips to Quang Ngai, three hours from here, and maybe Jon and Ada would like to join him. Explore the countryside.

Ada saw his eyes, blue with small pupils, black and clear. A shadow of a beard on his narrow jaw. Whiteness at the base of his neck indicated a recent haircut. He took his hand from Jon's elbow and spread out his arms as he described the moistness of the countryside.

Yen had disappeared. This was disconcerting for Ada. Jon said that it didn't matter; the boy would come back, too soon. They were standing outside the gate to Jack and Elaine's house. The wind came in gusts and blew Ada's hair across her face. She pulled it back and said, "You know Jack, don't you? It wasn't just a meeting at the post office."

Jon looked away. Then he faced Ada and said, "Yes, I know him."

"He lied," Ada said. "Right in front of everyone he made up a story about the stamps. And then he tells us, as if he knows, that Dad went south. What are you *doing*? The man's married. He has children. You're more interested in him than in finding your own father. Don't you want to know what happened to Dad? You're too scared, is that it?"

Jon walked away. The palm trees bent as the rain swirled. Ada caught up to him, but he pressed forward without speaking. Finally, rounding the corner onto the street that led to their hotel, he stopped and shouted, "*You* want to know, Ada. And because you're so desperate you think I should want the same thing. Well, I don't. Okay? I just don't."

In their room they dried off and Jon changed into jeans: his narrow thighs and the vulnerability at the backs of his knees, a hamstring moving, white legs disappearing as he straightened, his fingers dancing near his belt buckle, flesh and blood and bone.

They did not talk until Jon announced that he was going out. He wouldn't be late, and if the wind continued, he'd come back early. Ada said that that was fine. He was a big boy. She had put on pajama bottoms and was sitting cross-legged on the bed. When Jon left she remained sitting and she let the darkness fall into the room and even after it was totally dark she did not turn on the light as she listened to the approaching storm.

A memory from the mountain came to her. She and Jon had been playing in the woods behind the house when they found a nest of baby birds set in the small crevasse of two rocks. The birds were very young, their beaks yawning soundlessly at the empty air. The mother was nearby; she had a broken wing and she scolded madly and spun in useless circles. Ada squatted and studied the babies. Jon stood off at a distance. Ada told him to come look. He said no. He said the birds would die. Yes, she said, but you can still come look. He shook his head and left her there. A few days later, when she went back alone to find the nest, the family was dead. The mother bird had managed to spin her way to the rocks below the nest. The babies were featherless and curled into one another. Their chests were translucent, like blue glass.

ONE SPRING YEARS LATER, SHORT OF MONEY, CHARLES BOATMAN was hired on at a truss factory in the Valley. He worked the night shift and returned as the sun was rising, and there was always immense hope in that moment, though it didn't last. Sleeping in the daylight seemed to produce fewer dreams and for that he was thankful. One day after work he stopped at a travel agency and bought a ticket for Hanoi, through Bangkok. He didn't tell anyone about this plan, and if he'd been asked he wouldn't have been able to explain himself. He was feeling less and less connected to the world around him, and there were times when he would rise from his seat by the stove and say something just to hear the sound of a voice, and he would not recognize his own voice. Every so often he pulled out the airline ticket and studied it as if it were a precious relic, or as if it might offer him some revelation. Two days before the flight he cashed in the ticket and lost several hundred dollars on the transaction.

Sometimes he went down into the Valley and drank at a small bar close to the highway. One Saturday night he met a woman named Jill. They drank and danced and talked about nothing special and later she came up the mountain with him and spent the night. In the brightness of the morning he was sorry; all the noise of the previous night seemed excessive and false, and he supposed, based on her silence, she felt the same. He drove her down the mountain to her car, which sat in the bar's parking lot. They didn't speak, and he was amazed once again at how physical contact did not guarantee intimacy or even affection. He was glad to see her go, though he would recall, in later moments of lust, the tiny mole on her ankle and the manner she had of crouching over him and lowering her breasts into his mouth, as if she were feeding him.

The following year he quit the factory and took a job operating heavy equipment in the construction of a highway. It was easy work, sitting high up on the seat of a scraper, and he didn't have to converse with anyone, though the mindlessness allowed for too much wandering, too many detours into the runnels of his brain. He considered buying another plane ticket, even stopped his car outside the travel agency, but he didn't go in.

He saw Ada and Jon infrequently. Jon was living in Vancouver and working at an auction house. He phoned occasionally but he rarely came to visit. Ada came up the mountain every month. One time she brought a man with a goatee who owned several restaurants in Vancouver. They came for the day. The man, whose name was Jefferson, was well dressed and groomed, and he sniffed about the caboose and the outlying land as if attempting to connect the Ada he knew to the hardness of the place. When he finally got her alone, Charles told Ada she should have called first and he would have cleaned up.

"Oh, Jefferson gets freaked out by a little dirt," Ada said. "Don't worry about him." And she hugged Charles.

When she phoned Charles the following month, he asked about Jefferson and Ada said, "He's not my friend anymore."

Charles said, "It was the caboose, wasn't it?"

Ada laughed. "I love the caboose, Daddy." She paused and then said, "Don't lose sleep over it. Okay? I'm fine."

After Ada said good-bye, Charles hung on to the breathiness of her voice. Her self-possession always surprised him; it encircled her like a second layer of beauty.

IN THE SUMMER OF 1997, CHARLES RECEIVED AN UNEXPECTED call from Jimmy Poe, a fellow soldier to whom he hadn't talked in years. In Vietnam, Jimmy had been given the name Mister Book because he was a walking library, a man of quotes and titles and favorite passages, though Charles remembered Jimmy had been silent that day, after the attack on the hamlet in Quang Ngai Province.

On the phone, Charles said that Jimmy's voice sounded the same, it was eerie.

Jimmy said that that was the only thing the same about him. He was fatter and older and he had no hair left. The thing was, he said, he'd been doing too much thinking over the last year and it wasn't good thinking. "Vagaries of the past," he said.

"Speak English," Charles said.

"Whims and dreams. I keep seeing things. After all these years you'd think that the ugly stuff would disappear." He said that he was trying to make contact with some of the guys. "Do you ever see any of them?"

Charles said he'd talked to Harry a number of years back but it hadn't been useful. Then he said that if Jimmy wanted to fly into Vancouver someday, Charles would pick him up and show him his handsome house on the hill, which was actually a rebuilt caboose. "But, still handsome," Charles said.

Jimmy said that these days the only traveling he did was in his head. He didn't have the wherewithal to carry himself beyond his job and family and his armchair. "But let me tell you something, Charlie. I've got this novel I want you to read. It's something I stumbled across and I think it's important. It's right on. I'll send it to you."

Charles said that he wasn't a big reader, that he liked hunting books, or stories about horses.

"There're no horses in this one, but I'll send it. It's written by a former soldier from North Vietnam. You know, those guys we were trying to kill." Jimmy laughed and said that there was little in the novel that resembled what had happened to them, but in fact, it did feel right, there was a connection. "The madness. You'll understand."

"And what do you do with the madness?" Charles asked.

"Nothing. Have to wait till we die, don't you think? Look at Abel."

"But Harry or Alex B., they just float through it."

"That's because they don't think. And if you don't think, then everything's easy. Those guys'll always stay that way."

They talked about their children then, a commonsense conversation that whiled away the minutes and left Charles lonely and breathless. He wondered, after he hung up, why he couldn't see the world around him as whole.

Jimmy did as he promised. He sent the novel. It was called *In a Dark Wood*. There was a photograph of the author, Dang Tho, on the back flap of the book's jacket. He looked younger than Charles or Jimmy. He had a mustache and sad, intense eyes. There was a biographical note beneath the photo. It said Dang Tho was born in Hanoi in 1952. During the Vietnam War he served with the Glorious Youth Brigade and was one of the few survivors from that brigade. *In a Dark Wood* was a harrowing, nonheroic retelling of Dang Tho's own war experience.

Stuck inside the novel was a short note from Jimmy. He wrote that everything was running along ricky-tick, except he'd just been diagnosed with diabetes. Had to get more exercise and stop smoking. And he'd signed his name.

Charles put the book on the shelf.

He picked it up early one morning when he couldn't sleep. He had finished the first section by the time the sun fell through the window onto his lap. He looked up from the pages and heard the call of a crow, loud and raucous. For a moment, he was startled from his reverie. He returned to the book.

He came down out of the Central Highlands, avoided Kontum, and moved slowly toward the coast, walking at night, sleeping in caves and under heavy bushes during the day; as a deserter, if found, he would be shot. His clothes were dirty and worn; he carried a small bag tied in a knot, and in it was a bit of rice, some plantain, and a little salt that he had stolen from the abandoned pack of an American soldier, castoffs left in the haste of evacuation or death. It had been a lucky find; besides the salt he had found a pen and a sheaf of paper, as well as tins with fruit and some kind of bean, and a handgun, a small knife, some medicine with syringes, matches, and a green poncho. He kept everything but the gun, which might incriminate him in some way if he was captured. He had discovered boots as well, much too big for him, but if he stuffed leaves in the toes and tied the boots tightly around his ankles, they protected his feet, though they were heavy, clumsy, and inefficient. In the end the boots became a burden and he threw them away.

He walked for ten days, and during that time he had talked to only one person, a farmer east of Kontum who had offered him a place to sleep and some food. The food he took, but he refused the shelter. One morning he was nearly discovered by a group of thirteen North Vietnamese soldiers. They passed within a few feet of his hiding place. He woke and heard the soft pat of flip-flops and saw the thin ankles, and long after they had continued down the path, he lay there, hardly breathing. He had been dreaming and in his dream Tuan was calling his name, "Kiet, Kiet," and though he kept turning to find Tuan, he couldn't.

Tuan had been in his company. He had been killed in a

battle two weeks earlier. All over that hillside, men died. Men whom Kiet had fought with and slept beside and shared jokes with, most of these men died. They had been defending a hill. Had been dug in for months, with tunnels and a field hospital. Except the Americans had kept targeting the bunkers with gunships and bombers. In the end, it had been a slaughter, complete mayhem, men all around Kiet losing heads and arms, entrails spilling onto the earth. Kiet had been in a bunker with Tuan when Tuan stood up beside him and fell backward; a bullet had passed through his head, taking off half of his face.

Kiet, one of a few, had survived. At night, surrounded by the complaints and cries of the dying and injured, he moved down the hillside, made his way past the American lines, and carried on through the jungle toward Kontum and beyond toward the coast and then north. He had not planned to desert. It simply became a fact when he realized that he was walking away. The first few days, huddled in his hideouts, he would listen to the sound of his own breath, or study his hands and arms, and wonder how it was that he was still whole, that his fingers still counted ten, that his eyes were two, that he could chew and swallow and shit. He recorded these facts with the solemn astonishment of a man slightly mad who had not yet registered the guilt of survival. "You lucky bastard, Kiet," he muttered one day, and even the sound of his own voice surprised him.

He thought of his lover, Lien, whom he had left in Hanoi so long ago. He did not know if she was alive or dead. A year and a half earlier he had managed to put a letter into the hands of an injured soldier who was returning to Hanoi. In the letter Kiet told her that he was still alive and though she might be surprised by this, he hoped that it was a good surprise. He said more, much of it sentimental, and later he was sorry that he had written words that would seem self-pitying and unnecessary. How did one talk about love that had been untried for so long?

There had been no reply. If an attempt had been made by Lien, Kiet did not know of it. He wrote letters to her anyway, more specific and despairing, and he took these letters and stored them in a bag that he carried with him—tucked the bag inside his shirt and tied it round his neck. Always, sleeping or eating or fighting, he was aware of the bag and of the letters close to his body. Sometimes, he pulled these letters out and reread them.

On his fifteenth day he entered Hue Province, an area known for its sympathies to the South. He traveled carefully, still walking at night, but even so he sometimes caught sight of soldiers from the South Vietnamese Army, or he heard gunfire, or the passing of a fighter jet. Setting out early one morning, he bypassed a village north of Hue and came across a young woman washing clothes at the bank of the river. She looked up as he stepped along the path. She rose and gathered up a bundle beside her; turning to run, she called out. He caught her and covered her mouth as she struggled. Forcing her to kneel, he whispered in her ear that if she was not quiet he would kill her. The bundle she held was a baby. It began to cry and Kiet told her to make it stop. The woman sat and slipped out a breast and pushed the baby's mouth against the breast. Kiet watched. The woman whimpered. Kiet took the knife from his small bag and asked if she was alone. Was it just her and the baby? The woman nodded. Kiet looked around. In the distance was the village. Cooking smoke lifted to the sky. The shouts of children. A woman calling.

When the baby had finished, the woman set it down and took Kiet's hand, put it to her face, and held it there. She didn't say anything, just held his hand there. Then she moved it down to her breast and made him touch her. Kiet had not been close to a woman for two years. He touched her breasts, first the right and then the left. Then she lay back against the ditch and pulled Kiet down beside her and took his hand and placed it between her legs.

The baby began to cry.

"Make it stop," Kiet said.

The woman lifted the baby to her shoulder but it struggled and cried louder. The woman offered the breast but this was rejected by the baby, who began to howl. The woman shook it desperately. Kiet looked about. In the distance, three men from the village were standing on the trail, looking in the direction of the noise. They carried scythes. One had a machine gun.

Kiet took the baby from the woman and pressed his hand against the small mouth.

The woman cried out, "No," but Kiet pushed her away and took the knife in his hand. The white sky, the gray smoke, the blue pants of the men, the brilliance of the sun off the blade of the scythe, the thin red line at the baby's throat, an infant's howl descending into a mother's wail, and then that wailing, too, gone, disappearing like the pink bubble that rose from the opening at the mother's neck.

OVER THE NEXT DAYS HE WALKED QUICKLY, BYPASSING villages, halting at the sound of voices, circling well-worn paths, and keeping off all roads. A week later he crossed the Demilitarized Zone in pouring rain and dug himself a hole in a bamboo stand, covering himself with the poncho and leaves and dirt. He slept poorly; the rain pooled at the bottom of the hole, reaching his ankles and soaking his back.

He woke shivering, considered making a fire, and decided against it.

For the next while he followed the train tracks, slipping away as the trains passed. The southbound trains carried troops heading into battle; there was often singing, and sometimes soldiers sat on the roofs of the cars, smoking and looking out at the passing countryside. The northbound trains were full of the injured and dead. The cars were coffins; there was no singing. Men, if they were able to sit, rested their bandaged heads against the window, or cradled the stump of an arm or leg. Once, a soldier leaned out a window and called out to the emptiness, "Here, here," and then the train passed.

Early one morning, Kiet came across a soldier sitting at the edge of a path by a small stream. The soldier was very young, a boy really. Kiet circled the boy, studying him. He was gaunt and tall and claimed to be hungry. He was blind.

"Who are you?" the blind boy asked. Kiet thought that, based on the accent, the boy might come from a more northern province.

Kiet said that he was a man on his way back to Hanoi.

The blind boy looked up expectantly to the spot where he imagined Kiet was standing and said that he too was walking back to Hanoi. He had been blinded by a grenade, spent three months in a hospital, and was now going home. They could go together.

Kiet said that he couldn't. He was a deserter, and if it was dangerous for him alone, it would be even more dangerous if he traveled with a blind man.

The boy nodded at this. He said that he too was a deserter, but even so, what could he do if he fought? "Shoot at noises?" he asked.

They sat by the river. Occasionally, the boy tried to convince Kiet to take him along, but Kiet said no.

When Kiet rose to go, the boy stood as well. He swung an arm as if to seek out Kiet's location. Kiet said good-bye. The boy followed his voice. Finally, in disgust, Kiet agreed to walk the boy to a place where he could find shelter and food. They spent the day in the protection of a lee of rocks and in the evening set out. They made a wretched pair: a short resolute man called Kiet, and a much taller blind boy whose name Kiet did not know and who, at times, because of the darkness and the rain and mud, was tied to Kiet with a thin rope fashioned from the trousers of a man found dead at the edge of the train tracks.

THEY BEGAN TO WALK DURING THE DAY AND SLEEP AT night, and when Kiet slept he dreamed. In one of his dreams fire fell from the sky and Tuan's face appeared as whole and smiling, calling out Kiet's name and the name of Kiet's lover, Lien, and then Tuan asked, "What is that you're holding?" and Kiet looked down and saw the dead baby and he woke crying out. This roused the blind boy as well, who sat up and called, "What is it? Are you there?"

Kiet did not speak. He held his head and rocked in the darkness until it was time to rise and continue walking.

The dream came again and again. Sometimes he was holding the baby, sometimes the mother. Always, he woke shaking and calling out.

One night, rather than sleep and invite the dream, he stayed awake and watched the sky, trying to locate different constellations. The next day he was exhausted and when the blind boy suggested they rest, Kiet sat down with relief and fell asleep immediately, dreaming only briefly of Lien, who beckoned to him from across a wide river.

Kiet did not tell the blind boy about his dreams, nor did he tell him about the killing of the baby and the mother. What was there to tell? And if the story were told, how would it differ from any other that the war produced? He was not sure anymore what had actually taken place. He began to be convinced that a fever had produced the images and that, when he arrived home, all would be forgotten.

ONE DAY, WHEN THE RAIN HAD FINALLY STOPPED, THEY stumbled across a pig that had escaped its owner. Kiet chased this pig for an hour before finally trapping it in a slow-moving stream. The blind boy sat astride the pig and seized its ears while Kiet held the knife and considered the pig's heavy neck. He told the blind boy that he could not do what was required. As he spoke, the pig set to bucking and screaming. To stop the noise, Kiet searched desperately for some other weapon. He finally found a large boulder and dropped it on the pig's skull. They managed to bleed the pig, and then the blind boy sawed at the pig as Kiet called instructions. They fashioned pointed sticks and pierced large pieces of flesh. They built a small fire in the heat of the afternoon and around that fire the two of them squatted and had their first taste of meat in months. As they ate, the blind boy asked Kiet why he had had such difficulty killing the pig.

Kiet did not answer. He ate and looked at the sky, which had turned a bright blue. He told the blind boy about the color of the sky, comparing it to the bowl out of which he had eaten rice as a child.

Perhaps because of the heaviness of their meal, or perhaps because of the satisfaction taken in providing for themselves, when they had finished eating, they lay down near the bank of the river and fell asleep.

They were rudely awakened by a trio of soldiers who

stood above them, giants extending into the blue sky. Two of
the soldiers were young, one was old. The eldest spoke. He
accused Kiet and the blind boy of being deserters. He said
that he would have to shoot them.

They were bound and blindfolded. The blind boy said,
"Look at my eyes, you don't need to cover them." He offered them the rest of the pig.

The men laughed and said that they should be ashamed
of their fear.

Kiet, blindfolded, was aware of the sounds of the river
and the click of the magazine in the gun. One of the men
was chewing loudly. A match was struck. The smell of cigarette smoke. The blind boy said that he would like a cigarette. This was denied him. The blind boy said that he had to
urinate; he didn't want to soil himself. The men said he was
already soiled. Every time someone spoke Kiet tilted his head
to catch the timbre and tone of the voice; he listened for possible forgiveness, tried to sense which of the three men might
be most lenient. There was one man who had barely spoken.
Kiet called out that he had a story to tell. Would they please
listen to his story? And then they could shoot him. One man
was interested. He asked what the story might be. Was it an
important story? Was it erotic? Or was it tragic?

Kiet said that it could be whatever they wanted.

So it is not a true story? the men asked.

Absolutely true, Kiet answered.

Tell us then.

Kiet said that he could not tell a story in the dark. He had
to see his listeners. He lifted his chin to indicate his need.

It was the quiet soldier who removed his blindfold.

Take off the other's as well, Kiet said. The soldier standing before him was young and thin. He was barefoot and he
carried nothing except a stick that he used as a staff.

The young man freed the blind boy as the other two soldiers grumbled.

Kiet was prodded with the barrel of a rifle. Go on.

He said that the story was an age-old one. He asked the men if they had lovers or wives at home. Two of the men said they did. Kiet confessed that he too had a lover at home and it was the idea of reunion with her that kept his feet moving each day. He said that he carried in his mind an image of his lover and there were days when he was no longer sure if that image was true or not.

One of the soldiers interrupted Kiet. He said that the story wasn't a story at all but a confessional. He, personally, was hungry and interested in eating the pig and if Kiet had nothing better to say then he might as well be shot.

Kiet said that a story was only a story if it had a beginning, a middle, and an end. He was still at the beginning. And so he spoke. He said that there was once a young man from Hanoi who went off to fight in a war. He left behind a lover and a child. The lover was beautiful, but it was the child that remained forever in the soldier's mind. The child was his blood. The woman wasn't.

The man fought in many battles and learned that death was indiscriminate. In his last battle all of the men around him were killed. He was not. That night he left the battlefield and ran. He crossed rivers and mountains and bypassed cities and fled from bandits. He was going home to his lover and child.

Kiet paused. He looked at the soldiers and then continued. But at this point he began to tell his own story. He explained how the soldier stumbled upon a woman and a baby beside a stream. And how the woman tried to deceive the soldier, first by lying with him, and then by calling out for help. And so, said Kiet, the mother and child had to be killed.

He stopped. Looked at the three men, who had laid down their guns and were squatting near the pig. At that point, aware that the ending to his tale should remain as distant as the hills beyond the fields, he threw himself back into the story and discovered details he himself had not known. He described the woman's hair, her clothes, and the way she lay back against the grass and invited the young soldier to hold her. He detailed the length of her neck before it had been cut. He talked about the young soldier's grief after he committed the act. "Don't you see?" said Kiet. "He had no choice."

Kiet said he was thirsty. Could he take a drink from the stream?

The youngest soldier agreed. The other two said no. An argument broke out. The oldest soldier said that the story was almost finished and he wanted to hear the end. The thin young soldier said that if the teller of the story was thirsty, certainly he should be able to drink. And besides, he was not sure if the story was nearing completion. He asked if it was.

The three soldiers looked to Kiet, who shrugged and said that though all endings were elusive, a conclusion was inevitable. In the distance, beyond their backs, a small black figure ran toward the group, brandishing a gun. He was not noticed by anyone except Kiet, who thought it might be a comrade of the three bandits, or another wandering madman, or perhaps someone sent to save him. In any case, understanding that fate could not push him any nearer to death, he said nothing until the figure in black, who turned out to be the farmer, stood before the five men, pointed his gun at the oldest soldier's head, and asked who had killed his pig.

Kiet was aware of the sun behind the farmer's head. He was aware that the first to speak would save himself. And so, he spoke. He said that he and his blind friend had been lost

and had come across these three men feasting on this pig. He
motioned at the pig, and then at the soldiers, who stood and
backed away. Their guns lay on the ground and they glanced
at them as if gauging distance and opportunity.

In a rage the farmer shot above the heads of the soldiers
and chased them off. Then, without another word to Kiet
and the blind boy, he contrived a way to carry the dead pig
home. As he tied a rope around the pig's rear legs, Kiet took
the blind boy's hand and led him down the stream and out of
sight.

"We are alive?" the blind boy asked. Kiet said that they
were, though barely.

IN ORDER TO PUT DISTANCE BETWEEN THEMSELVES AND
the farmer, they walked through the day and the night until
heavy rain forced them to take shelter in a cave. They stayed
there for three days with a monk who was traveling south.
The monk did not speak for the first two days and on the
third day he woke from what appeared to be a deep sleep and
he asked Kiet and the blind boy where they were going. Kiet
talked about finding the blind boy and he told the story of
the three soldiers and the accusation of desertion and the
blindfolds and the rescue.

The monk listened to Kiet and then, as monks are wont to
do, he spoke in riddles and half-truths. He wondered why it
was always necessary to cover the eyes of a man you were
going to kill. He said that sight was not everything; in fact,
the blind often saw more than those with two good eyes and
it was unfortunate that this was not understood. He talked
about life and death. He said that there is always a yes and a
no and that you cannot have one without the knowledge of
the other. He said that life feeds on death and death on life.

"Look around you," he said. The monk had some fruit and some cooked rice and the three of them shared this food until it was gone.

At the end of the third day the monk disappeared; Kiet woke from a sleep and saw the blind boy lying on his back, but he did not see the monk. The boy said that he had heard him leave several hours earlier. Then the boy asked Kiet to complete the story of the woman and the baby.

Outside the rain had stopped. The leaves were still dripping but the sun was shining and Kiet saw the light as it fell through the trees. He said that there was nothing to tell. The story wasn't finished yet.

The blind boy considered this information and then said he preferred stories that had doors on them, so that when you were finished, you could shut the door and be done with it. "Did you make it up?" he asked.

Kiet said that the story was true.

The blind boy nodded. He did not speak for a long time after this.

Four days later, in a small village outside Dong Hoi, they passed a school courtyard where a beauty contest was taking place. Kiet and the blind boy stood back from the crowd and listened to the girls recite poetry and sing. Kiet described the movements of the girls and the color of their *ao dai*s. He said that the most beautiful girl was perhaps the oldest; when she moved it reminded him of water flowing over a smooth rock. He said that her neck was long, her back was straight, and her breasts were barely visible.

A week later they slept close to the bank of a fast-flowing river and in the middle of the night were set upon by a lone crazed soldier who waved his pistol in the air and demanded they feed him. They had not eaten in three days, not since a farmer and his wife had offered them manioc and a few grains of rice. Kiet told the madman that they had nothing. Nothing to eat. Nothing to offer.

He did not believe them. He had them strip. He went through their rags and, finding nothing, circled them. He waved his gun before the blind boy's eyes and elicited no response. He repeated the gesture. He turned to Kiet and asked if he was a soldier.

Kiet said he wasn't. He was aware of the blind boy's thinness and of his own nakedness.

"And this one?" the soldier asked.

The blind boy answered that he had been a soldier with a North Vietnamese battalion fighting near Saigon, but that he had been discharged because he had been injured. He said that a blind man could not shoot a gun.

The soldier leaned toward the boy as if to sniff him. He touched his scars and pushed a finger against one of the milky eyes. Then he said that a blind man could shoot a gun, he just had to practice. He took the boy's hand and put the gun into it and raised it so that it was pointed at Kiet. He said, "Shoot."

Kiet did not move or speak. He saw the barrel of the gun and the blind boy's finger on the trigger. He felt nothing. A few days ago—or had it been even longer?—he had decided that death might be preferable to wandering the countryside, being pushed about by the whims of man and nature. His hunger had left him weak. He no longer had a conscience; he was a rat tunneling his way from one disaster to another.

The blind boy did not shoot.

The soldier became impatient and told the boy, once again, to shoot. He had stepped back and was midway between the boy and Kiet. The boy's hand, the one that held the gun, began to shake. He said that he did not know where his friend was and he did not want to hit someone by accident.

The soldier laughed and said that there would be no accident.

Kiet spoke then. Very calmly, he told the boy to shoot the soldier. He told him to aim at the voice. "Aim lower than the voice," he said.

The soldier laughed, thinking this impossible, and the boy, hearing the laughter, pointed the gun at the sound and pulled the trigger. He shot six times. The first bullet hit the soldier in the chest and the rest of the bullets missed because the soldier had fallen immediately with the first shot, which had killed him.

They buried the soldier in a shallow grave near the fast-flowing river. He wore boots, possibly stolen from some poor victim. These they shared, switching left for right and so on as they walked. Two days later, the blind boy announced that he could not walk further. Kiet said that he would carry him. He sat down, pulled the boot off the blind boy's left foot, and put it on his own. Then, he stood and picked up the boy. It was like hefting a sack of chaff. There was no weight. As Kiet walked he talked to the blind boy. He said that soon they would find someone to feed them. They would eat and drink and they would sleep under a roof and when they had regained their strength they would carry on. He told the blind boy that he knew a girl in Hanoi and that he loved the girl very much and that he had promised her he would return.

The blind boy answered that there were many men who had promised the same thing but they were dead and would not return.

Kiet said that he would return. He would not die.

He carried the blind boy for three days until, on the evening of the third day, the boy died. He must have died on Kiet's back because, when they stopped for the night and

Kiet rolled the boy off his shoulders onto the ground, there
was simply a loosening of the body and a snapping back of
the head.

Kiet stood and looked down at the boy. He did not need to
test for breath or pulse. He knew. He slept that night beside
the boy, waking often to see if perhaps the boy had not been
dead at all but only sleeping. In the morning he picked up the
body and continued north. He walked alongside the rail
tracks, waiting for a train. When one finally passed it did not
slow down and he saw that the cars were full and that some
men were sitting on top of the cars. He waved with one hand
and even dropped the boy and chased after the train, but it
eventually disappeared and he returned to retrieve the boy's
body. He was weak and had to rest often, sitting beside the
tracks with the boy at his feet. There was a sweet smell rising
from the boy, and as he walked, the boy's arms and legs
draped over his shoulders, Kiet knew that the boy was de-
caying and that soon he would have to bury him.

He did this one evening in Quang Binh Province. Near
a small river he set the boy down and piled rocks on top of
him. He worked through the night, pausing to sleep and then
waking to seek out more stones. By morning the cairn was
complete. He left the boy and retraced his path to the rail line
and sat down to wait. A woman passed by and gave him a
piece of bread. He chewed slowly and felt the ache of his jaw
and stomach. He saw the bones in his hands and arms and
legs. The boots he wore were too large, and the legs and
ankles that protruded from them were the limbs of a small
bird.

He slept. And in his sleep he saw the blind boy and the pig
and the beautiful girl with the small breasts and the dead soldier's mouth moving, commanding the boy to shoot, and he
dreamed of the girl to whom he was returning and he woke

from his dreams believing that he had crossed over and that
all was well.

THE SUN THAT FELL ONTO CHARLES'S LAP WAS WARM. IT WAS
early morning. There was no fire in the stove and so the cold of the
night had crept into the house and touched at his feet and hands
and seeped up under his shirt and the sun was a blessing. He stood
and laid the book down. Looked out the window at his yard, the
pickup, the stack-log shed, the one goat grazing beside it.

He would not have been able to explain, to anyone who asked,
why this particular story had moved him, but he felt kinship with
something. Perhaps it was Kiet returning from the war only to find
he was alone, or the disappointment in the betrayal of a lover, or
the shedding of innocent blood, though in Kiet's case it seemed
less random and more necessary. The fact was Kiet was a creation,
a ghost wandering north toward Hanoi. Charles was intrigued by
the author of the novel, by his brooding photograph and the sadness that seemed to hover behind or above him. Charles set the ket-
tle on the stove and turned the element to high. He thought about
his children. He thought how lives could slip away, undiscovered.
He saw himself as a liar, though he didn't know that the truth
would necessarily help anyone.

All through that day and the next he worked around the yard
and pondered different possibilities. Then, on Friday, when the
sun was trying to appear but not quite managing, he called on
Tomas and, for the first time in all the years he had known him,
asked if he wanted to go hunting over the weekend. He told Tomas
that it was time to build a little trust and there was nothing better
for trust than hunting. They were standing in Tomas's kitchen and
Charles was looking at the décor, the cement walls and the metal
conduit for the wiring, and he imagined he was in a prison. Tomas
grinned and put his arm around Del's small shoulders. She was

twenty-five now and had filled out happily, though sometimes she came back to the caboose for the night to get away from the moodiness of Tomas, who because he was an artist, thought he had the right.

Tomas gave Del a squeeze and said, "I'd like that, Charles."

They left on a Tuesday morning. Drove up Highway 97 toward Prince George and stayed in a motel with two single beds. At night Charles woke and he heard Tomas breathing deeply, with a slight whistle at the intake. He thought of Del lying beside this man. The evening before, they had eaten dinner at a restaurant in town, and they had talked about Tomas's art and about luck and about Del. Tomas claimed it was all luck, his success, his meeting Del. "I was invited to a dinner just by chance, and at that dinner I met a girl who happened to like me and I happened to like her and from there love took its own route. It's funny, but I'm certain that we can't plan love." He had been eating asparagus in hollandaise as he spoke, spearing tails and folding them into his mouth, and for some reason Charles pictured the asparagus as intimate parts of his daughter. Then Tomas talked about the gift shop Del was running in the Valley and how they planned to sell some of Tomas's art down there. It was Del's idea. "The smaller pieces," Tomas said. "She figures there's a market, that I should be selling as well here in Canada as I do in Europe, and who am I to argue with that?"

Charles finished his baked potato and drank the last of his beer and said that he had had his doubts but it was obvious Del was happy and he, Charles, wasn't a destroyer of happiness.

Tomas said, "There was a time, at the beginning, when you frightened me." He smiled slightly and eyed Charles. "That day you came to visit me in my shop. You remember?"

"Of course, I remember." Charles sat back. He said, "She's still my daughter."

"But older now."

Charles didn't answer. He realized that he still harbored a dislike for this beefy man who not only had money and confidence but seemed to take it for granted that success was his right.

But now, lying beside Tomas and listening to him breathe, Charles was enveloped in a sadness that went beyond his daughter and the man she had chosen. He had hoped, as he always did when he went on hunting trips, that the prospect of stalking a wolf or bear through the bush would carry him away. But more and more, this journey took him into a darker place. It would be after this particular trip, on the following Saturday, that Charles would drive down into Abbotsford and buy another ticket for Hanoi, via Bangkok.

In the morning they drove to see the outrigger, a friend of Charles's. They set their route and rented an ATV to drive up into the woods. Charles handed Tomas the 300 Winchester and showed him how to load and fire. Wrapping his left hand around the barrel, he said, "This is a semiautomatic hunting rifle. It's extremely accurate up to seven hundred yards and it'll kill animals both big and small. Never aim it at anything that you don't want to shoot." He looked at Tomas and said, "And it's got some good recoil. Here." He patted his shoulder. "So hold on to it."

They rode several hours that morning and saw quail and an eagle high above, and when they stopped for lunch, a fox crossed in front of them, lifted its nose, skipped sideways, and disappeared. Charles had to point this out to Tomas, who seemed incapable of seeing what was in front of him. Charles said, "Look for the shape of something, not the actual thing. An animal is in its natural habitat and has disguises. The only thing it can't hide is its shape."

Toward evening, they saw a wolf just above the tree line. It was cutting across the mountain with an easy lope. Without a word, before Charles could call out that it was too far, Tomas raised his rifle, sighted, and fired. The wolf went down and got up immediately and continued running toward the tree line, where it disappeared. They rode for a day. Followed the tracks and the blood. Late that evening they came to a small stream into which the tracks disappeared. Charles crossed over and walked one bank while Tomas walked the other, looking for the place where the wolf had exited. The size of its paw prints indicated it was a large animal, bigger than anything Charles had ever seen, but he didn't tell Tomas this. They walked for a mile and then, finding nothing, turned back.

The next morning, Charles woke early and climbed the trail above the camp. Reaching a point where he could look down on the camp, he sat on a rock and watched the smoke from the fire curl upward. He saw Tomas climb out of the tent, stand, and stretch and look around. Tomas called out, a faint "hello," and Charles thought, in that moment, that the man was a fool. He sighted the scope of his Browning and laid the crosshair inside Tomas's left ear. He felt nothing, just a slight breeze on his neck and the smoothness of the stock against his cheek.

Once, out hunting alone a few years earlier, Charles had felt like he was walking point again and he had heard a sharp crack and panicked and dropped and covered his head. When he'd looked up from the mulch of boughs and wet leaves, he saw a pheasant staring at him. It was shaped like a pear; one eye opened and closed sleepily. Charles had laughed, and the pheasant had thumped its wings and exploded upward.

Now, his back against the flat rock, Tomas's ear in his scope, he was taken back, and he felt the easy power and the fear. He could shoot the man. He wanted, for a small moment, to shoot the man. But he didn't. He swung his scope and sighted the ATV and the tent and then, further east, he located the trail they had descended the day before. Upwind, just at the edge of the trail, he saw the wolf. At first he thought it might be a grizzly, because of the size and silver fur at the neck, but then it began to limp down toward the camp and Charles recognized the long lope. He watched it approach the camp, sliding west and then east, favoring its right front leg. He imagined that the wolf had found their day-old scent but hadn't yet caught wind of the camp. Tomas was moving around, laying out a larger fire, cooking.

Charles thought that as soon as the wolf heard Tomas or smelled him, it would retreat. Still, he watched through his scope. About two hundred yards from the camp the wolf stopped and smelled the air. Backed up slightly. Then it swiveled and slid through the brush and disappeared.

When Charles told Tomas about the wolf later, Tomas wanted to know why he hadn't killed it. "Too far? Was that it?"

"No, I could have shot it," Charles said. Then he said, "Could have shot you too."

Tomas looked up. His head turned and one eyelid fluttered and he put a finger up to stop it. "You're crazy," he said.

"I didn't shoot you, though, did I? You're still sitting here, eating bacon, drinking coffee."

Tomas didn't speak.

"That's what happens," Charles said. "We make certain decisions and the decision takes on a story and the story has a history of its own and the history becomes fact. Might be warped, but it's fact. Not a whole lot different than luck."

For two more days they tracked the big silver-backed wolf. At one point they came across a fresh kill, a young doe that had been hauled down by another animal, and they sighted a few black bear that were too young to shoot.

On the last night of the trip, after a few drinks of whiskey and a quiet evening around the fire, Charles climbed into the tent and fell asleep to the crack of the wood burning and the rustle of Tomas moving about the campsite. During the night he woke from a dream in which he had come face-to-face with the wolf and shot it between the eyes. He lay on his back in the dark, his hands clutching the sleeping bag. In the dream, just before he killed

THE TIME IN BETWEEN 93

the wolf, it had called out in a language that was mournful and ancient.

WHEN JIMMY POE HAD SENT CHARLES THE BOOK, CHARLES HAD read it over the period of a day and a night, and then, almost immediately, he had begun to read it again. In some ways he was like a man who had lost something of value years ago and had just now become aware of that loss. At the end of the novel Kiet has just come back from the war to a city that is ghostly and alien. He wanders the streets, calling out for a lost lover. He suffers from nightmares and takes solace in sleeping with a woman who lives near him. There is the gray light, the rubble in the streets, the green of a tree growing out of a bomb crater, the scent of a light rain dusting the street.

Charles imagined himself falling out of the sky and landing in that place. He did not see the impracticality of that. And so in October, twenty-eight years after leaving Vietnam as a young soldier, Charles made the return trip, thinking that in some way he might conclude an event in his life that had consumed and shaped him. He was not entirely hopeful; in fact, because of this lack of hope, he cheerfully told his children that he would be traveling as a tourist. There would be no real intent, he said.

In Hanoi, upon first arriving in Vietnam, he found a room in a run-down hotel with uneven stairs and cold-water showers. For the first two days he suffered from jet lag; he slept during the day and at night he looked out through dirty windows to the neighbor's balcony and beyond into a badly lit room where a man was reading. One evening, late, he left his hotel and walked down to Hoan Kiem Lake. He remembered, in Dang Tho's novel, that there were scenes in and around this lake. However, the description of the city and the lake was different from what he was seeing now. In the book, the city was harder and dirtier. It had just survived massive bombing, and people wandered around in a wasteland.

His third morning in Hanoi he bought a train ticket for Danang, and then he spent the remainder of the day wandering the old city. At a sidewalk restaurant he ate a soup with things he didn't recognize floating in it, and the hawkers called out to him as he passed them by. Once, out of curiosity, he had his shoes shined and he found himself mesmerized by the quick hands and the dark head of the young boy working at his shoes. A girl wearing a gray felt hat rode by on her bicycle, in her basket a bundle of pink flowers. The light was dusty. The air was cool. He sat in a coffee shop and drank iced coffee. In his bag he had the novel. He took it out, and on one of the blank pages at the back he wrote down that day's date and beneath it he wrote "Hanoi." He looked up and saw a woman in a red *ao dai* hang laundry off her balcony. He wrote down what he saw, describing the woman's fluid movements and the color of the sky. He wrote that the blank page was daunting and whatever he chose to write would seem unimportant. Later, he bought three postcards and sent them to his children, saying that never had he seen so much activity and that everyone, except for him, seemed to move hastily and with great purpose.

He left Hanoi by train and traveled through the night, riding second-class. At each stop, girls with platters of sticky rice and sweet treats passed through the car or called out from beneath the open windows. Candles were mounted on the platters and so the effect was sacred; the flames waved and beckoned and in some cases died, and then were instantly reborn.

He slept and when he wasn't sleeping he watched his companions. Across from him there was a young couple with a newborn. The baby was silent and at one point Charles thought it might be dead. But the mother, a girl of shocking beauty, held a bottle against the baby's mouth and it stirred and sucked and the girl raised her eyes, caught Charles watching, and looked away. The husband slept and woke occasionally, only to rise and stand by the open doors, at the back of the car, and smoke. When he returned, he ate an orange and then slept some more. He had a perfectly groomed mustache and he wore shoes of brown leather and dark slacks that were badly pressed.

It was a slow trip south with numerous stops. Charles dreamed on and off. They were surprising dreams, in that they were neither dark nor troubling. Laughter figured in some, and singing. In one dream he was young and marrying a girl with red hair and the girl was not Sara but she said his name, Charlie, as Sara had. They danced while a violin played a jig and at the end of the dance the girl turned to him and said his name again and she kissed his chest, just below the throat. Then the train stopped and he woke. The mother across from him was sleeping. She had placed the baby between herself and her husband and she had curled up her legs to stop the infant from rolling onto the floor. It was awkward and impossible, but still, she slept.

The couple with the baby left the train at a midmorning stop. They were replaced by a grandmother and a child of about twelve, who was carrying a bamboo cage with two birds. The child talked quickly and the grandma told her to shush. The child stuck a finger through the bamboo and the birds went wild and pecked at the girl and she laughed. Her black eyes sought out Charles and she said, "Hello, how are you?"

Charles said he was fine and asked, "How are you?"

"I am fine," the girl announced, and she giggled.

Later, at the request of her grandma, she put a brightly colored cloth over the cage and the sound of the birds disappeared.

At the station in Hue, Charles bought an iced coffee from a boy passing through the train. It was in a glass, and the boy disappeared and then returned to retrieve the glass just before the train left. Coming down through the pass beyond Hue, Charles saw the mountains falling away into the ocean and he could not remember such magnificence. Sometimes, their train passed another passenger train going in the opposite direction, and through the windows he caught flashes of families and children and groups of men dressed in army uniforms and old women smoking homemade cigars. The girl across from him played a game with two sticks. She talked to herself as she played. At one stop Charles bought her a yellowish candy that looked like peanut brittle. She took it and turned to her grandma, who was sleeping. Then she nodded and sucked on the candy.

When they arrived in Danang, he took a room at the Binh Duong Hotel. It offered a view of the river and the harbor and at night he sometimes woke to the desolate call of a ship. When he couldn't sleep, he stood by the open window of his fifth-floor room and he watched the city and listened to the noise of the traffic and he saw the lights of the boats far out at sea. He took his meals in small restaurants, usually eating dinner late and then walking back to the hotel. Sometimes he stopped close to the tennis courts on Quang Trung Street and smoked and watched the prostitutes. He wasn't lonely, but he thought that if he ever was, he would come back and hire the girl in black stockings.

Then one day, he met an American couple, Jack and Elaine Gouds. They found him; talked to him in a restaurant one evening and invited him to join their table. He agreed. There was Jack and Elaine and their daughter, Jane, and their son, Sammy, who thumped his fists against the table and called for noodles. He was introduced to Vo Van Thanh, a translator who was sitting with them. Charles explained that he was visiting Danang because this was where he had been stationed during the war. "I'm one of those burdened ex-soldiers, I guess." He lit a cigarette, blew the smoke to the ceiling, and shrugged. He held out the pack of cigarettes. Thanh waved a hand. Jack shook his head. Elaine looked at Charles, and then away, bending toward Sammy. She was brusque; when Jack asked her a question, she ignored him or answered curtly. She had a lovely neck, and when she looked up from Sammy's furrowed brow, Charles saw the pulsing of a vein. Her daughter, Jane, was more like the father, softer.

Jack said that Thanh would be a good man to hire if Charles needed a guide. "He's experienced. Knows the temperament of the West. Understands nuance. Isn't that right, Thanh?"

Thanh deferred. He shook his head and said, "Not right."

"See?" Jack laughed. Put a hand on Thanh's shoulder.

Charles learned that the Gouds were in Danang because of Jack. He had taken a year off work as a salesman to live in Danang, where he said the average man had no idea who God was. He said that the Vietnamese authorities saw him as a teacher of English, but this was simply a way to obtain visas. "We have work to do," he said, and as he spoke he looked down into his glass of beer and then he lifted his head and said, "I love this country. But it is aimless."

Elaine said, "Jack has a mission." She shook her head as if the four words she had just uttered were the engine that was pulling the family to some unforeseen and terrible doom. Jane was eating ice cream out of a small glass bowl. She was watching her father and mother. Her face was round and morose.

Thanh listened to the conversation without any expression. He drank slowly, and his eyes moved from Jack to Elaine to Charles. He had a high forehead and what hair he had left was dark. Charles wanted to ask him questions but didn't.

When they left the restaurant, Elaine paused at the entrance and told Thanh to bring Charles over the next day. "Okay?" She said to Charles, "He'll pick you up and show you where we live. Come by for a glass of wine or something to eat." And then she left, as if she were used to giving orders and having them obeyed.

Thanh rode Charles back to his hotel. It was warm. The taillights of many motorcycles lit up the streets. Close to the hotel Thanh stopped at a kiosk and an old woman poured a whiskey bottle of gasoline into his tank. He stood beside his motorcycle, a small man wearing gray slacks and a white shirt with short sleeves. His shoes were worn and scuffed.

The next morning Thanh did as Elaine had asked. He took Charles to the Gouds's house. They sat on the balcony and looked out over the smoke of a misty morning. After a while Jack stood up and said that he and Thanh had to run some errands. When they had gone, Elaine served Charles coffee. She drank juice and chased it with coffee. She was wearing a loose-fitting black dress of a light material that fell to just above her knees. She was barefoot, her legs were bare as well, the dress was sleeveless; her mouth went up on one side in a sort of half smile.

She said, "Jane and Sammy are out at the market with the nanny."

Charles sat in a wicker chair with a soft cushion. He was surprised by the comfort and the amenities and he called the surroundings lavish. Elaine laughed and said that opulence was relative. There was a brief silence, not awkward, and then Elaine asked Charles why he was there and where he came from.

Charles talked about his children and about his life in Canada and as he spoke he saw how easily history could be related as both unblemished and inconsequential. He said, "Because I was a soldier here when I was young, I have memories and other things to settle. So, you see."

And she did seem to see. She was not as harsh as he had initially believed. When he smoked, she touched his arm and asked for a cigarette, bending toward his proffered light almost clandestinely, explaining that Jack disliked her smoking, and of course, she didn't want the kids to know.

There was something wistful about her. During his subsequent visits, he found himself drawn to her, to the oddity of her gestures and her habit of throwing her hands in the air as if she could not believe her circumstances. "Stupid country," she said, and her hands went up. Or at dinner, after several glasses of wine and an argument with Jack, she turned to Charles and whispered, "Jack be nimble." And her hands went up.

One Friday, late afternoon, he called on the family and she was alone; Jack had taken the children to the roller rink. She was on the balcony, sitting in her usual chair. Her bare legs, the half full glass of wine, the magazine in her lap—he noted and found pleasure in these things. She'd cut her hair. He mentioned this.

"Do you like it? Sort of flapper."

It was. The bangs highlighted her green eyes. He nodded and sat. He said that he was lost.

THAT DAY, HE HAD RENTED A CAR AND DRIVER AND ARRANGED TO go with Thanh down the Number One Highway, south into Quang Ngai Province. About an hour out of Danang they had turned onto a side road and had driven toward the mountains until they came to a small village. They got out of the car. There were a few houses made of wood and corrugated tin. A crowd gathered. Dogs and women and old men and young children. The children pulled at Charles's pants. Thanh pushed them away and spoke sharply, but no one listened to him. During the walk through the village the children kept pushing against Charles, and at one point a young boy wearing only shorts tried to put his hand in Charles's pocket. Charles grabbed his shoulder and said, "No."

He asked Thanh if this was it. Was he sure this was the village Charles had asked for.

Thanh addressed an old woman. He asked her a question and the woman looked around and said something. Thanh turned to Charles and said that this was the village.

Charles said, "Ask her if she was living here during the war."

Thanh did this. The woman shook her head and spoke quickly. Thanh said, "There is only one family left from the war. The mother is in Danang today with the grandfather. The son is at work. There is nobody else."

They walked through the village and then turned and walked back toward the car. Charles looked for the road, the rice paddies, the ditch. Nothing was familiar. He pushed the children away and walked out toward the fields and then stood and looked back at the village. The children had followed him. He told them to go away. They laughed and one boy kicked dirt at Charles's feet.

In the car, driving back, he asked Thanh how he had survived the war.

Thanh said that the story of his own life was insignificant and he went on to say, "It is just my life."

Charles asked him again what he had done. How he had lived.

They were sitting in the back of the car. The driver was an older man who wore a chauffeur's hat. Thanh placed a hand on Charles's forearm and leaned into him and said that his story was meager, that it was one thing to survive the war but another to survive after the war. But if Charles insisted, he would tell him.

. And so he told his story. In May 1975, Vietnamese civilians and soldiers who had fought for the South were ordered by the new government to register and attend reeducation camps. Each person was to appear with enough paper, pens, clothes, mosquito nets, personal effects, food or money to last ten days. Thanh, who had served with the South Vietnamese Army in Danang as an air-traffic controller, did not trust the promises of the new government, and so he left his wife and three young boys and ran into the hills and hid. He survived on roots and manioc and the occasional bowl of rice from a farmer. In March 1976, he was turned in by one of these same farmers, and he was placed in a reeducation camp.

He was in the camps for two years. There was constant hunger, he had to work six days a week, autobiographical essays were written in which he confessed to atrocities that he had not committed, he was beaten, his fellow prisoners were beaten. They were given one cup of water per day, and with this one had to quench his thirst, bathe, and wash clothes.

But it was the hunger that consumed the prisoners. Thanh said that when he slept, he dreamed of food. He would wake, and all around him in the dark was the sound of chewing and he realized that the prisoners were chewing in their sleep and that everyone, like him, was dreaming of food. He killed mice and slipped them into his trouser pockets. He ate them at night, his knees curled up to his chest. He ate the head first and then the feet and tail, and finally the body. He chewed slowly, and when he was finished he was even more hungry than before. All prisoners caught both mice and lizards, but eventually these disappeared and then the prey became centipedes and worms and spiders. Early one morning, Trinh Bao, a doctor who would die within the week from an infection, roasted a lizard over a fire and slowly ate it while the other prisoners squatted, coveting his feast.

Everyone talked of eating: while they worked, while they walked to and from work, and always before sleeping. When they did not talk of food, they thought about food. Thanh remembered his mother's barbecued pork with the finest slivers of ginger. One night he heard Hien, his neighbor, chewing quietly on something. Hien was weak and small and, during the day, was expected to dig up large roots with a small wooden spade. Thanh tried to help him, but it was difficult. The guards were not sentimental and disliked one prisoner helping another. Thanh touched Hien's back in the dark and whispered, "What are you eating? Be more quiet, or you'll be heard."

Hien stopped chewing, but later in the night, Thanh heard him again. In the morning Thanh noticed that the tip of Hien's finger was missing. Hien had eaten it. That day, Thanh caught a small snake and crushed its head with a shovel. He carried it back to the camp and tried to share it with Hien, but Hien refused. Again, at night, Hien chewed at his hand. Madness settled in like a fog.

Thanh did not know who was mad, he or Hien. During the day Hien wrapped his hand in a dirty cloth and during the night he ate. The hand became bruised and swollen. Thanh told Hien to go to the clinic. Hien laughed at him. His teeth were falling out, his hair was thin, his knees were bigger than his hips. He had been a pharmacist in Hue and he had four daughters and a wife who were waiting for him. His pharmacy had been turned into a government office. One night, in a moment of clarity, he told Thanh that he would not see his daughters again. The following morning he attacked a guard who was using the South Vietnamese flag as a dusting rag. Hien was beaten and then tied to a pole in the middle of the camp. He died two weeks later.

Thanh said that everything seemed distant. "Like Hien. I talk about him, but with little passion. He is dead. I am alive. And every day I need to feed myself, to feed my children. History does not fill my stomach."

Charles was aware of Thanh's affect, of the movement of his hands as he spoke. He seemed both animated and sorry, as if his desire to speak should be a cause of shame. He asked Thanh what had happened. How did he survive?

Thanh said that yes, he had survived. Obviously, he said, look at me. I am here sitting talking to you, Charles. He said that he was moved to Dong Hai, another prison outside of Hue. There he worked all day and through the night, slinging pieces of clay. When he was released in 1978, he went back to Danang, and to his wife, Nguyen Linh, and his three sons, who were now three and five and seven. He did not want revenge.

He taught his sons English. He read to them from books that he had stumbled across, or from books that his father, a former university professor, had kept from among his large library. He read *Tess* and *Hard Times*. There was a tattered copy of *The Old Man and the Sea* and this he read over and over again. *Ivan Denisovich* he read once, and he learned that all prisons are the same, only some are a little bit worse.

Of his three sons, he said, one would run to America, where he would study architecture at the University of Michigan, one would move down to Ho Chi Minh City to study medicine, and the youngest would stay in Danang and become a teacher and a boxer.

Because of his politics Thanh said that he could not go back to the job he had left. So, he acquired a small shack on Ong Ich Khiem Street and he set up a hardware store. He sold nails and turpentine and screws and lightbulbs and electrical wire of various gauges and brushes and bolts. He did not make enough to support his family. His wife worked as a cleaner at the hospital. His mother-in-law took care of the boys when they were young. And Thanh worked as a translator; for the Gouds family, sometimes for other foreigners. A sister in Canberra sent twenty dollars a month. He saw himself as defiant; sometimes he told friends that he was the true proletariat—he had no car, no real business, and no home. He had nothing to lose.

But still he behaved. Because to behave was to survive and survival was something he had learned while in prison. Survival required patience and a subtle cunning. And loyalty, Thanh said. When the last U.S. helicopters had prepared to lift off from the airport in Danang, Thanh had been on one. He had stood in the open doorway, the downdraft beating at his hair, and he had looked out at the city in the distance and the crowds of Vietnamese pushing against the wall of soldiers and he had thought of his mother and father and he had thought of his wife and he had turned to his friend who was also on the helicopter and said, "I cannot." He had climbed off the helicopter and walked back into the city. Two months later he fled into the hills.

WHEN CHARLES HAD TOLD ELAINE THAT HE WAS LOST—A CON-fession for which he was immediately sorry—she had not said anything, simply offered him a drink. She poured him a beer and handed it to him and he was aware of the shape of her body beneath her dress. He thought that he might be attracted to her and this was alarming. Here he was, sitting across from Elaine Gouds, and they were drinking together, and in his mind he was removing her dress while her husband was off roller-skating with their children. Becoming involved with an American woman from Kansas City had not been the goal of this trip.

He stood and looked over the balustrade at the street. He said, "Thanh told me his story today. About his life after the war."

"Oh," Elaine said. "I have heard bits of it. It sounds so sad."

"I don't know if he would put it that way."

"You're right, I sound patronizing."

"He was so matter-of-fact."

"Jack is convinced that grief and despair are a luxury and that a man like Thanh does not have the money or time or even the physical space for that luxury."

"He may be right," Charles said. Then he told her that he had traveled to a small village with Thanh. He had hoped to find something there, perhaps recall a memory, and he had found very little. He shrugged and said that the village had been tiny and dirty and nondescript, not the kind of place where anything momentous would have happened. "It felt small," he said. "Really small." Elaine crossed her legs. Her right sandal hung loose and Charles saw the narrowness of her foot. She seemed to be considering what he had just told her. She said that Jack and the children would be returning soon and did he want another beer. He accepted.

While she was gone he wandered from the balcony into the adjoining room. It was set up as a guest room, with a small cot and a side table and bamboo dresser. There was a photo of Elaine as a younger woman, standing beside a horse. She wore riding gear: the breeches, the boots, the hat, the gloves. The horse stood high above her. The shape of her bent elbow and the tightness of the breeches around her calves. The hat shadowed her eyes. He recognized the posture, the same one she used when she and Jack were at each other; sardonic and skeptical, yet precise too, especially in the way she held her head.

Elaine came back and touched his shoulder as she handed him another beer. She said, "What you were talking about. Being lost. Every morning I wake and imagine that today my life will tip over into chaos. And then when it doesn't, when I come safely to the end of the day, I am so relieved that I begin to think that Vietnam is not such a bad place and that any fear I might have felt must have been my imagination."

Charles watched Elaine carefully as she spoke. She had moved away from him and he saw her profile and the movement of her mouth. He wondered what it would be like to kiss her neck.

WHEN HE MET THANH, THE NEXT TIME, AT A CAFÉ NEAR THE harbor, Thanh was sitting with another man, whom he introduced as Hoang Vu. Thanh said that Vu was an artist, quite well known, but not as well known as Pablo Picasso. He chuckled, called for more iced coffee, and then lit a cigarette and studied Charles. "It is a fact," he said, "that a man from North America would not know many Vietnamese artists."

Charles had to admit that this was true, though he had just read a novel written by a Vietnamese author. "Dang Tho," he said. "Do you know it?"

"Everyone has read Dang Tho's novel," Thanh said. He confessed that he had certain misgivings about the novel. "This is a book that wants to say it is telling the truth, but it is very individualistic. Dang Tho took all those horrific years and said, 'This is about me.'"

Charles said, "The author had a story he needed to tell. Besides, any war and any suffering is about the individual. When I read the book it was like the author was sitting beside me and telling me secrets that he had not told anyone else. A young soldier starts out naïve and then realizes what he's gotten into, the danger, the chance, the throwing of the dice, which are probably loaded, and all he wants is to get back to Hanoi, to his lover. I haven't been able to climb up out of it." Charles paused, tapped out a cigarette, lit it, and exhaled.

Vu had been sitting with his legs crossed, looking out at the street as Charles and Thanh talked. He was a thin, sharp-featured man with long dark hair. Now he said, "Poet. That is what Tho means. His novel has been banned here in Vietnam. Some say that it didn't recognize the glory of the North's victory, or the sacrifices, others say it was too bleak." He shook his head. "An artist shouldn't try to please the public, he simply tells the truth as he sees it. Dang Tho wrote the novel five years ago, became famous, and since then only his close friends see him. He is, what is the word, a hermit?"

Charles said that *hermit* was right. Or *recluse*.

Vu repeated the word *recluse*, emphasizing the first syllable. "Sort of that," he said.

"Though," Thanh told Charles, passing a hand across his glass, "Vu here has met him."

"Once or twice only," Vu said. "In Hanoi. I know that he lives with his parents in an area close to the university, and that he has two children and that he cannot find work because his book has been banned. He also drinks at a certain café every evening until nine. His wife is an artist, this is how I met him. She is ten years younger than he is." Vu looked up. "A good artist."

For a moment, knowing this man had met Dang Tho, Charles felt estranged, as if the author had become suddenly separate from his character, Kiet. An image had been presented of a man who was cut off from the world and he imagined Dang Tho flailing helplessly.

Vu studied Charles. He leaned forward and confessed that Charles appeared to be a man who was more serious than most vis-

itors. He was curious if this was true or not. He would like to talk
more. He took from his bag a pen and paper and he wrote down his
address. He handed it to Charles, who slid the paper into his
pocket.

Thanh, as if to reenter the conversation, said that there were
two things to remember in Vietnam. "First, everyone you meet
will promise you things that they cannot give, and second, do not
let this country defeat you."

He said, "Let me tell you a story. About me. About Vietnam.
My son was to go to America on a scholarship. University of
Michigan. We had the airline tickets and everything was set except
for the final approval. A signature of course. Well, I had a friend
who could get the signature for me. He said, 'Thanh, you will have
to do this and this and this.' I said, 'No.' He said, 'Thanh, you don't
understand.' And this friend, this colleague, then refused to help
me. Over a six-week period I went back to him again and again,
and still he refused. Then two days before my son's flight I returned to this man and I said, 'I need the signature tonight or it is
too late.' We stayed up till midnight talking. Then at the end of the
evening he leaned forward and said, 'Thanh, I trust you, you are
my friend. I will get the signature for your son.' I was surprised. I
said good-bye, went home, put some money in an envelope, and
returned to this man's house under the pretext of having misplaced
my motorcycle keys. I knocked on the door. He let me in. I pretended to search. I slipped the envelope under his pillow, I found
my keys, and we said good-bye."

Thanh paused here.

"Did this man know you had given him money?" Charles
asked.

"Of course."

"And how did you know how much to give?"

"I gave as much as I had."

Walking home later, Charles put his hand in a pocket and felt the piece of paper that Vu had given him. Back in his room he slid it into the novel and then he sat at his desk and began to write a letter to his children. He spoke of the sights and smells and sounds of the country, of the old women who called out for rubber or glass or paper. He said that just today he had passed by a man wheeling a cart in which there lay a whole fish the size of a couch. A marlin, he thought, or perhaps a kingfish. It had shone silver and black. He said that in the late afternoons, down by the tennis court, young boys in their school uniforms played soccer barefoot, and their brown skinny legs reminded him of when Ada, Del, and Jon would run through the forest on the mountain, their voices calling out, and with each cry he'd known where they were.

ONE EVENING, LATE, HE PLAYED SCRABBLE WITH JACK AND ELAINE out on their balcony. The mosquitoes were persistent, so Jack lit some coils and placed them near Elaine's ankles. As he squatted he put his hand on Elaine's thigh, very lightly, very briefly, and then he stood. Charles realized that he had never noticed any physical contact between Jack and Elaine before. He suffered a moment of jealousy and pushed it away.

Elaine served Brie and crackers. She was quite happy to have found the Brie. There was a store down the street that catered to Europeans, and she had bought the Brie and some dark chocolate. She had also found a bottle of Beaujolais that tasted slightly sour. Still they drank and ate. Jack talked about his vision for the people in the province of Quang Ngai. It was an area of the country that during the war had been sympathetic to the North and to Communism. They still were, and the challenge excited him. He said that two Vietnamese pastors had been beaten there a few days earlier. He related this with a certain glee.

Elaine said, "Jack wants to be a martyr."

Charles didn't want to talk about Jack, whose religion bored him. Charles said once, after too much to drink, that the Vietnamese should be left alone to find their own god.

Jack shook his head and said that the incredible mishmash of animism and ancestor worship and Buddhism only served to confuse the people. Clarity was needed. He said that there was nothing stronger than a church that was persecuted. The world was full of complacency.

That evening Jack saw Charles to the door. They stood on the sidewalk and looked out over the street to the noodle stand where a man berated a woman and waved a flyswatter in her face. The woman swung a fist at the man and someone laughed. The man fell down. The woman walked away, the glow of her white shirt disappearing into the darkness. Elaine called down from the balcony to say that Sammy was awake and asking for Jack. And Charles had forgotten his cigarettes, she would bring them down. Charles could see her face and her arms and part of her neck as she stretched over the balustrade. Jack sighed and said good night. He touched Charles's arm and went inside.

Charles waited. After a while Elaine appeared. She stepped out of the door and shut it quietly. She carried the cigarettes and a key. She touched Charles's arm very near the spot where Jack's hand had lain and said, "I wanted to smoke. Do you mind?"

And so they stood under the overhang of the building, side by side, and Charles leaned forward to light Elaine's cigarette. She steadied his hand, though it was not necessary. The glow of the match accented her eyes and nostrils. She tossed her head and stared out at some point in the darkness.

Charles considered what he might say and then found himself referring to the last conversation they had had. He said, "And the chaos, how is it?"

She said, "Right now, I can't think of a safer place to be." Then, as if embarrassed by this confession, she said, "The wine was a bit off. Didn't you think?"

He said it was fine. Better than whiskey.

She said she didn't like whiskey. She asked, "Did you ever think, when you came here, that you would be playing Scrabble with a couple from Kansas?"

Charles did not answer. Across the street, at the noodle stand, someone had lit candles in buckets. The light flickered and waved.

She looked at him. "What you said, a few days ago, about being lost? I am lost, too." She shook her head quickly. "Oh, God. That sounds so melodramatic. I'm not trying to outdo you."

Charles said that he didn't see it that way. He imagined he should say something else but he was not sure how to move beyond the obvious, so he just watched her in the shadows.

She said, "Everyone loves Jack. He comes to this country and within days, hours even, people are fawning. He's like a magnet that attracts both good and bad. There's always someone at our house, for dinner, for drinks, whispered discussions. Sometimes it feels like I'm standing outside of a life that is his making. Not that I want what he has." She put out her cigarette. "I must smell like smoke now. Jack will notice. Do I?" She put her face close to Charles's. "Do I?" she said again. He was almost touching her jaw and neck. He breathed in and said it was hard for him to tell. He said that she smelled nice, if that was any consolation.

She put the key in the lock. Turned it. Opened the door, and without looking at him said, "Good night, Charles," and then she went inside.

He walked back to his hotel. It was late on a Saturday night and the traffic was still busy. Young people on motorcycles, taxis, bicycles. He walked past the museum and the wharf. On past a restaurant where the lights were glowing and a party was taking place. On the open balcony upstairs men and women were drinking and dancing. For the first time in a long while, he imagined a woman in bed beside him.

.   .   .

FOR SEVERAL DAYS HE KEPT TO HIMSELF AND STAYED IN HIS room. He took his meals in the vegetarian restaurant down the street from the hotel, and then he returned to his room. He slept poorly. One afternoon, Charles called Jon in Canada. Jon lived in downtown Vancouver with a man who was older than Charles. Jon had met him at the auction house he worked at. Just last spring Jon had come home for a visit and he had brought the man with him. Introduced him as his friend and said his name, Anthony. The three of them sat in the sunshine on the roughed-out deck that Charles had been building and they drank beer and made small talk. Anthony asked questions about machining and electricity and clearing the roads in winter. They were practical questions, and Charles had to give the man some credit. He wondered if Jon and Anthony would touch each other, show some affection, but they never did and Charles was relieved. He told Ada later that he was working hard at being open-minded, after all Jon was his son, but he still couldn't get his head around the physical relationship. That was a tough one.

Ada had said, "Dad, you don't have to make love to Anthony," and they'd moved on to other things.

Now, calling Jon, Charles wondered if Anthony would answer. When he heard Jon say hello, Charles took a quick breath and said, "Hey, it's your dad." He heard his own voice arriving as an echo, slightly late, and he imagined their words overlapping.

"Dad? It's three in the morning."

"Is it?" Charles said, "Jesus, I didn't realize. You want to hang up I'll call tomorrow."

"No. I'm awake. Is something wrong?"

"No. Nothing. I'm here, in Vietnam, and I missed you."

"Is it good? What you thought it would be?"

"It's okay. Nothing's the same. I mean the light is the same and the sun comes up and sets in the same place and the language is the same but everything else is different. I don't know what I was thinking. What I was expecting."

Jon was quiet. Then he asked, "How long do you think you'll stay?"

"I don't know. Maybe a few more weeks. It's up in the air."

"What do you do all day?"

"Huh, lots to do. I sightsee. I eat. I sleep. It's all quite relaxing. I eat clams down by the beach and then sit in a hammock and drink beer. I'm spoiling myself."

"That's good. Ada was asking about you. If you'd called. You should phone her. She worries."

"I've started a bunch of letters, but I haven't sent any. I'll phone. Tell her. Have the postcards arrived?"

The phone crackled and the connection fell away and then came back.

"You there?" Charles asked.

"I'm here."

"I'll let you go back to sleep."

"You okay, Dad?"

"Great. Just great. In the lap of luxury, son."

"That's good."

"I love you."

"Me too."

THE NEXT DAY ELAINE CAME TO VISIT. SHE BROUGHT FLOWERS, A bouquet of orchids. Sammy was with her. They went up to the rooftop. While Sammy played with the rainwater in the barrel, Elaine sat across from Charles and asked him why he was hiding. "We haven't seen you. I leave messages at the front desk but you don't return my calls. Even Jack noticed. Jane, on the other hand, asked me, 'What's with you and that Mr. Boatman?' I said that you were a friend. Wasn't that okay? And she looked at me like teenagers are wont to, with suspicion." Her hand was resting on her leg.

He said, "I'm not hiding. You found me."

Elaine said that she and Jack were going up to Hue for the weekend. "He's got people to see there. The children are staying home with Ai Ty. Why don't you meet us there?"

Charles said that he didn't know, though he had always wanted to go to Hue. Elaine said that the train ride was spectacular. She stooped and dried Sammy with a towel, her hands quick and her movements efficient. She stood and faced him again, stepped forward. She was wearing a simple sleeveless print dress, and as she came closer he noted the scent of some kind of powder and bath oil that seemed familiar and made him lean forward slightly. She took his hand and put her mouth close to his right ear. She would be lonely in Hue while Jack was busy, she said. If Charles came they could visit the Citadel together and play at being tourists. "You should try to be a tourist for a few days." He recognized the scent now, it was something his daughter Del had used long ago, when she was young and still lived with him.

Elaine was still holding his hand. Sammy was behind her, peeking around her hip, as if this were a game.

Charles said, "He's watching."

She smiled and turned and scooped Sammy up and moved toward the door of the rooftop stairs, whispering in her boy's ear. Just before she left she looked back at Charles and her mouth went up on one side, as if she were communicating something, or as if she knew something about the two of them that he didn't yet understand.

The following morning Jack came by and asked Charles to join him for breakfast. With Jack was a young Vietnamese man who wore leather shoes, no socks, and tight jeans. He deferred to Jack, who called him his helper. He introduced him as Lan.

Lan drank coffee while the two men ate. Jack asked Charles

if he had found yet what he was looking for here in Vietnam. "Everybody's looking, of course. The expatriate community is a soup of bewildered souls. Nicky, the handsome Italian with the Vietnamese wife, who would rather be floating down some mosquito-infested river in Africa than running a bar for Americans in Danang; Miss Hereforth, who works for the UN as a dentist but spends her evenings dancing with young Vietnamese men. Haven't you noticed the sexual energy one gets from this country?" He pointed his chopsticks at Charles's chest.

"What do you mean?" Charles asked. He wondered if this were directed at him, some allusion to the time he had been spending with Elaine.

Jack said, "Perhaps it's the heat, which leads to torpor, and the torpor leads to indolence, which in turn leads to desire." He drank his coffee. He turned to Lan and said something in Vietnamese. Lan stared at Charles with his dark eyes. Then he touched the table with his little finger.

Across the street, in midday's white light, a mother followed a toddler following a dog. Lan stood and wandered off toward the motorcycles parked near the sidewalk. He leaned against the wall and began talking to a waiter. As he talked he laughed, and once he touched the waiter's shoulder and then his face.

Jack asked for the bill and said, "Elaine told me you might be coming up to Hue this weekend." He studied Charles's face. "I think that would be good. You haven't been there, that's what she said. Though it's cool this time of year, the trip alone is worth it."

"Yes," Charles said. "We talked about that." Outside, against the wall, he saw the boy, the movement of his eyes and mouth, a slight knowing smirk. He paid for the meal, even though Jack protested. "Please," Charles said, and he pulled out his wallet and laid the money on the table. As he did so, he said, "If your offer is genuine, I'll come to Hue. I'd like that. Elaine said that I needed to be a tourist for a bit. So, why not with you two?"

"Excellent. I'll tell Elaine. I'll be busy, so she'll be happy to have someone to spend time with." He took a napkin and wrote down the name of the hotel where they were staying, and the restaurant where they could meet on Saturday night. Outside, Charles saw the young man, Lan, push away from the wall and leave without saying good-bye. Jack didn't seem to notice.

IN THE EVENING CHARLES TOOK A CYCLO UP TO THANH THUY Street and stopped at a painted green gate and looked in on a garden where a dog slept. He called hello. The lights in the house were on and the door was open and inside the first room Charles saw a couch and a coffee table and a cup of tea that was still steaming. He waited and eventually a woman appeared. He called out again and she looked into the darkness, holding her hand up as a visor. She was dressed in jeans and a button-down white shirt. She wore cloth slippers. She walked toward Charles and said, "I do not speak English." She opened the gate and said, "Come in, please." Charles stepped inside and said, "I'm looking for Hoang Vu, the artist."

The woman bowed slightly and left him standing in the courtyard. The dog lifted its head and blinked.

A young girl entered the room, stopped, and stared. She was wearing shorts and a big T-shirt and her hair was in braids.

"Hello," Charles said.

The girl said hello. Her pronunciation was exact. She asked, "Are you rich?" and then laughed and backed out of the room as Hoang Vu appeared. He was wearing a white shirt and black polyester pants and socks with broad stripes of white and baby blue. The elastic was gone on the socks and they had drooped at his heels.

"You have come," Vu said. "Good, good." He motioned at the couch and told Charles to sit. He sat across from him, lit a cigarette, and said that he had many friends in many places, in London, in Montevideo, in Paris, but it was always nice to meet someone new, and that was why, that afternoon with Thanh, he had asked Charles to visit. He stood and excused himself and left the room, and in a moment he returned with two glasses and a bottle of whiskey, which was a third full. He poured generously, handed Charles a glass, and said, "To new friends." They touched glasses and drank. Vu finished his and poured himself another. "I know a little about you," he said. "Tell me more."

Charles talked about his life back on the mountain and about his three children, and then he said that almost thirty years ago he had fought in Vietnam and now he was coming back for a visit. He said the country surprised him. He didn't really know what he had expected.

"This is the case, isn't it?" Vu said. "We set sail in a particular direction, certain of the route, and then find ourselves loose." He paused and tilted his head. "Or adrift. That is more correct. Yes."

Charles said that it was, and he complimented Vu on his English.

Vu dismissed this. "As I said, I have foreign friends, and with these friends I must speak English. How many people from Uruguay know Vietnamese? You see." He drank and then leaned forward, elbows on his knees, and said that it was to his benefit to meet people who came from another place, because that could only add to his artistic vision. "Imagine sitting in a room by yourself with nothing to look at, no one to talk to. I need other people. I need images. I need the solid world. I am asked sometimes why I don't move to another country where there is more freedom, and my answer is that I cannot be an artist elsewhere. How would I remain faithful? From which place would I tell my story? Finally, of course, the artist is alone, like Dang Tho, the writer we talked of the other day. I feel great envy and great pity for him. He has succeeded in angering the authorities, but he is also separate. This is what happens, isn't it? A man has a vision which is not political, but others make it so, and so the vision is made smaller because some person of little consequence decides that the man with the vision is too big, too proud."

Vu stopped. "I am talking too much," he said. He drank quickly and then said, "Dang Tho's answer to all the attention around the novel was to turn away. He did not write another book. And of course, though the war did not kill him, the time after the war probably will. He is a man bathed in a sad blue light."

He stood and left the room once again, coming back a few minutes later with a plate of satay pork garnished with mint and wrapped in rice paper. Vu began talking about his time after the war, about returning to Hanoi and the difficulty of life. He said that his niece—he lived with his sister and her daughter—had been born a long time after the war, good for her, and with fortune she would never have to suffer. He had run out of cigarettes and he called for the girl. She left and returned some time later, handed him a pack of Raves, and moved sideways out of the room, her bare feet brushing the tile. Vu poured more whiskey for them both, lit a Rave, and closed his eyes. He said, "I love everything. Art. Books. Women. There is an Indian writer, Tagore, a poet. I love him. I love languages. French. André Gide. Sinhalese, German, Arabic." He paused.

"You speak Arabic?" Charles asked.

"Maybe. A good poet is Nguyen Du. 'In another three hundred years, / Will anyone weep, remembering my Fate?' Or Tan Da, he wrote about getting drunk. Do you like poetry?" He was looking at Charles. Then, before Charles could answer, Vu was off on several more lines, from *Hamlet* this time, and then back to a Vietnamese poet, Nguyen Khuyen, and he recited in a soft voice, and though Charles did not understand the words or their deeper meaning, he felt that he had arrived at some unlikely place.

Vu got slowly drunk. His conversation began to meander. He

quoted both Kahlil Gibran and Ernest Hemingway. He said, "I read *The Prophet* years ago when I was in school. How do you say his name, Kawleel Zibrun? Like that. And Hemingway, you know that one about the fish where the old man comes back with nothing? That's it. You fly over things, you must, and you arrive on the other side with nothing. You ask me, do I believe? I love the tiniest flower, that rock, that tree, the indigo moon. I am not a Communist. I can believe. But that's a big question. Everyone's question."

They drank and when the whiskey was gone Vu wandered into another room and came back with a bottle of brandy and poured a little into their glasses. He raised his glass, studied it, and then he ducked his long face and drank quickly.

At two in the morning Charles shook Vu's hand by the green gate. The moon was full and the streets were bright. Vu offered Charles his bicycle, even began to set off to find it, but Charles stopped him, saying he would walk up to one of the busier streets until he found a taxi.

He did not know when he lost his way but he supposed it might have been just after he turned off Thanh Thuy Street. He had come down a small lane that he did not recognize and he had arrived at a beach. He did not know this particular beach. It was different from the one at My Khe; debris floated on the water. He walked and he was aware of his own breathing and the roiling of his stomach. He passed shuttered shops and he wandered through small streets and crossed large thoroughfares. Always, he looked for the bright neon sign of the Binh Duong Hotel, but he never saw it.

He walked by an old man sitting in a metal chair by a child's swing. Charles tried to talk to the man, but he was sleeping. On a dead-end street, near a cluster of buildings that turned out to be a carpet factory, he was set on by a man brandishing a long knife. The man talked to him quickly and moved the knife in short thrusts through the air. Charles backed up until he was at the gate. He took out his cigarettes and offered the man the pack. The man put the knife in the waistband of his shorts, took the pack, and lit a cigarette, all the time watching Charles. The man made a motion with his free hand, a curling of his fingers. The knife was still tucked away. Charles was drunk. If he had not been drunk he would have swung at the man, who was small and thin. His shorts were dirty and his T-shirt was torn. Charles stepped forward and in a single motion the man pulled out the knife once more and swung at Charles's waist. The knife slit his shirt. Charles looked down. Put his hand to his waist and felt something wet. "Fuck," he said and he looked at the man, who clicked his teeth and circled Charles and passed the knife by his face. In the darkness the man was a black ghost, and it came to Charles, in the haze of his drunkenness, that he was going to die. The man crouched and muttered some words that were foreign and fluttered about in the air. There was the knife in one hand and the cigarette in the other and as the man shuffled clockwise he drew on the cigarette and then exhaled at Charles. Charles thought of the money in his wallet. He reached for it and the man cried out and lunged forward. Charles swiveled and watched the knife slide past his rib cage. The man stumbled and fell. Charles knew then that he should kick the man in the chest and in the head, but instead he stood there, offering his wallet. The man rose and was going to reach for the wallet when from the courtyard of the carpet factory there came a whistling sound, a shout, and the rattling of a gate, and the man fled.

It was the night guard of the factory who beckoned. "You, come," he said, and he led Charles through a small metal gate and into the showroom. He made Charles sit on a rolled-up silk rug. He returned with a glass of water and handed it to Charles. "Okay?" he asked.

Charles looked at his stomach. The knife had barely scratched his abdomen, leaving the slightest trace of blood. He nodded and thanked the guard. A single light shone down on the spot where he sat. The night guard was an old man with bowed legs. He carried a magazine and a cup of tea. Keys hung from his belt. He spoke quickly and then left and returned some time later and directed Charles out to the taxi he had found. Charles offered the guard money, but he moved his hands back and forth and said, "Happy, okay?" and he closed the taxi door. Riding home through the quiet streets, Charles saw the moon and the clouds around the moon. His chest hurt. He could not remember if his attacker had hit him in the chest. He didn't think so, but he could not remember.

In his room, he showered and then lay on his bed in shorts and waited for a sleep that would not come. He recalled the attack as something that had happened quickly and with little warning. He had been more curious than alarmed, as if he were a spectator at the scene of his own execution, and he wondered at what point indifference had set in. He saw Vu's long face, the dark high cheekbones, heard the soughing of his voice.

And then he sat up, as if from a dream, though he had not been asleep. Thoughts had been dipping like swallows in and out of his head. He had discovered a kind of narrative but the story had turned out badly. He put it down to a brief sleep that had produced a nightmare in which his attacker, just before sticking him with the knife, had whispered in his ear, "What we have on our hands is always enough."

He was shaking. His mouth was dry. He got up and drank some water. The manner of his own death was an important one. To be killed by a wastrel and a drunk in the dirty streets of Danang was not what he had imagined. The man had been missing two front teeth, and contrary to the dream, he did not speak English, neither was he any sort of a philosopher.

Charles sat in a chair and watched the sun rise. It came quickly, red turning to orange and then yellow and finally white. He recalled mornings like this on the mountain when the children were younger, mornings when he sat and waited for their voices or the padding of their feet, and always it was Ada who came to him first, settling into his lap, the smell of sleep on her breath, her bare arms around his neck. "Daddy," she said, and nothing more. She didn't need more. Sitting there, her head pressed against his neck, was enough.

ON THE WEEKEND HE TOOK THE TRAIN UP TO HUE. FROM HIS window seat he saw the occasional aqueduct and the cliffs falling away into the fog below and then the ocean breaking through that fog.

In Hue it was cold and windy and raining. He found a small room for ten dollars a night and then walked the streets close to the Perfume River. As arranged, he met Jack and Elaine for dinner. They ate noodles and tiny whole fish fried in garlic. Jack drank Festi, Elaine and Charles ordered beer. The restaurant was cold; rain drove against the shuttered windows. Elaine said that the car ride up had been beautiful. She described the hairpin turns and the color of the ocean far below. Charles watched her as she talked. At her neck was a silver necklace and as she talked she fingered the necklace and sometimes it seemed that her hand wanted to reach across the table, but it didn't. Jack seemed distracted. He looked out the open doorway or he watched other customers and, once, he struck up a conversation with the owner of the restaurant, a tall man wearing a beret. Later, Charles complimented Jack on how well he spoke Vietnamese.

"How do you know?" Jack asked and grinned.

"Don't listen to him," Elaine said. "Jack always says that a good ear helps you hear the tones. Jack thinks he is a singer."

"And you?" Charles asked Elaine.

"She doesn't want to speak the language," Jack said. "Anything that smells of this country, she throws away or deliberately ignores."

Elaine moved her food around on the plate with a fork. "I enjoyed this fish," she said. "I like being here, right now." Her head lifted. "Jack likes to show off, to use his halting Vietnamese, which is really quite elementary. And he thinks that talking to a restaurant owner who wears a beret, that this somehow raises our estimation of Jack Gouds. May I?" She reached for Charles's cigarettes. Took out one and lit it. Her hand was shaking.

Jack watched her. He said, "When did you pick that up?"

Elaine exhaled. "Oh, long long ago. Before we met. Millions of years ago, in fact."

Jack said to Charles, "She's impossible."

Charles took a cigarette for himself and shrugged. Beyond the open door he saw the rain and a cyclo driver curled up under his canopy.

Elaine said, "Charles and I are going to see the Citadel tomorrow. Aren't we."

Charles said that that would be fine.

Jack nodded and said, "Good, good," and then explained that both tourists and locals were pillaging the grounds of the Citadel, prying up ceramic tiles that had been laid a thousand years earlier. It was a shame, he said.

Elaine said, "We are not the kind of people who plunder. Are we, Charles?"

Charles, trying to save Elaine, said that he knew nothing about the history of the Citadel. He said that history was not his strength, but still he liked walking through castles and museums.

"Well," Elaine said happily, "that's exactly what we'll do." And she told Charles they should meet there at noon. It was easy to find, in the middle of town.

On parting, Jack seemed to want to repair the evening. He held an umbrella above Elaine's head and said that he had been bad company. He was sorry. Charles waved the apology away. In the driving rain, he was aware of Elaine studying him, and then her mouth moved and she said, "See you tomorrow."

THE TIME IN BETWEEN

He rode back to the hotel by cyclo. His feet and hands were cold, his head felt light, and he saw the images that passed as if they were happening elsewhere and at another time: a man leaning over a pool table; a child crying beside a chicken; a woman sleeping inside her jewelry shop; a boy being beaten with a stick by two other boys while several people looked on and laughed; a basket of bread; a man and a fridge on a bicycle.

That night he sat at a small desk and opened Dang Tho's novel to the blank pages at the back where he had written the few lines in Hanoi and the date, October 4. Now, he wrote Elaine Gouds's name. And then he wrote, "In Hue. It is raining. The room is damp and chilly. Ate fish the size of pencils. She is sharper than him by far. Than I am, as well."

AT THE CITADEL THE NEXT DAY, CHARLES WALKED PAST SMALL iron cannons and foundering sculptures, on down the walkway between two shallow pools, and came upon Elaine sitting in an alcove full of sunshine. He said her name and she looked at him and said that the sun's heat was making her sleepy. They sat and looked out at the grounds. Several French tourists took photographs of their group by the entrance to the Midday Gate. Elaine said that she had thought of Charles all night. "I couldn't sleep. The room was cold. I imagined a day of looting." She laughed. Closed her eyes. Her hair was pulled back in a short ponytail. The marble spiral of her ear. Her eyes opened, caught him looking. He shifted, aware of the sun on his knees.

"Sixteen years I've been married to Jack," she said. "We met in college. He wrote for the paper, I was on the debating team. We moved around a lot at first and finally bought a house in a suburb outside of Kansas City. And then about a year ago Jack started to get restless and to talk about going overseas, doing something different with our lives. We went back and forth, with him really pushing and me resisting. I loved my life. I had started up a small catering business with a friend and I didn't want to walk away. And then Jack suggested Vietnam and I said, Okay." She paused and whispered *okay* again. She removed the cap from a bottle of water and drank. Then she said, "I was thinking about you being here so many years ago. How old were you?"

Charles hesitated, then said, "Eighteen."

Elaine considered this. "I was ten when I first heard about it. I remember things. Or maybe I think I remember. The television reports. The images. That little girl running down the road screaming. The helicopters lifting off of roofs." She touched his arm.

"I saw that photo," Charles said. "The one of you with your horse."

"Albany. I was older there."

"Did you know Jack already?"

She nodded. "I did."

"You had a good life."

"You mean spoiled."

He said he didn't mean that. He said that there were times when he wished his own children could have had more.

She asked him then about his children and he gave her the bare facts of his life. Sara, the mountain, the twins, Ada. He said that he had just talked with Ada the week before and that hearing her voice from such a great distance had carved out a space inside him. "Maybe it was her worry for me. I don't know." He paused and then said, "We used to go duck hunting together. She didn't like to shoot very much but she always said if she was going to eat the duck, she might as well kill it. Not a hypocrite, that one."

"You're lucky," Elaine said. "I can't get anything out of Jane. Sometimes she'll talk to her father. Never to me. I think she's afraid that she *is* me. Or will be me. And she loves Jack. I remember my own father, waiting for him to come home from work. The smell of him, something like ink, the feel of his suit jacket, the way it hung like a real person across the back of the chair. Sometimes I would wear one of his jackets around the house." Elaine folded her hands and slipped her feet out of her sandals. "I don't eat duck," she said.

The heat of the sun had pushed Charles down into himself and her words floated about, here and there, landing, slipping away, returning. He thought she might be waiting for him to jump so that she could catch him.

She said that she and Jack would be taking the children down south to Dalat for a two-week holiday. They'd planned this a while ago. Then she said, "You get to go home soon."

He shrugged and said he had no immediate plans. He had a three-month visa.

"So, two more months," she said. Her voice was brighter. She stood and pulled him upward and hooked an arm into his as they walked through the grounds.

Charles said that he didn't know much history and he would be hard-pressed to explain why the Citadel existed. Elaine said that if Jack were present he would give a running commentary on wars fought and each emperor's most important lover and the succession of rulers. She said that she preferred it with Charles; she liked the absence of noise. "Jack likes to trample on other people's space."

They walked along the gravel lanes into the grassy areas and up onto a plateaulike structure that used to be a courtyard. It was a peaceful place in a state of disrepair. Further on, they found an old man working in the sun, refashioning clay carvings of swords and cannons. They stood and watched him work. A young girl sat beside him drawing in the mud with her finger.

Elaine asked Charles why he was sad. What secrets did he have?

He was quiet for a while and then said that his secrets, if he had any, were small and unimportant. "I don't know that I am any sadder than other people. Than you, for instance."

"I'm not sad," she said. "I refuse to be. I think you are mistaking sadness for longing. I was imagining your caboose. How romantic it must be." Then, before he could respond, she said that she had had enough of Hue and she thought she might return to Danang before Jack. By train. "We could travel together," she said. "If you like."

Charles turned, looked at her for a moment, and said that she should do what she wanted.

"You know what I want," she said.

"Come with me, then," he said, and he was immediately sorry. He felt he had nothing to offer her.

"That's better." She took his hand and held it.

ON THE TRAIN, COMING DOWN THROUGH THE PASS FROM HUE, Charles said that when he had first arrived in Vietnam he'd come down by train through Hue and on to Danang, and so he'd taken this leg of the trip before. He remembered a young girl on the train, with two birds and her grandmother. The girl had chattered. The birds were noisy. The grandmother was affectionate and seemed happy. Charles said that at that point everything felt normal and good and he'd been quite hopeful. He hadn't known what would happen.

Elaine looked at him. "What I like best is figuring you out."

Charles said, "The first time I saw you I thought that you were beautiful but I also thought that you were very self-centered."

She said she was. "Always have been, in some ways."

"And that you loved your children more than you loved him."

"You saw that?"

"I did."

She said, "I imagine standing at the edge of a rift, and far below there is a deep gorge. You are at one edge, I am at the other and attempting to cross a narrow and treacherous bridge." Elaine seemed pleased by this image. She sat up and asked, "How far am I on the bridge? Near the middle or just at the beginning?"

They were seated across from a girl who wore tight white cor-
duroy pants. She had a round face with a jag of red lipstick, and an
older man, with a thin mustache, was talking to her as if he had
hopes of something more than conversation. The girl's hair was
long and dark and Charles was reminded of his daughter Ada.

Charles took one of Elaine's hands and held it. Her knuckles,
the sharpness against his palm. He said, "What you want, I can't
give you."

She turned quickly and said, "A few nights with Charles Boatman. That's all I want. I don't expect anything else."

"You know that's not what you want."

Elaine stood and said she was going for a cigarette. She slipped
by Charles, stepped out into the aisle, and walked toward the end
of the car. The girl in the facing seat was watching. She probably
didn't understand English, but she was watching and Charles was
aware of her curiosity, of how she feigned sleep and shifted in her
seat.

Charles rose and joined Elaine, who was standing by the open
door of the car. The greenery rushed by and fell toward the ocean.
Elaine turned to Charles and began to finger the buttons on his
blazer. Then she dropped her cigarette on the floor and ground it
out with the toe of her shoe. She put her head against his chest.
"Oh," she said. Then she lifted her chin and kissed him on the
mouth, tentatively at first, then deeply. Charles kissed her back.
After, she stood hugging herself and said, "I'm shivering." Far
below them the water was green and azure and white and then
blue. "Come," he said and guided her back to their seats, and they
sat and after a while she leaned her head against his shoulder and
fell asleep. He wanted to wake her, but he didn't. The girl across
from them was still watching.

IT WAS MIDAFTERNOON WHEN THEY ARRIVED IN DANANG. THE
station was cool and wet. A family of six was gathered near the last

car, all dressed in formal wear. Elaine held Charles's arm as they walked out onto the platform. She said that she wanted to see him. He could come by for dinner that night.

He felt the pressure of her hand and he lifted his head to look past her and he said, "I'm not sure."

She did not respond, simply hailed a taxi and then pressed her cheek against his and said, "Charles." Then she got into the taxi and was gone.

He took a cyclo to the hotel. He could still feel where her hand had touched him. Later, in his room, he lay in his underwear on the bed. He watched the ceiling fan slowly turn and recalled her expression on the train as she pushed her head against his chest and said, "Oh." After she had kissed him and drawn away, he had seen the wet inside of her lower lip and her perfectly straight teeth and the flash of one silver filling. He fell into a light sleep and woke to the ring of the phone and the clear image of himself as a dentist bending toward her and extracting a flawed tooth. Above him the fan still turned. The phone rang and rang. And then stopped.

Much later, he sat up. Poured himself whiskey and drank. Then he dressed and went down the stairs and out into the street and walked toward the harbor. He followed Bach Dang Street till it curved with the waterfront and then he turned and walked back, stopping at a restaurant that extended out over the water where he had a beer and watched the lights of the boats in the harbor, the ferries passing by.

After he had paid he left the restaurant and followed the walkway, the water on his left now. A strong wind was blowing and bits of garbage blew across his path. For a moment he paused at the edge of the harbor to light a cigarette, and as his hands cupped the match he saw the corpse of a dog, hugely distended, moving back and forth with the waves. Footsteps behind him. He turned as three men in suits passed by. Charles stepped back. He heard the men's sudden laughter and the wind and the clicking of the palm trees. The bloated moon. A hole had opened up before him.

In his room, with trembling hands, he took out a small pipe and a package of tinfoil, crumbled bits of hashish into the pipe, and lit it and drew. He lay on the bed and ascended with the twisting smoke, up, past the swirling fan, beyond the ceiling and into a night sky hurled through with celestial beings that blinked and disappeared and then blinked again.

THE FOLLOWING MORNING THE HOTEL CLERK HANDED CHARLES an envelope. Charles folded it into his pocket and went across the street to the café and ordered a coffee. Then he took out the envelope and opened it. It was from Elaine. She'd written, "Charles. Last night during that fierce wind a lamp standard was knocked down just outside our house and a loose wire danced across the pavement. It was all chaos and pandemonium. And the largest moon ever. Over there. Don't be so sure that you know what is at stake here. I can look after myself. You know where I am. Elaine."

Charles laid the note on the table. Her handwriting was lovely, black looping threads like the strands at the back of her neck when she pulled her hair up. All chaos and pandemonium. He wondered if she was aware of her own perfection. Such ease with herself and the spaces she moved through, the effortlessness of language, the expectation that she should get what she wanted. This frightened him. Outside, on the street, a boy walked by carrying his shoeshine case and Charles thought of Hanoi, of sitting by Hoan Kiem Lake and of having his shoes shined, while above him in a blue sky a balloon had lifted into the air. The night before he had had a vivid dream in which a man whom he thought looked like Dang Tho was standing and staring across a river. If Charles was in the dream at all, it had been as an observer, but he had woken shaking, his mouth dry. He put the note back into his pocket and left the café and found himself at the airline office, where he bought an open ticket for Hanoi.

The next day he rented a motorcycle and rode up past Monkey

Mountain and walked down to the empty beach that curved between two points of rock. In a grove of small pines, he sat on his
jacket and watched the fishermen out at sea. Several times over the
next week, he returned to that same beach. Once, a young soldier
approached him and said, in broken English, that he must pay.
Charles said that he did not understand. The boy was carrying a
machine gun and he shifted it and stared out toward the sea and
then turned back to Charles and repeated that payment was needed
to sit on the beach. "One thousand dong," the soldier said. Charles
considered this and shook his head. The soldier moved a black
boot through the sand and then turned away to walk up the beach.

That afternoon, returning to his hotel, Charles saw Elaine step
through the lobby doors and out onto the street. Her back was
to him and she walked purposefully, a black bag swinging from
her left hand. She turned the corner and disappeared. In the hotel
the desk clerk handed him a piece of yellow paper, folded once.
He climbed the stairs to his room. Inside, he sat down and unfolded the paper. She wrote, "I came by and, again, you were gone.
Where are you, Charles? Why are you doing this? We are old
enough to follow our feelings and I sense that you have certain
feelings. I have no patience for games, if that is what you intend."
She said that they would be leaving for Dalat the following morning. "This is childish," she wrote.

He put the note down and then picked it up and reread it. Then
he took a piece of blank paper and responded. He said that his
fifth-grade teacher, Miss Everly, had looping handwriting just like
hers. And in the early afternoons, during quiet reading, when the
sun poured through the venetian blinds, dust motes floated around
Miss Everly's head. He said that only recently had he become
aware of the mercilessness of time, of its cruel push. "I'm sorry,
Elaine," he wrote. And then he signed his name.

He put the note into an envelope and wrote her name on the
outside. Then he went down to the lobby and asked the desk clerk

to deliver the envelope to Mrs. Gouds and he described the house and the street it was on. He gave the clerk a sum of money and asked, "Do you understand?" The clerk said that he understood. He knew the house, and he knew the American family that lived there. The letter was safe.

Charles spent the next days wandering the city. Once, he found himself in her neighborhood and he went by her house. The windows were shuttered and the front door was padlocked. One evening in a small restaurant at the north end of the city Thanh walked in and sat with him and drank iced coffee. The night was humid. Moths banged against the glass of the lanterns that hung above the tables.

"You have been absent," Thanh said.

Charles said that he had been walking, and then sleeping, and then walking some more. "I saw Dang Tho in a dream," he said. "He was melancholy. He was standing and looking across a deep river. There was no view of the other side." He shrugged and said that it was, in the end, just a dream.

"Yes, but dreams can warn us," Thanh said. "Or indicate something." He looked at Charles and said, "You are sad."

"You sound like Elaine Gouds," Charles said. "She says the same thing."

Thanh offered him a ride back to the hotel but Charles said he would walk. He was slightly drunk, but this time he did not lose his way. On a corner close to the hotel a prostitute in magenta tights and a blue skirt teetered toward him and called out, "How many days?" Then she said, "You have hunger?" and she pointed at her legs. She was close to him and he saw her dark eyes, the light powder on her cheeks and forehead, the strap of her silver purse against her wrist. In the distance, leaning against the wall of the hotel, a boy was smoking and watching. Charles led the girl back to the hotel. He was aware, as they walked, of the boy following them. They passed through the lobby, where the night clerk, lying on the vinyl couch by the fish tank, raised his head and observed Charles and the girl and then put his head back down.

They climbed the stairs to the room. Inside, he turned on a lamp and the girl sat on a chair and crossed her legs. He took out the package of tinfoil and prepared his pipe. Lit it and inhaled. After he had released the smoke he asked her if she liked to smoke. She smiled and got up and began to lift her top. "No, no," he said, and he went to her and took her arm and led her to the bed, where they sat, side by side, and shared the pipe. She did not seem to be a novice; she held the smoke and exhaled carefully. He saw that her fingernails were dirty.

When they'd finished the pipe, Charles stood and went over to the desk and laid it down beside the lamp. He turned and said that he was glad to be with her. Her skirt was short and she wore a black tank top with small rhinestones sewn along the edges. He told her his name, Charles, but she had a hard time pronouncing it. She tried, giggled, and tried again. Her voice was high-pitched. She uncrossed her legs and said the word *want* as if she were trying to capture Charles. He went over to her, touched her face and her hair, undressed her, and then undressed himself. They lay on their backs beside each other for the longest time. Their hips and arms touched. The fan above them seemed to turn slower and slower. At some point she lifted a bare arm and pointed at the ceiling, and his eye followed the line of her forearm and beyond to her index finger.

He rolled onto his side and studied her. Her breasts were small, almost nonexistent. He lifted himself onto an elbow and traced her collarbone with a finger. Her eyes were wide open and showed no emotion. Then, he put on his pants and stood by the open window, smoking a cigarette. She went to the bathroom and returned and slipped back into her clothes, and when she was ready to leave he handed her one hundred dollars.

She was surprised and perhaps even a little frightened by this, but she put it into her purse. When she left he stood by the open window and waited. It took a long time, but finally he heard the sound of her heels on the sidewalk below, and then nothing.

HIS DREAMS IN THOSE LAST DAYS WERE DARK. IN ORDER TO ES-cape he fell back on drink and hashish. He found that the drug helped him float and the dreams that came to him then were softer and more fluid. He tried not to sleep, exhausted himself, and ended up on his bed in the late afternoon, waking to the sound of nightlife and the flashing of the hotel sign, disoriented, his mouth dry. He would walk then. Up and down the streets of Danang. He became familiar with the landmarks, the different shops, and came to know certain restaurant owners. Bartenders welcomed him as a regular. He tried not to think of who he was, of his children, of his past, of Elaine, or of anything else that might press some sort of anguish upon him. He grew to appreciate White Horse cigarettes. He became fond of a certain Vietnamese whiskey. He knew where he was going.

One night, at a small restaurant on Bach Dang Street, Charles ordered an iced coffee and smoked the last of his cigarettes as he sat and watched the fishing boats enter the harbor. He spoke to no one except the waiter, an older man who occupied his own table in the far corner and drank something dark and viscous from a small glass. When he finally rose and paid the bill, it was near midnight. A solitary cyclo was waiting on the sidewalk. He waved the driver away and walked up toward his hotel. The evening was warm and there was still some bicycle traffic and the occasional taxi. Other-wise it was quiet.

Close to the hotel he passed three prostitutes, who called out to him. One he recognized from the previous week. Her face was powdered white and the magenta tights she wore now seemed ex-cessive. She called out his name, "Chawz," and began to follow him, but he shook his head and passed on. She said something hard in Vietnamese and laughed and the other two women laughed as well.

He climbed five flights of stairs to the room. Inside, he turned on a lamp and sat on a chair, took out a glass, and poured whiskey and then drank. Then he went over to the small desk and opened a drawer and took out his pipe and prepared and lit it. His hand was trembling. He steadied it and focused on the small glow of the pipe. He went to the window and looked down at the three women on the corner. A motorcycle pulled up and idled, and when it left it took along the girl who had mocked Charles.

He put out the pipe and lay down on the bed and watched the ceiling fan turn. He closed his eyes and slipped in and out of sleep. From a great distance he heard rain and voices and then rain again and the banging of the shutter in the wind. He saw his children lined up, their faces pressed together, clamoring for his attention. He saw all the women he had known. He saw Elaine. She was standing under her awning, and she was telling him to step carefully. He began to speak and then he woke to the backfire of a motorcycle in the street. He sat up and saw the dark sky beyond the window.

It was very late. The wind had pushed the rain through the open window. He closed the window, and some time later he went to the desk, wiped it off with a towel, and began a letter. He addressed it to his children. He told them about himself. He told them what they had never known. He apologized, and then he folded the letter, placed it in an envelope, and put the envelope into a pouch inside his suitcase.

It was the middle of the night when he left his hotel and walked out onto the street. He was carrying a tote bag and in the bag were a rope and a ten-pound cinder block, which he had found at a construction site a few days earlier. The streets were empty and the rain and wind had let up. He walked up toward Bach Dang and finally found a driver sleeping in his cyclo. He woke the man and told him, "My Khe."

The ride to the ocean was quiet, though roosters crowed and occasionally the soft echo of voices carried over onto the street. A ship sounded its horn and Charles heard the creak of the pedals on the cyclo and the deep breathing of his driver. He saw his own hands and considered them for a while and thought about how easily one could choose this path.

From the cyclo now he saw the outline of Monkey Mountain. He dismounted on the beach road, paid his driver a good amount, and then walked toward the shore. A dog appeared out of the darkness and stood before him, growling. Its rear end was furless and as the animal circled Charles could see it favored a hind leg; a reprobate creature that saw an equal in Charles. Charles picked up a stick and swung out, hitting the dog across the snout. It howled and backed away, its rear furrowing the sand. "Get lost, you piece of shit," Charles said, and the dog tilted its head, as if the language it heard was unexpected. Charles continued toward the water. He intended to take a basket boat out past the breaking waves. There were numerous boats along the beach and he chose one close to the shore. It was heavier than he had imagined and he had to rest as he dragged it toward the water. More than once he went down on his knees and had to catch his breath. When he did this, the dog slid in closer and Charles threw things—sand, rocks, shells, empty cans—to keep the mongrel back. Even when the boat was in the water the dog sat near the shoreline and lifted its head and howled, as if aware of what was to pass.

Pulling the boat out into deeper water, Charles had difficulty fighting the surf. The waves kept pushing him back toward land. When the water became too deep, he hoisted himself up into the boat and landed heavily against the cinder block in the tote bag. He sucked air through his teeth from the pain. The boat rolled with the ocean. He took a paddle and worked his way past the breakers, out toward the open sea. He struggled for a long time and when he finally paused and looked back, the lights of the houses at My Khe were distant and foggy. The dog, both sight and sound, had disappeared.

He put the paddle down and looked at his bag. What he did next he did with speed and clarity. He opened the bag and took out the rope and the block. He tied the rope to the block, fitting it through one of the small openings, and he fastened it with a taut line hitch. Then he took the other end of the ten-foot rope and looped it around his left ankle. This too he tied with a hitch. Finally, he stood, picked up the block, and threw himself and the block overboard. The water was warm but even so he felt a quick shock and he sucked in air. He thought, briefly, of his children and he pitied them.

When the rope uncoiled to its full length, he was pulled down. He did not panic but sank with the weight of the cinder block. If he had wanted he could have loosened the rope and swum to the surface, but he didn't. As he felt the pressure build on his ears and temples he released the air in his lungs and swallowed the ocean water. His last sensations were a burning in his chest and things brushing either side of his face. These were his arms lifting past his head and reaching toward the surface as if to grasp at the last of the bubbles that floated upward and broke into the night air.

The block hit the ocean floor first. Then Charles's heels touched and his legs buckled slowly and he came to rest on his back. A school of blowfish circled above him and moved on. Within a few hours a cuttlefish had found him and slid past his mouth and ears and finally settled in beneath a raised shoulder. The following day, a tiger shark would stray from its group and nose the man's leg, finally settling on the right foot, working the teeth through the canvas shoe into the flesh. But the man's eyes would go first, nibbled at by the smaller animals on the ocean floor, until a blue swimming crab would appear and pry free first the

right eye and then the left. Sea horses would study the holes, and
then slide away.

On the surface, the basket boat would disappear, carried by the
tides toward the shore. A Russian oil tanker would anchor above
the corpse for several days. The stern anchor would land beside
Charles Boatman and catch the rope and drag his body along for
several hundred yards. For over a month the currents would toss
the body until, finally, Charles Boatman would be delivered up
onto the land from which he had come.

PART TWO

THE TYPHOON ARRIVED DURING THE NIGHT AND CONTINUED
until early morning. All through the following day, the sky remained dark and the wind still blew and tossed muddy water onto
the wreckage of the beach. Two days after the storm, midmorning,
a local fisherman pulled his basket boat down toward the water and
saw the movement of a large object in the waves. He thought it
was a dead marlin or a dolphin, but as he approached he saw the
arms and the head of a man. One of the legs was bent backward in
an awkward position; there was a frayed rope tied to the left ankle.
The man's face was gray and bloated. The arms were swollen.
Something had eaten away at the right leg; the foot was missing. The man wore jeans and a black T-shirt. No shoes. He had a
watch, and the fisherman looked around and then bent quickly to
remove it. He patted the dead man's pockets, found his wallet,
pulled out several waterlogged hundred-dollar bills, and put the
wallet back, which was difficult because the body kept rolling with
the tide. The fisherman saw the corpse's face, the holes where the
eyes had been. He stood and looked up the beach. Then he moved
away toward his basket boat. He had been planning on going out

for the day, but now he wouldn't. The dead man would weigh on the fisherman's thoughts. His money would weigh in his pocket. Still, he would keep the money; for him, it was the equivalent of a year's salary. He walked back up behind the restaurants that lined the beach and stepped over into the bushes and urinated. Then he climbed onto his bicycle and returned to his house. His wife was in the back, squatting and fanning the coals in the barbecue. He walked past her and she looked up but she didn't say anything. He went into the room where he and his wife slept, took out the money and studied it, and slipped it into his dress shoes, the ones he wore for weddings and funerals. Then he went outside and got on his bicycle and rode down to the police station to announce that a white man had drowned at My Khe.

THE MORNING THAT CHARLES BOATMAN'S BODY WAS FOUND, A young policeman who barely spoke English knocked on Ada's hotel door and announced that Lieutenant Dat required her to come down to the police station. The policeman, a boy really, had taken off his cap and lowered his head as he spoke. He talked too quickly, slurring his words, getting them all out in one breath, as if they had been memorized. Ada asked him to repeat himself. The boy looked horrified but said again what he had been told to say.

Ada was still half asleep. She noticed the boy's eyes move up and down her bare legs and then he turned his head away.

Ada rode behind the boy on his green Czech-built motorcycle. He had on a wool jacket, and when she brushed against it with her arms and wrists she felt the roughness. At the police station, he led her straight to Dat, who was in his office. He told her to sit and then he announced that her father's body had been found.

"How do you know?" she asked.

"His wallet was still in his pocket. I am sorry. It is your father." He pushed a small hand up his forehead and through his hair. "In any case, still you must identify him."

He offered her coffee. She refused. He asked if she wanted her brother to be present. She said that she did not know where her brother was. He had not come home the night before. Dat raised his eyebrows. He seemed to want to say something but didn't.

Ada looked at her watch and then called the hotel and let the phone ring and ring but there was no answer. She hung up and said that she didn't know what to do.

"You can wait for your brother if you like. Or you can identify the body by yourself. It appears to me that you are old enough to recognize your father. Yes?"

She heard Dat speak, and she knew that his words were cruel, but she did not acknowledge them. She asked where her father's body had been found. Dat said that a fisherman had found him at My Khe that morning. Ada nodded. Saw Dat's small head, his dark shirt. Beside him a blue ashtray on a gilded stand, the polished desktop. She said finally that she would go with him and look at the body.

At the hospital she was led down many hallways and through rooms that were full of crying children and sick people on small cots, down the stairs to the morgue, where a doctor in a lab coat took her to a gurney and pulled back a sheet to reveal her father's face. It was swollen and the head had been rotated slightly. She saw his left ear, a distended mouth. She turned away. Looked again. Then she nodded and the doctor drew up the sheet.

Back in the hallway, she asked about her father's eyes, what had happened. The doctor explained in perfect English that sea animals had probably viewed the body as a form of shelter and food. He shrugged, said, "I'm sorry."

She put her hand to her mouth. She was panicking. She swallowed and said, "How did he die?"

"He drowned."

"But was he killed?" she asked.

The doctor looked at Dat, who said, "We don't think so." He said that there was no reason to suspect this. "And so we believe he may have killed himself." He squinted, as if trying to see a small object from a great distance. "He tied something to his ankle. I do not know how he got out into deep water. Perhaps a small boat." He shrugged again and sighed, as if to say, "And that is that."

Ada realized that what she had wished for earlier, for someone to climb the stairs and give her the news of her father's death, had now happened.

The doctor shook his head and then said in English, "I beg your pardon."

Once outside the hospital, Ada said that she wanted her father's belongings, and so Dat rode her to the police station on the back of his motorcycle. As she held on to the edge of the seat, her eyes were level with the back of his hairline and she saw his neck and the mole close to his ear. A long black hair grew from the mole.

She had felt nothing at the hospital. She still felt nothing. What she had seen was simply a corpse. Of course, she was willing to accept that it was her father: his wallet had been found; the ring he wore on his right hand was still there. But the fact of his death was like some far-flung tragedy that had befallen someone else. It did not matter.

Dat proved to be unexpectedly solicitous. At his desk he sat her down and gave her a cup of tea, saying he would be back in a moment. He disappeared for a long while and returned with apologies and her father's suitcase. He said that this was everything. "So," he said. He removed his glasses and cleaned them with his shirttail. He tucked his shirt in again. "There is a small café close to your hotel. I will take you there for a drink."

Ada was unsure. She had no desire to spend more time with this lieutenant, but perhaps he had some extra information. She asked, "Do you have details? Do you want to tell me something?"

"Tell you something? No, no. I have nothing. I simply want to be of assistance. Your father drowned. You are unhappy. You need a drink." He said, "Please," and he picked up the suitcase and led her out to the motorcycle. The sun was shining now after the storm, but the streets were still littered with toppled electrical poles and palm trees and sheets of plastic roofing. At the café, Dat walked in without a word, carrying the suitcase, leading Ada toward the back and into a garden, where he pulled out a chair for her. There were two birdcages hanging nearby. A parrot talked to them in a language that Ada thought might be Vietnamese. "What did he say?" Ada asked.

"That you are beautiful," the lieutenant said.

She did not respond but thought that Jon should be with her now, not this lieutenant with his black suit jacket, small shoulders, and breezy innuendos. She ordered a Pepsi and the lieutenant asked for a whiskey. He said, "In your father's suitcase you will find nothing important. There are clothes and a passport and some Vietnamese money and there is a novel, by a Vietnamese writer, and in that novel someone has written some notes. I do not know what they mean." He shrugged. "We found the remains of some drugs, but they are gone now. Hashish."

He said this word quickly, slurring the *s*'s, and then leaned toward Ada. "I must warn you that if you have drugs you will be arrested. It is a serious crime here in Vietnam."

"I don't. My brother doesn't."

"But your father did."

She lifted her shoulders, as if to say "So?" and then she said, in a tired and distant voice, "I didn't know."

The drinks arrived. The waitress wore a tight uniform with a Tiger beer insignia on the chest. Dat eyed the waitress and then he spoke sharply to her and she bowed her head and turned away, but there was a slight smile on her face. When she had gone, he said, "It is easier to be a man than a woman in Vietnam. That is a fact, but it is our culture, our way. I think it is quite possible for men and women to be equal, though not in a Western sense. Equality here has to do with respect for one's place. Take my wife and me, we respect and trust each other. We were, what do you call it, high school sweethearts. But in the end I am the provider, I allow her independence by making enough money. I want my wife to behave the Vietnamese way, to show her thoughts and feelings through actions and not words. I do not want to come home and have her say, 'Oh darling, you look so tired.' No, I want her to offer me soup or get me a cloth, or guide me to a chair. Words do nothing. In Vietnam, actions are more important than words. Respect. For each other. You are married?"

"No."

"In Vietnam a woman over thirty is too old."

The waitress placed a plate of clams on the table. Dat leaned back, lit a cigarette, and exhaled upward. "Please," he said to Ada and motioned at the plate.

She turned away from the gray flesh of the clams and said no thank you.

He watched her, then said, "And so you will go home now."

"Yes, I suppose."

"I would advise it. Your brother." He shook his head. "It gives me a hard time to say this but I must. What your brother does is dangerous." He lifted his head and stared at Ada, who wanted to leave.

"I'll take care of my brother," she said. She stared back at Dat, expecting him to argue.

He said, "Your brother took a car to Quang Ngai. He went with an American man. Did you know that?"

Ada was surprised but did not want to show her surprise. She said, "My brother can make his own decisions."

Dat smiled. "Of course he can." He said that he wanted the best for her, that he liked her. "If you are going to stay, you will need a translator and guide. I have the man for you."

"I have someone already, thank you," Ada said.

"Thanh?" He smiled.

"Yes."

He raised his eyebrows and then licked his lips. Then he said that perhaps she misunderstood. Every stranger who came to Vietnam misunderstood. "I have come to see that you think differently from the way we do. And sometimes you do not think at all. You believe that if you want something you will ask for it and it will show up. Nothing is that simple. This is not Paris. It is not New York. Vietnam is an unusual place, and people who come here, strangers like you, they arrive naïvely, with all kinds of plans. There is a word that I have heard used. Nostalgic. That is a good word. To be nostalgic is dangerous. The Vietnamese have no time for the past. We are too busy trying to survive. Do you understand?"

Ada shrugged. She was aware of the suitcase at her feet. She said that she wanted to go back to her hotel now.

Dat said, "You expected that your father was dead."

Ada said she had, but even so it was difficult.

Dat dropped his eyes to the table, where the clams lay untouched. He moved an index finger in a small circle. "If you want something," he said, "you must come to see me. I speak English almost as well as Thanh." And then he said, as if thinking she might not have heard him, "And, please, if you want something more." He finished with a grand gesture of his hand, and for a moment Ada saw his vulnerability, the pleading of a man who was trying to survive.

Ada picked up the suitcase, dipped her head slightly, and left the café. She walked over to the hotel and climbed the stairs, resting on every landing, until she reached her room. She thought about Jon, who had run off to Quang Ngai with the American. Obviously it was Jack Gouds. She was angry, at Jon, at Jack, and at Elaine for her blindness.

Ada placed the suitcase on her bed and studied it, running her hand along the metal ridges and over the snaps. Then she opened it. On top were clothes, neatly folded. She took these out and placed them on the bed. Several T-shirts and underwear and pants. A dress shirt that had never been worn. An older blue blazer with a button missing. She lifted one of the T-shirts, smelled it, and was overwhelmed by the latent scent of her father. She composed herself and took out her father's notebook and his passport. She found a letter from Del that was illegible except for a few words and Del's name. A plane ticket to Hanoi whose date had expired. A credit card with the magnetic strip washed away, a few Canadian coins, no other money. The novel that Lieutenant Dat had mentioned. It was black, with no dust jacket. It was called *In a Dark Wood*. Her father had written on some blank pages at the back: dates, disconnected sentences, the odd name. Some scraps of paper fell out. There were a few Vietnamese names in handwriting she didn't recognize, and some addresses. She slipped the pieces of paper back into the book, and as she laid it back in the suitcase she noticed the corner of something and discovered a sealed envelope stuck in one of the pouches. She took it out, opened it. In it she found a letter from her father, which she unfolded and began to read.

The letter was addressed to the three children, and in it her father was matter-of-fact, almost cold in his writing, and yet poetic and wistful as well. He talked about sitting at the desk in his room, looking out over the harbor of Danang, and contemplating, with great peace, his own death. He described the call of a ship out on the ocean and, on the street, the sound of a bicycle bell, or voices and footsteps. He said that he had imagined coming back to this place and solving some mystery, that then he would understand what had happened to him. But it was not the same place. Oh, the streets were familiar and he recognized certain buildings and the landscape, but everything else had vanished. All the inside things, the things felt when he was an eighteen-year-old, that was gone.

He said that he had gone back to some of the places where terrible acts had taken place and all he had found was grass and fields and dirt roads and young children tugging at his pants and small hands pulling him. Nothing made sense.

This place, he wrote.

He said that he was uncertain of how much knowledge about him they needed, or how, when that knowledge arrived unexpectedly, they would respond. Several times he had tried to tell them what happened but then he had stopped because it had seemed selfish and almost untrue. And so, he was telling them now because he didn't want them to have to enter into a strange place in search of something that wasn't there.

He said that a few months before he had finished his tour in Vietnam, his section had been sent into a small village in Quang Ngai Province. The village was supposedly sheltering the enemy, and their group was supposed to go in carefully, make contact, kill whatever enemy was there, and then get out. It was intended to be simple, but it wasn't. There was no one in the village except women, children, and old men, and it was some of these people that they ended up killing. Not all of them, but he got scared and heard gunfire and shouting and everything went to hell.

He shot a young boy. The boy was standing in the doorway of a hut and he shot him. That's what he did. He wrote that he couldn't tell them anything different because there was nothing different to tell. He said that he saw right away that it was a young boy and not a soldier. And then, immediately after that, he said he shot a pig and a dog. The pig had been squealing between the houses and he shot it. And then the dog as well. About all of this he had nothing to say other than to say it. He said that after the shooting stopped—and there had been other innocent people killed by other soldiers—they chased the remaining villagers out into the fields and called in an air strike. And everything disappeared. The boy that he had shot. The old woman that someone else had shot. All of that disappeared.

Only it didn't.

He wrote that things were never what they seemed. Still, he wanted what he had written to be clear. He said that he loved all three of them.

When she was done, Ada folded the letter and stood and went over to the dresser. She put the letter into the top drawer and picked up her cigarettes and lit one and stood by the window and saw the sky and the sea. Her hands were shaking. A woman passing by on the street below called out for something over and over again. When Ada began to cry, she let the tears come. After, she went to the bathroom sink and washed her face, changed into a clean shirt and jeans.

She climbed the stairs to the rooftop and sat back on a wooden chaise longue. The sky was milky and deep and far above her, in the middle of all that depth, three birds hung in the air as if dead. She had been watching them for a long time and during that time they had not moved. She closed her eyes and opened them and the birds were still there. A baby cried from the street below. A dog barked. She thought the birds might be carrion eaters and were waiting for her death. Or they might be hawks seeking out some small animal, though she was not aware that this country had hawks.

She heard quick soft steps on the stairs, the jangle of keys, and then Jon's voice. "I looked for you in the room," he said, "but you weren't there."

She turned to look at her brother and said, "Dad's dead. I just saw his body." Then she went to him and they stood there on the rooftop and he held her and whispered her name. When she pulled away he looked smaller and worn out and his voice was weak as he said, "Tell me what happened."

"His body's at the hospital," she said. "I just got back from there. They took me to identify the body."

"What happened to him, Ada? What are they saying happened?"

She paused, then said, "He drowned, probably a month ago."

"That long? All that time."

In the street below, a horn sounded. Above them, the birds had disappeared and a few clouds, white and oblong, had replaced them. Jon went over to stand at the edge of the roof. Ada waited for him to turn or say something, but he didn't. She saw Jon's outline against the sky. She began to speak. She talked about the hospital. "His eyes were gone."

He turned. "Christ, Ada."

"You should have been here. I was all alone, Jon. Looking at our father dead."

"Are you sure it was him? There couldn't be a mistake? A body that's been in water."

"I have his wallet. His ring."

"So, all this time we've been looking, he's been dead. He was already dead when we arrived in Vietnam."

"Jon," she said. "Dat told me, you know. He told me you were with Jack Gouds."

Jon nodded. He sat down in a chair and lit a cigarette. He said, "Was he swimming or what?" Then he asked what they were going to do.

She closed her eyes. Her mouth was dry, she could hear her own heart. She said, "I don't know, Jon, you tell me. I've never done this before, you know." She rubbed her temples and said that she had a headache. She wanted to go down to the café for something to drink. He took her by the arm and led her down the stairs, through the lobby, and out into the late afternoon light.

The noise and the people in the café seemed distant, muted. There was a monkey chained to a nearby chair and it tilted its head and looked at Ada and grinned. Jon began to talk. He said, "I didn't mean to be gone. He invited me and I went. We weren't planning to stay for the night. It got late, he called Elaine, I should have called you. No one knew that any of this would happen."

The monkey held out a paw, blinked, then screamed and tried to hide behind a leg of the chair. Ada wanted to say something about the letter and the notes but the monkey was chattering and the waiter arrived carrying a yellow drink for her and somewhere nearby a man was singing about a hotel in California and her brother's hand appeared holding a cigarette and Ada shook her head, no, and she closed her eyes and opened them again and the monkey was gone. Her headache was worse, it pushed against her temples. The beer tasted bitter and even the bottled water was foul. She made a face and said, "I'm getting sick. It started last night." She wiped at her face with a wet napkin and put her head in her hands. "People are simple," she said. "Everything we do. What Dad did, what you do, Mr. Dat, myself, Del and Tomas. We are all simple. Our waiter. I looked at his hands when he put down the beer earlier and I was thinking about where he came from, and if he had a wife and children or if he had a lover or another job or maybe he gambled in his off hours. Simple. We do things because we have needs. We feel something, and then we act."

Jon held Ada's wrist. "You don't know what you're saying. It's your fever."

They left the café, and once in the hotel he half-carried her up the stairs, holding her under her arms. In the room he covered her with the thin sheet.

"I'm so cold," she said, and she pulled her knees up to her chest. She was shaking. Jon told her not to worry. He pulled a woolen blanket over her and said he was going downstairs for more blankets.

When he returned he knew she was sleeping, though her body was still shivering wildly. He sat on the edge of the bed. He rubbed her back and said her name, but she did not answer. During the night she called out and he woke and sat by her. He pressed a cool cloth against her forehead and forced her to drink water.

"Tastes like shit," she mumbled, and then she slept.

THE TIME IN BETWEEN

In her sleep she was falling, but she never landed; she would
drop with great speed and then stop and float and rise a bit and then
fall again. She saw things: her father holding an ax; Del standing
naked with no breasts, kissing Tomas; herself kissing Jon; Mr.
Dat's gold tooth; a bird dropping out of the sky; her father's eyes.
She woke and called out for water, and when Jon brought it to her
she swallowed and complained and asked for Tylenol. "My head is
being cut in half," she said as she sucked on the Tylenol and then
washed it down. She lay back and said, "What time is it?"

"Almost morning." Jon said she needed to see a doctor. He
seemed worried and it was strange to be looking up into Jon's face
and seeing the fear.

He touched her neck and said, "Is this sore? Stiff?"

It wasn't. She just wanted to sleep and so she turned over and
closed her eyes.

At some point he pulled her from the bed and dressed her. Led
her down to the street and put her into an air-conditioned taxi and
they went to the hospital. There was a waiting room with cement
walls and wooden benches and there were many people. Ada
leaned her head against Jon's shoulder and watched a baby wearing a wool cap crawl over the floor, chasing a line of ants. The
baby talked and drooled and his mother, a girl really, squatted in
her *ao dai* and plastic sandals and talked softly to him. An old
woman coughed and coughed, and the man with her, her son perhaps, kept stepping outside into the courtyard to smoke. He wore
a blue uniform, like that of a janitor or an electrician, and he stared
at Ada and Jon.

The boy Yen appeared. He stood before them and said, "Hello,
Miss Ada." He stuck his hand out at Jon but Jon didn't take it.

Ada stared at Yen with feverish eyes. She said that she was sick.

"I can see that," Yen said. "And I will do everything to help
you."

Jon told him that they didn't need help, that his sister would be seeing a doctor. Yen agreed and sat down on a bench not far from Ada's side. He said, "Remember the day I took you to the American woman's house? That night the typhoon came and much has happened, hasn't it? Your father I heard about. For that, I am very sorry. And now Miss Ada's sickness." He took a book out from inside his shirt and placed it in Ada's lap. "Thank you," he said.

Ada looked down at her lap and said, faintly, "You stole my book. I was looking for that."

"No, no, Miss Ada. No, I didn't steal it. The book was in the sand after you left. I meant to give it to you, but I began to read and it was like a hook and I was the fish." He opened his mouth, clicked his teeth, and shook his head back and forth. "Unfortunately, there were many big words and I grew tired. It is yours." He whistled as he sat there and then he took some bread and a Coke from a plastic bag and offered them to Ada.

"She's not hungry," Jon said.

"She can decide for herself," Yen said. "Please?" he asked Ada. She waved him away.

So, Yen sat down and ate the bread and drank the Coke, and he did this slowly, as if it were a communion of sorts. He told Jon, between bites, that he would be happy to get him whatever he wanted. He said he knew a woman who was experienced in herbs and potions and tinctures, and if science did not work, he would be glad to guide the two of them to the woman's house. And she was not expensive.

Ada listened and was surprised that Yen would know the word *tincture*. She repeated the word to herself, as if it were something novel. She was dimly aware of Jon's voice and she thought she heard him tell Yen to fuck off and then there were apologies and she felt Jon's hand touch her arm and the sun fell through the openings along the top of the concrete wall and made egg shapes on the floor, eggs that the wool-capped baby broke and then put back together again.

When she woke, Yen was gone. Finally, a man approached and said he was Dr. Bang. In a small room in the back of the hospital he took her temperature and looked down her throat and then held his stethoscope to her chest and her back. He asked questions that, to her, seemed to arrive in waves. Had she been bleeding from the gums or the mouth? Had she traveled in the countryside? Was she using a mosquito net?

She was lying on a small cot and she saw his thick glasses and soft mouth and she felt safe. Behind his head was a poster on AIDS and condoms. She turned but could not find Jon. "Jon," she said, and he answered, "Here." He was standing in the doorway. A small woman wearing a stiff white nurse's hat sat beside her and took blood from her arm. Ada watched the dark blood swirl up the container. The nurse pressed a cotton ball against her arm, held it there for a while, asked Ada to press against it, and then walked away.

The doctor talked in a slow but clear English about Japanese encephalitis. He said, "Pigs, bats, and egrets are all conduits, and there is a correspondence to the lychee season." She heard the word *conduit* and thought at first that he had said *condom*. Vaccines were mentioned, and Dr. Bang shook his head. He said it was rare to see a case in the city. It might be dengue fever, he said. This was passed on through mosquitoes. He said they should always use nets.

A dullness had settled over her that wouldn't allow her to speak or move. She slept in the taxi back to the hotel. As soon as she climbed into bed she slept. When she woke it was light and Jon told her that the doctor had called to say it was dengue fever. He would watch her. She heard him deliver the message and then she slept again. And woke. And slept.

One night she woke with a sudden clarity and called out for Jon. He came to her and she said, "Dad's dead."

"I know," he said. "I know, Ada." And again, she slept.

At one point she saw her father holding Jon by the ankles, dangling him above the rug in the living room. Jon's mouth was an O, and their father was laughing and Del was dancing to "American Woman." The tune flitted above Ada's brain and then disappeared. She heard Jon's voice but it was too deep for a seven-year-old's. She lay back and called his name. He didn't come. And then a softer voice, with a slight accent and perfect sentences. She saw Thanh. He was introducing a young man who held out his hand. She closed her eyes and opened them again and the two figures were gone.

She coughed and wiped her mouth with the sheet. Spots of blood. Not much, just a bit. She waited, and while she waited she slept, and then when she woke she turned and saw Jon sitting in a chair reading, and she said, "I'm bleeding."

He got up and asked her to open her mouth. With his hands he held her jaw and she was surprised that she couldn't smell him and she realized that some of her senses had been erased with the fever.

She reached for water and rinsed her mouth and spat into a bowl. Jon went out to find the doctor, and much later when he returned he forced her to swallow several pills. When it was dark again there were more whispers like mice scrabbling over paper and she called for water and was given some.

"The letter," she said. Jon touched her forehead and told her to sleep. She did and in her dream her dead father came to her and sat beside her. They were in the kitchen back on the mountain. The fire was burning in the stove. She was drinking coffee, but he had nothing in his hands, which were folded. She knew that he was dead because his skin was gray like that of the man she had seen on the gurney at the morgue. She wondered if he understood that he was dead. They talked then of different things, in a manner that they had never done when he was living. She asked him about the boy and he said that there was not a day he did not think of him. He said that a human was more than just a collection of atoms, that people were not just bugs. He talked about the soul of the boy he killed. He said that he had been looking for him in the place where he was now staying. Ada understood then that her father knew he was dead. She asked him what place that was. She tried to touch him but could not lift her arm. She said that she had seen him dead at the hospital and that he had had no eyes. Can you see now, she asked, and when he turned toward her she saw the holes in his face and she woke with a tremendous thirst and called out for Jon. When he came to her and she had finished drinking, she told him about the dream. Her telling was convoluted and erratic and he did not seem to understand. He shushed her and laid a cool cloth across her forehead and she thought of his hands sliding across the body of a stranger.

The next day, a rash broke out over her body. Jon told her this was good, it meant the fever was breaking. She still slept. She saw her father; he was holding a gun and pointing it at something that was at knee level. She knew what he was aiming at but she didn't want to look and so, in her dream, she forced herself to turn away and as she turned she saw a pig and a dog lying in a ditch. Then her father spoke. He was standing on a beach, in water up to his ankles. His mouth was larger than normal and he was holding the dead pig. "I'm sorry," he said. He was crying and he was young and he looked like Jon. Dr. Bang arrived. He had grown to over six feet and he said that there were two provinces in North Vietnam where the disease was endemic. Ada said, "We have pigs next door." He said, "Everybody has pigs next door. In any case you must have a combination of three of those factors. For example, pigs, egrets, and the lychee fruit." "I've seen egrets as well," Ada said, "standing on and eating from the back of a water buffalo." Bang gestured with his hand. "Two million people died from bombs and guns and you worry about an egret." He laughed and he had a gold tooth that Ada had not seen before and when she reached out to touch it she was riding on a bicycle past a woman selling flowers.

On the day the fever broke she drank from the bottle that Jon handed her; the water tasted sweeter and she finished it and asked for more. He told her that she had been sick for nine days. Her mouth was still sore and her joints swollen, but she sat on the rooftop and a breeze moved across her face and lifted the hair on her arms. She ate some rice and drank a 7UP. She had lost weight; her jeans hung loosely from her waist, and her breasts, when she looked at them in the mirror, were smaller.

The next morning when she was on the roof again, Yen appeared, startling her. She had been washing her hair, standing over the rain barrel, scooping the lukewarm water with a dipper and pouring it over her head as she bent at the waist. She was wearing shorts and a tank top, and when she thought about it later, she realized that the boy must have seen her from behind, as she was bent forward. He would have seen her bare thighs and the edges of her buttocks and the undersides of her arms. She had noticed him only as she stood and wrapped a towel around her head and turned to go down the stairs. He said, "Hello, Miss Ada."

She paused, looked about, and then said, "What are you *doing* here?"

"Checking on you."

"Go away." She motioned at the rooftop, the space around them. "This is private. My place. I didn't invite you here and you aren't to come here, ever again. Do you understand?" She stepped toward him.

"I came to your door and knocked. And then I heard water splashing and I knew that there was a body up here. And it was yours."

"I don't want you sneaking around this hotel looking for me," Ada said. "Do you understand that?"

Yen walked toward the table and the chair. He tapped a hand against the tabletop and plucked a single cigarette from his shirt pocket. He asked if it was true that her father had drowned. That his body had been found on My Khe Beach.

Ada said that it was not his business.

Yen nodded. He said that everything was quite clear. It was clear that she had lost what she loved, and now did not believe that she could love anything else.

The base of her neck hurt with a fierceness that she had not experienced even at the height of her sickness. She whispered that he should leave. "Go," she said. She closed her eyes and waited for him to disappear.

He walked toward the door, and just before he went down the stairs she heard him say, "Miss Ada, my father is dead too." Then he left.

Later, Ada was sitting in a chair looking out over the harbor when Jon came up to find her. Far out at sea the contour of a distant island rose from the water. Jon sat beside her. He said he had been at Christy's. Had a beer. And then another. He pulled an envelope from his pocket and laid down their father's letter on the table. "And I read this."

She looked at him, and then away.

"Why didn't you tell me about it?"

"I wanted to." She stopped talking.

Jon lit a cigarette, watched the smoke rising upward, and said, "So, you knew all along that he killed himself."

"Lieutenant Dat said they believed it was a suicide."

"How could you not tell me about it?"

"I don't know, I was going to but I was sick. I wasn't sure how you would handle it."

Then he said that he could handle it just fine. Look at him. Wasn't he fine? He said it almost made sense that their father had killed himself. It didn't surprise him. Not really. "Does it surprise you?"

Ada said that she just felt really sad.

Jon said, "Remember those times he took us into the bunker and told us his war stories? Well, I guess they weren't all true, were they. Or he didn't tell us everything. Did he."

Ada said that he had told them everything he was capable of telling. "He must have been tormented."

Jon said that even if he was tormented, he shouldn't have confessed like he did, in a letter. "What does he want us to do? Forgive him? For what he did, for what he's now done? As if it's that easy? Like a coward he tosses all this shit at us and then doesn't hang around to discuss it. He didn't even tell us why."

Ada said that a person's private horror wasn't something to throw out for group discussion. The only reason he had confessed to them was that he knew he was going to kill himself. Ada talked about her sickness and the dreams she had had of their father, and how his voice had been so familiar and so lifelike that when she woke from the dreams she did not know what was real and what wasn't. "Of course, I was feverish, but I still remember everything so clearly. I was holding a bucket and as it filled and water spilled over the top Dad took a large basin and held it under the pail and caught the water. He said that memory was precious and we mustn't waste it."

Jon didn't answer. He waited and then asked, "What are we going to do?"

Ada said she didn't know. She couldn't imagine going home yet. "It would be like running away. He's still here. The things he saw, what he was looking for, the people he talked to, they're all still here." She asked him if he wanted to go home.

He said that he couldn't think beyond the moment. They sat there then and did not speak save for the occasional observation about their father, which evoked a memory and a rush of commentary, so that by the end of the evening they had exhumed a few scraps of their father's life. It was, Ada said at one point, as if they were trying to pin him down.

That night Ada took out the novel her father had carried with him and looked more closely at the notes he had written. A few dates, the name Elaine Gouds, a sketch of a map of Danang, and some lines that read, "In Hue. It is raining. The room is damp and chilly. Ate fish the size of pencils. She is sharper than him by far. Than I am, as well." Ada wondered if "she" was Elaine. One of the pieces of paper had the name of the author of the novel she was holding. And another had a street address, in Vietnamese hand-writing, and a different name. Her father had never been one to write down his thoughts, and so all this recording, this keeping of notes, surprised her.

Over the next two days she read, and all the while she thought about her father and about his letter and the confession. When she was finished reading, she was not sure where or how the story fit into her father's history. He had given no indication. He had been searching for something, she felt that. She imagined that he had sat on this very chair and looked up at the same sky and at some point he had moved in a direction of his own choosing.

A breeze passed over her neck. She shivered.

MR. THANH HAD VISITED WHEN SHE WAS SICK. HE HAD COME WITH his son, Trang, and so the feverish memory of the two figures had not been a dream at all. Thanh had left her a marble ball the size of a baseball. It was black and red, and when she held it in her hand, it felt solid and smooth. He had also given her a note in which he said that he was very sorry about her father and that he hoped she would feel better soon.

He came again with his son one morning. Stood by the stairs that led to the rooftop and called out her name. She was happy to see him. He gave her gifts of mulberry wine, lotus tea, and fresh figs. He folded his hands and said, "How are you, Ada?"

She was sitting in a chair and she called him closer. He took two steps and stopped and then half-turned, gesturing at his son. "Have you met Trang?" Trang shook hands with Ada, and she apologized for her paleness, for her lack of strength.

"No, no," Trang said. "My father keeps dragging me along, hoping that I will meet you. It's all rather embarrassing. I am sorry."

Ada waved this away, turned to Thanh, and asked if he knew

anything about a boy called Yen. A boy who seemed to be around constantly, she said.

Thanh said that he didn't know any Yen but that he might be a pimp or an orphan or a scoundrel or a beggar. "Or he might be all four," Thanh said, "which is more possible. If you like, I can find the boy and have a word with him."

Ada shook her head. "No, that's not a problem. He seems so precocious and yet so helpless."

"Boys like this are always seeming helpless. They aren't," Thanh said.

A light wind blew across the rooftop. Thanh held up a palm to the sky and commented on the sun and the lovely plants beside the table and the good fortune of being able to sit here with her. He said that the figs he'd brought were very special. His wife had found them in the market. Ada thanked him again and then she held up the novel she had found in her father's suitcase and said, "My father was interested in this book and, I think, in the man who wrote it."

"I know this." Thanh took his glasses from his shirt pocket, put them on, and lifted his shoulders.

"My father. Did he tell you anything about himself?" Ada asked. "About who he was and what happened to him during the war?"

Thanh said no. Though they had gone to a village south of Danang at the base of the mountains, in Quang Ngai Province. Charles had wanted to go to a village there. They had hired a car. "He did not say why he wanted to go there."

"He had been there before. This would have been a difficult thing for him. He didn't tell you this?"

Thanh said, "His face was the same face. He walked slowly. He did not talk much. He might have been worried. On the way home he said that there had been nothing to indicate the past. He said it quietly. I think he was talking to himself and so I did not ask him what he meant." He studied Ada and then said, "I want to invite you and your brother to eat with us on Sunday afternoon. There will be others, and my family wants you both to come. You have had a loss." Then, brightening, he said, "Trang will be there. He will be delighted to see you again." He looked over at his son, who was standing beside the rain barrel. Thanh continued, "It will be special. We will meet at my sister's house on My Khe."

"Okay," Ada said. "Thank you." And she smiled at Thanh's enthusiasm as he wrote down the address and explained how she and her brother should get there. And then he excused himself and said good-bye, backing away and turning at the last moment as he guided his son through the narrow doorway that led down the stairs.

THE ROAD TO THANH'S SISTER'S HOUSE PASSED THROUGH AN AREA where merchants sold wicker furniture and artists displayed water-colors of Vietnamese scenes. Close to the mattress factory a fruit vendor squinted out into the harsh sunshine as she held a baby in the doorway of a shop. On past a metal factory and across the Han River into My Khe and then along the sandy road where boys played soccer with a tin can and the brown waves of China Beach roiled in the distance.

Ada and Jon were squeezed into the narrow seat of the cyclo. They did not speak. That morning they had phoned Del and told her everything they knew. Del said that this was what she had feared, that their father had seemed so distant in the last year, and why hadn't they done something. She said she felt so removed from everything. "Are you all right? It must have been just awful for you both," she said.

"I've been ill," Ada said. "I've been floating in this delirium." She looked at Jon. "Dad's death is hovering somewhere beside us. It all seems untrue. Though, of course, it's all terribly true."

"I should be there," Del said.

"No, there's no need."

"Tomas will pay."

"He's already given enough and anyway there's no point now, Del. We'll be home soon."

"I should be there with you. I *am* a part of this family. I want to see my father."

Ada said that she understood Del's frustration and that she must feel helpless and far away. But they would be coming home soon. Their father had written them a letter in which he had explained some things about who he was and what he had become. She said that he had chosen to come to Vietnam and that he had chosen to die in this place. And then Ada said that they were going to leave the ashes in Vietnam.

"They're only ashes. They're not our father," Del said. Then she asked, "Are you sure I shouldn't come there."

"No," Ada said. "You shouldn't. We're fine. We'll be home soon." There was a delay and then a hollow chime and the word *soon* was repeated and then repeated again.

AT THANH'S HOUSE THERE WERE THIRTEEN PEOPLE. ADA AND JON, Thanh and his wife and his mother and Trang, and the American family, Jack and Elaine Gouds and their children, Jane and Sammy. Nicky, the bartender from Christy's, was also there with his wife, Delphine, a Vietnamese doctor who had trained in France, and their child, Colin. Delphine was sharp featured and thin; she and Nicky spoke French with each other. Ada was introduced to a man named Hoang Vu, an artist, who was dark and silent, quite a bit older than Ada, and whose thin long face kept turning in her direction. He smoked and watched her.

Nicky, when he greeted her, had kissed her first on one cheek and then the other, and whispered that he was sorry. She said thank you and turned away, not knowing what to say. In the front room, before they sat down to eat, Jack looked at Ada and then at Jon and said that he had heard about Charles and he offered his condolences. The artist was sitting beside Jack and he simply nodded. Ada lifted a hand from her thigh and then let it fall back. She was aware of her mouth moving oddly. She said they were okay. They would be fine. And then Thanh said that he felt he had known Charles as a brother. "Older," he said. He touched Jon's arm and smiled and then told the group that they were ready to eat.

Thanh's wife served tripe and headcheese and spring rolls and salad. There was also noodle soup, bread, watermelon, pickled carrots and cauliflower, and a certain dish of pork bits and sticky rice wrapped in banana leaves. Ada nibbled at rice and prawn chips and she drank Coke through a straw and watched people silently. Trang was across from Jane and he went to great efforts to pretend he wasn't watching her. Jack Gouds was sitting beside Jon. Once in a while he whispered something in Jon's ear and Jon smiled and responded. Elaine Gouds was busy following her son, Sammy, who wandered from the table to the outside courtyard and then back again. When the children said they wanted to swim, Elaine volunteered to take them down to the beach. Ada said she would go along, and she got up from the table. Thanh motioned at Trang with the back of his hand and told him to go along. Nicky called out to be careful of the undertow. "No deeper than your waist."

Elaine held up her glass of wine and said, "I'll be doing this," and as they followed Jane and Sammy and Colin out of the house she took a bottle from the table and carried it with her as well.

Out on the beach, when they were sitting on the sand, Jane took off her shorts and pulled her T-shirt over her head. She was wearing a red bikini that was strikingly brief. Trang, who was in pants and a dress shirt, kicked off his shoes and ran toward the water, stopped at the edge, and then ran back to the group. Jane glanced at him and then sauntered over to Sammy, who was digging in the sand close to the shore.

Elaine said, "I tell her to dress properly but she doesn't listen. It's as if she thinks we're still living in Kansas City, where girls can show their navels and not be seen as easy. The men here are awful to her. I'm afraid to let her go out on her own. Of course, Trang is an angel." She refilled her wineglass and held up the bottle to check the level. She called out for Jane to watch Sammy.

"About your father," she said.

Ada, as if she had been expecting this, looked up and said, "Thank you."

"You're going home then?" Elaine asked.

Ada looked down the beach. Two men had squatted at a distance from Jane and were watching her as she played with Sammy. "Yes, but we haven't made any arrangements yet. Does one ever get used to this place?"

"I hate it here. We had this vision, or at least my inspired husband did, to start a church here. My husband, you know, is a man much given to grand plans. Everything is such a struggle. I'm terrible with the language, and I abhor the market and the people clutching and grabbing, and I miss my friends. We have eight months left and then our visas expire. Sitting here, with you, this is nice. And every third Monday of the month I see some of the other women at Christy's, but I can't survive on that. Jane is suffocating. Sammy's happy as a clam. He jabbers away in Vietnamese with Ai Ty, his nanny." She began to cry. She looked straight ahead and made small noises and tears ran down her cheeks but she didn't wipe them away. She held her glass of wine and her bottle and she sat with her back perfectly straight and she cried. Then, just as suddenly as she began, she stopped. She wiped at her eyes and said after a moment that Charles had spent a lot of time with them.

"We knew him. Better than I let on the other day when you came to visit. I didn't know what you wanted that day. I thought,

These are Charles's children, how odd. The thing is I didn't want
to know his children. I wanted to remember him as I knew him.
Though I guess I didn't *really* know him." She said that Thanh had
come to their house to give them the news, two days after Charles's
body had been found. She said the word *body* softly.

Then, as if she needed to step backward onto more solid
ground, she said, "When your father first came to Danang, we saw
him. On the streets walking. A few times at China Beach. Then
one day we were in the same restaurant. He was sitting in a corner
by himself, wearing a blue blazer—I remember that because it was
very hot and I thought he must have been uncomfortable—and we
asked him to join us. He didn't jump at the invitation, but in the
end he did sit at our table and I asked him, just before we said
good-bye that day, whether he always wore a jacket in hot weather.
He smiled. After that, he started to come over to our house for
drinks and meals. Sometimes, in the afternoon, I'd sit with him on
the balcony and we'd talk. I have very fond memories of that. We
met at different restaurants. Jack was usually there, of course. One
time, your father and I rode down by train from Hue. Jack and I
were going up there and so we invited Charles. Jack had to stay on,
he had some work to do, so Charles and I, we traveled back to
Danang together." She stopped.

Ada saw the redness of Elaine's mouth and was astounded at
this carefully worded confession. She saw that sex could leap out
of nowhere and obscure people, make them stupid. She imagined
her father's hands holding Elaine's thin calf.

Jane came running up from the shore, carrying Sammy. Colin
followed, being chased by Trang. Jane sat Sammy down and then
lay on her side in the sand and pushed a hand under her mother's
foot.

"Jellyfish," Sammy said. He held up his arms in a circle.

"Are there, dear?" Elaine said. She put her bottle down and
held the ends of Jane's wet hair.

Jane lay on her back and shielded her eyes with one hand. Her belly was smooth and dark. Ada could see the tan lines where her bikini had slid down.

Jane turned her head toward Ada. "Jon said he might tutor me in math. He said he was brilliant. Is he?" She squinted. Her mouth was round and full and it made Ada think of Del.

She said, "More brilliant than I am. But then, I'm awful. Who teaches you, normally?"

"My mom and dad. But they're tyrants."

"Aaw, sweetie." Elaine looked away. She wiped her raw face and then stood and brushed the sand from her legs. "Sammy," she called. He ran to her and she lifted him up. "Big beautiful boy," she said and began to walk back up toward the house. Colin tagged along, running circles around them. Trang said that everybody should come up to the house for a drink. Then he turned and followed Elaine and the children.

Jane had sat up and was studying her legs as if to check for flaws. She lay down on her stomach and pushed the side of her face against the warm sand. "Nice," she said.

"How is it here, in Danang?" Ada asked.

"It sucks. It's boring. My mother? She's so depressed. And my father rides around on his motorcycle and takes nothing seriously. He knows it's illegal to be preaching but still he does it. He wants to get caught."

"Caught?" Ada asked. She was intrigued by Jane's voice. It was husky and low and cynical.

Jane lifted a shoulder and tugged at her bikini top and then settled back in with a satisfied sigh. "Yeah. Like he was a spy or something," she said. "Am I burning?"

When they got back to the house, Elaine was standing by the doorway, looking down the lane toward the road that led to the bridge to town. She said that Jon and Jack had taken Thanh's motorcycle into town; Jack had wanted to get more beer. They would be right back.

The rest of the guests had moved into the front room that

looked out toward the ocean. Hoang Vu was sitting by himself on a wicker couch and Ada asked if there was space for her. "Space?" he said, and then he said, "Oh," and slid over and said, "Please." He crossed his legs and Ada saw his delicate ankle showing between his pant leg and sock.

Delphine suggested they play charades; Colin loved the game. Jane, who had changed back into shorts and a T-shirt, stood and divided the group into two. She said that they should do movie titles. Thanh said that he didn't know American movies, except for Sylvester Stallone. He laughed and Jane said she would help him.

As the game progressed, Ada was conscious of Hoang Vu, of his alertness when she called out a response, and his hands resting on his thighs. As they played, Elaine stood off to the side, lifting her glass and lowering her chin ever so slightly. Every few minutes she would walk to the doorway and look out. Once, she stepped outside, and when she returned, her face was wet and she said, "It's raining."

The games ended, cake was served, an hour or more had passed and still Jon and Jack had not returned. Sammy had fallen asleep on Thanh's sister's lap. At one point Vu turned to Ada and said that he had met her father. One night Charles had come to Vu's house and they had drunk a lot and talked late. Vu confessed that he had done much of the talking.

Ada wanted to pursue this, but she couldn't keep her eyes open. The remains of her fever tugged at her brain; she felt as if she were seeing through a fog. Nicky began to tell a ribald joke, moving his hands about. Ada lost track of the joke. She yawned and covered her mouth and found herself leaning against Vu's shoulder. He didn't move.

A voice woke her. She saw Jack standing in the middle of the room. Jon was behind him. Jack was explaining that Thanh's motorcycle had broken down. Elaine cried out "Like hell it did," and she hit Jack across the face and Nicky grabbed her and held her.

Jack shuffled his feet and reached out for her but Nicky waved him back. Jane leaned against the far wall and bit at a hangnail, her eyes moving from Jon to her mother, and then back again. Jon held up his hands and said, "I think I should go." He turned to Thanh and said thank you, and then he glanced at Ada, grimaced, and left.

Thanh was very officious and apologetic. He said sorry to Ada, to Elaine, Jon, and to Nicky and Delphine. He clasped his hands and said that the motorcycle was old. It was Russian-built and very prone to breakdowns. He said *prone* carefully, and he seemed aware and pleased that he had used the word correctly.

The light in the room was dim, people seemed to disperse and then come back. Ada apologized to Thanh for her brother's rudeness. She said that she was still feeling weak after her illness and thanked him. She turned to Vu then and asked if he could take her home or maybe find her a taxi. He stood and said that he had his bicycle and if she didn't mind sitting on the carrier, he would take her back to her hotel.

The rain had stopped, the sky was gray, and a warm wind came off the water. Vu rode her up the small lane to the ferry landing, and together, sitting on a wooden bench, they waited for it to pull in. It was not late, but darkness had fallen and on the other side of the Han River the lights of Danang glowed.

When the ferry arrived they crossed the gangplank and Ada walked to the bow and sat. Vu stood beside her, holding his bicycle with one hand. She tried to keep her eyes open but did not succeed. Her head dropped and lifted and dropped. She heard Vu light a cigarette, looked up, and saw his hands and his dark face. When they had exited the ferry, she again sat sidesaddle on the bike's carrier. She put her arms around Vu's waist and pressed the side of her face lightly between his shoulder blades. He didn't seem to mind and as they rode she felt the movement of his shirt against her cheek.

.   .   .

ADA WAS ASLEEP BY THE TIME JON CAME BACK TO THE HOTEL, AND in the morning neither said a word about the night before. But while they were eating breakfast Jon told Ada that he was going to fly up to Hanoi for a while. "I want to see the city," he said. He sat back and ran a hand through his hair. "And there's not a lot left here. For me."

"And for me, Jon, you think there's a lot for me here? The hospital called again about Dad's ashes. We have to face that. We told Del we'd be home soon."

"We'll figure it out. It just doesn't have to be done at this moment. I'm going up to Hanoi to be on my own for a while. Will you let me do this."

Ada stirred sugar into her coffee. She did not respond.

Jon sighed and said, "Yesterday was kind of lousy."

"Kind of?"

"It wasn't planned. And then Elaine lost it. Came out of nowhere."

"Really." Ada shook her head. She lit a cigarette and said, "You want to break things into pieces but what you're really after is attention."

"I didn't break anything. Dad did."

"No, Jon. Dad made a choice for himself. I know that you were hurt by Dad, that you didn't feel he praised you enough, or that he didn't admire you or accept your lifestyle, but what he did here in Vietnam is about him, not you. He didn't kill himself so that you would be left without a father. That's just wrong thinking."

Jon called the waitress over and paid for the breakfast. He said that he didn't owe their father anything else. He would be moving on.

"You're going to Hanoi alone?"

"I'm going to Hanoi alone." He looked at Ada and asked

whether she would be lonely by herself. He worried that she might do something rash.

"Uh-uh," she said. "I'm fine. Really."

They left the restaurant and walked down the sidewalk, past the post office, and across the street to the harbor. While they walked Ada said that there had been something between Elaine and their father. "Elaine talked about him yesterday. I could see that she liked him."

"Elaine Gouds. Well, well. I wonder if Jack knew."

Ada said that she liked the idea of their father spending time with Elaine Gouds. Elaine was clever and she had a privileged woman's allure and their father must have been intrigued by her confidence and her sharp beauty. They were quiet for a time as they walked alongside the river.

"What will you do while I'm gone?" he asked.

She said she didn't know. "Wait for you."

Later, they went up the street to the airline office, where Jon bought a ticket to Hanoi for the following morning. Ada stood there watching him and was aware of the sharpness of his shoulders and the soft bristles of his freshly cut hair.

Jon left for the airport early the next morning. Ada said goodbye to him at the hotel entrance and then went to the café across the street. At first it felt good to be alone, but back in the room later she saw Jon's empty bed, panicked, and wondered why she had let him go. At loose ends, she read and then showered and read some more. At one point she thought of Thanh's party and of Jon and Jack, and she recalled Vu riding her down the lane to the ferry and how his silence had made her feel safe. She thought that she wanted to see him again. She liked his presence and that he had known her father. His address was among her father's things.

That afternoon, she took her map and walked up Quang Trung Street, past metal forges and a glass blowing factory. She paused at Ong Ich Khiem Street. It was a hot day, and she had forgotten her hat. She stood in the shade of an awning. The sun had tired her out. She sat down on a red plastic stool and took a bottle of water from her backpack and drank slowly, watching the street. A bread vendor passed by, a woman on a bicycle.

When she stood finally and continued walking, she found that she had lost her sense of direction. She stopped a young boy, pointed at the map, and said a street name. The boy grinned at her and spoke quickly in Vietnamese and pointed in the direction Ada had been going. The boy asked for a cigarette. Ada gave him one, though he must have been no more than thirteen. She left him squatting by the gutter, smoking, hugging his bare knees. She carried on and eventually came to the street she had been looking for. She followed the small lane and found the number on a green gate. Everything appeared locked, the gate, the door beyond the gate, the shuttered windows. She called out and from inside the house came the sound of barking. She looked around for neighbors, for movement, but saw nothing. She stood close to the gate and waited for a while and then, disappointed, found her way back to the hotel.

That evening it began to rain and she ate in a small restaurant that was actually a boat on the harbor. An old man, who might have been a waiter or the restaurant owner, sat in the corner, his head on the table, sleeping. There were no other customers. She drank a beer and ate crab and fried vegetables with rice that was full of small pebbles. After dinner she found herself in a taxi going back to Hoang Vu's house. She believed that, if she remained here in Danang for a while, she would be able to discover something new and essential about her father, something previously concealed. With the conviction of these thoughts she experienced a strange feeling of hope. The slap of the windshield wipers in the rain lulled her into a sense of calm and safety.

The green gate was unlocked and the shutters of the house were open now and lights glowed from the front room. Ada asked the driver to wait. He didn't understand. She moved her hands out toward the house and said, too loudly, "I will go out. I will come back. I will check."

"Chick," the driver said. He held out his hand for the fare.

Ada paid him and said, "You wait. Right?"

The driver grinned and nodded.

She got out of the taxi, closed the door, and the driver left. Ada raised her hand to call out but at that moment a dog rushed at the gate and snapped at her. She jumped back and said, "Shoo," but the dog kept on barking until a young girl appeared. The girl said something and threw a rock. The dog yelped and circled to the back of the house. Behind the girl was Hoang Vu. He asked Ada in. Ada said that she had been there earlier in the day, and that she wasn't usually so impatient, however she had been free for the evening. She shrugged and smiled and waited to see where her explanation would fall. She had come out of the rain but still her hair was wet and she brushed at it with a bare hand. They were standing in the sitting room; the doors were open and gave out onto the garden. Vu, when he said her name, stretched out the first vowel. His voice was low. He asked her to sit.

In the room there was a cello case and a piano and there were also many paintings and sculptures. Ada was sitting beside one of the sculptures, made from what looked like concrete and iron, which depicted five men bent over and carrying enormous weights. Vu said that the name of the piece was *Carrying Cannonballs up to Dien Bien Phu*. His name was scratched onto the base.

Ada said she liked the shapes of the heads. "My sister lives with an artist," she said.

Vu took in this information. He smiled and said that her sister must have good taste. He offered Ada a beer. Or whiskey. She noticed his arms, the thinness and the veins against the dark skin. His shirt was unbuttoned and she saw his narrow chest.

She said she would prefer whiskey. He stood, and as he left the room she noted that he walked carefully as if judging each step, and that he held his hands slightly out from his body, a kind of balancing act. When he returned and handed her a glass of whiskey, she asked about the little girl. Was that his daughter?

His niece. "My sister lives here as well. I don't have children." He called out, twice, and the girl appeared. She wore a yellow dress with white lace trim. Black flat shoes. Her hair was in braids. "This is Phuong," Vu said.

Phuong clasped her hands and said, "How do you do?"

Ada smiled and said hello.

"Phuong plays piano. Would you like to hear her?" He made a motion with his fingers and spoke quickly. Phuong shook her head.

"Yes, yes," Ada said. "Please."

Phuong nodded this time and went over to the piano. Lifted the cover, pulled the bench toward her, and sat. She played a short simple piece that Ada recognized. Phuong's back was straight, her toes barely touched the ground. She played by memory and when she was done she stood and curtsied and then stood off to the side, sneaking looks at Ada as Vu explained that his sister taught music at the local high school. "Flute, cello, violin, piano. She is very talented and so, as you can see, is her daughter. Bach. I love Bach."

Phuong slipped from the room and returned with a plate of chocolate wafer cookies. Held them out to Ada, who took one. Phuong turned to her uncle, who waved her away. Mouselike, her small flat feet barely scraping against the floor, she left the room.

Vu leaned toward Ada. "Now, tell me, what brings Ada Boatman to see Hoang Vu?"

Ada said that she was interested in finding out about her father. "He'd written down your name. You told me that you met with him. So here I am. Silly me."

"There is nothing silly about this. It is wonderful to spend time with the beautiful daughter of Charles Boatman." He said this plainly, with no hint of flirtation. His hands were at rest on his knees. He explained that he had met her father only once and that they had spent the evening together. "A good man," he said. He lit a cigarette. Offered Ada one. "I never saw him again," he said.

"My father died," Ada said.

Vu said that he knew. He had heard this at the party and also again through Thanh just recently and he had not been happy to hear this news. He was looking over her head when he said this and then he sighed and his eyes met hers and then moved over her face and took in her shoulders and arms and the rest of her body. He looked at her face again and said he was sorry. Ada said thank you.

Vu said that it was an odd thing to thank someone for expressing sorrow about a father's death. Did she not think? He said, "Two nights ago, on the ferry, you were not well. And so we couldn't talk. But now, you are better."

Ada said, "I was wondering if my father said anything. If he told you something about himself."

"When your father was here I am afraid that we drank a lot. And that I did most of the talking. Even so I would have a difficult time relating what I said, let alone what he said, but we talked of many things. Of poets, of your country, of his children, yes, of his return to Vietnam. He told me he had read and admired a certain novel by one of our best writers."

"That's the novel then. By Dang Tho. I've also read the book, thinking I might find something in it to explain my father. Or what he saw in himself."

"And you have found this something?"

Ada shrugged. She said that perhaps all men who had fought in the war would find something in the novel to relate to. "It's a very strong story, full of sadness, and I know that my father's experiences in Vietnam produced sadness."

"Dang Tho writes with great certainty and brilliance. He tells his own truth. However, I have a brother in Hanoi who works at the writers' association, and he says that there is more than one fish in the sea, that Vietnamese literature has many very good books, and isn't it too bad we can't translate those for the foreigners." He held up the bottle of whiskey. "More?" Ada nodded, and as he poured she saw once again the thinness of his wrist. The whiskey, the warmth of the room, Vu's physical proximity, all of this gave her a feeling of comfort. She raised her head and leaned toward the intimacy of Vu's voice and said, "The police believe that my father killed himself."

Vu made a humming noise that was almost inaudible. He said, "I had heard that. It was told to me and I thought that this was possible but it was not from the horse's mouth. Is this what you think? That he killed himself?"

"Yes," Ada said.

"I am sorry about this. I saw unhappiness in your father." As if considering this, Vu paused, and then he said, "Several years ago I met an artist from Chicago. There happened to be an exchange of Vietnamese and American artists and she came to Danang. We fell in love. It was foolish love, but it was love. She wanted me to come to America. I said, 'I cannot leave my country. I love it. This is my place. Why would I want to live in Paris or L.A. or Chicago? What language would I speak? No, Vietnam is my country, and though it has its faults, I will stay.' I suggested that she stay in Danang. She did not like that idea. So, she left.

"When I told my sister, she laughed. She said this: 'That woman will pull your heart from your chest and leave it on the floor. You are the jasmine sprig, she is the field of buffalo dung. She will betray you. She will love you and walk away. She has a passport. You don't. You are making a fool of yourself. She has white hands that are smooth and her soft skin is seducing you. Marry a Vietnamese girl, they do not smell like cheese and sour milk. A Vietnamese girl will wash your face and take off your shoes when you come home from work. This girl will run off with

other men. She will dance to the Bee Gees late at night in small
bars and then come home and expect you to have dinner prepared.
She will buy jewelry and waste your inheritance. She will take you
away to Chicago, where they eat food from tins and women sleep
with men who are not their husbands and large groups of people
have sex. She is too beautiful. She doesn't speak our language. She
wears short shorts and her legs are long and white. Other men will
want to touch those legs and she will let them. You are Vietnamese.
You eat *pho* for breakfast. She eats cornflakes. If you have children, they will speak English. She is not a good artist.' " Vu paused
and smiled. "My sister has strong opinions." He lit a cigarette.
Said, "Most of this was not true, of course. Except for the last part.
Her art was not the best."

The dog had come back into the room. It nosed Ada's leg and
flopped over. Ada was quiet. She had listened to Vu talk and she
had smiled. She didn't know why he had told her this story; it
seemed too comical, too far-fetched, too self-centered, and maybe
even made up. It seemed more like some set piece that he recited as
a sort of warning to every foreign woman he met. Still, his voice
had taken her to another place and she wanted to stay in that small
room with Hoang Vu, she wanted him to tell another story. He
showed little curiosity about her and this was disappointing in a
way. She tried to imagine him falling in love with the artist from
Chicago. She wondered if he fell in love only with other artists. At
the end of the evening, when he said that he would take her home,
she said there was no need.

"Of course there is a need," he said. "It is raining and a taxi
will be difficult to find and you cannot walk at this hour." He disappeared and came back wheeling his bicycle. "My car," he said,
and he laughed.

And so, she sat with one of her hands on Vu's waist, the other
holding an umbrella, the rain nevertheless dripping onto her back.
Vu weaved through the streets. He did not speak. At one point he

sang a brief song and then stopped. Ada wanted to rest her head against Vu's back, but this time she had no excuse, she was not sick. And so she held his small waist and felt him breathing in and out. She imagined a wraith.

At the hotel she handed him the umbrella and thanked him for the evening. For the ride. Vu nodded. His face was dark as if carved from some ancient and nearly extinct wood. Then he was gone. His shirt glowed in the dim light of a streetlamp, and then he disappeared into the black rain. Ada climbed the stairs to her room. She undressed and showered. Passing from the bathroom to the bed, she saw herself in the mirror, her shape, fleeting proof of her own existence.

SHE SAW HIM AGAIN THE FOLLOWING MORNING. THE RAIN HAD stopped during the night and the sun was out but even so it was a cool morning. He brought her the bicycle and said it was hers to keep until she left the country. He had painted it black. She asked him when he had found time to do this.

"At night," he said. "I do not sleep well. Sometimes I don't sleep at all."

They were sitting in the café across from the hotel. As Ada ordered a breakfast of eggs on rice and coffee, she noticed Yen standing in the café entrance, talking to one of the waiters. She turned to look at Vu and then shifted her gaze back to Yen, but he had disappeared and only the waiter remained.

Ada felt a brief moment of pity for the boy but then shrugged and asked Vu if he was hungry.

He said no and lit a cigarette.

She said, "You smoke too much. You should eat instead."

Vu said that the cigarette was a friend and it was hard to give up a friend. Besides, he had eaten early in the morning with his sister.

Ada imagined him sitting across from his sister, bending over a bowl of rice, the lines of the chopsticks dissecting his wrist. She could smell him. A breeze passed across the table and it carried his scent and she smelled soap and something else, a hint of some spice, cilantro perhaps, maybe ginger. He had a beautiful face. She tried not to stare, then she said, quite abruptly, that she wanted to go out to the village her father had visited. "I guess I could ask Mr. Thanh to take me there, but I thought you might want to come instead and translate for me."

"I'm not a translator. That is Thanh's job."

"I know. It's just, I don't know, I thought it would be easier with you." She was embarrassed and wondered if Vu could notice this.

That evening, he called on her. He gave her a Chinese ink drawing of three boys squatting and playing marbles in the dirt. The lines were uncomplicated and round. "Very simple," he said. "Not brilliant." She said she loved it. She had seen boys playing in the street, just like this. She invited him up to the rooftop and they sat at the table. A breeze came in off the harbor and brought with it the smell of fish and salt water. Vu said that he had found out where the village was and they could drive out the following morning.

He said that the light was different from this height, that there were fewer shadows and the lack of shadows changed the colors of objects and the sky itself. He said that even her skin was a different color.

She said that she didn't know how to see color or light.

"So," Vu said suddenly. "What do you think, do you want to go dancing?"

"With you?"

"Of course. I don't dance, but we can watch other people dance."

"Wait here," Ada said, and she left Vu on the rooftop and went to her room. She changed into a red dress whose hem was possibly too short but she liked the idea of dancing and the dress was suitable. When she climbed the stairs she found Vu leaning over the balustrade, gazing out at the city, and she stood beside him. He turned to look at her and he lifted his right hand and lightly touched the back of her neck.

The club was in the back of a restaurant. Through the kitchen, past an old woman boiling lobster in a terrifically large pot, and into the din of recorded music and flashing lights. They sat at a corner table and drank Singha beer. It was very dark and loud, and occasionally Vu leaned over to say something into Ada's ear. There was his mouth, the rasp of his solicitous voice, and a hand on her arm. "Go ahead, dance."

She tried to pull him up, but he refused. And so she danced alone, to music of the seventies, and in the midst of the crowded floor she caught glimpses of Vu in the corner: his dark suit, the flashing lights revealing his face, his hand at his brow, the glowing cigarette. She could still feel his hand brushing across the back of her neck. When she returned to the table, Vu was wistful. He said, "Ten years ago I would have been severely questioned for talking to a foreigner. Today we can sit here and you can dance and then come back to talk to me and nobody bothers us."

He paused, lit a cigarette. He crossed his legs and clasped his hands. "This is good," he said. "You and me. Now."

A boy, probably no more than eighteen, approached Ada and asked if she wanted to dance. She shook her head. He looked mournful and asked, "Are you sure?"

She shook her head again.

When he was gone, Vu said, "You see, everyone envies me."

She did not dance again but instead watched Vu as he talked to her and she thought about his hand touching her face. Here, in the bar, he seemed more cautious, and once, when she put her head close to his, he smiled and pulled away and said that the beer was making her too happy. They left the bar late and walked up toward

sure this is it?" and then she looked about and walked the length of the village and then down a footpath to the stream at the base of a small hill. At the stream a young woman squatted on a rock. Vu said something to the woman, and she looked at Ada and then looked away. She picked up the clothes she had been washing and left, pressing a large bowl against her hip.

Ada walked back up the path, followed the swaying hips of the woman. There was the sound of the wind. Nothing but the wind. The palm branches moving above her. It might have been here, or here, or here. There was the sky and the earth and up from the earth popped a little boy, a chicken tied to his shorts with string. The chicken was upside down, its head brushed the dirt. A girl in bare feet who touched Ada's kneecap. The top of the girl's head, the flat crown. And then a multitude of children, swarming her, calling her names, and she turned and turned again, calling out for Vu, who waded into the pack and took her arm. He pulled her into some shade, close to several old men. Ada caught her breath and then asked if Vu thought anyone here remembered the war.

He shook his head. "No one knows anything. There're all too young, and if they're old enough, they don't want to remember."

Ada said, "Ask them."

Vu lit a cigarette and spoke to the men. One of them began to talk and his voice went up and down and he gazed out over the treetops and sometimes he closed his eyes. When he was done, Vu said, "He remembers fire coming out of the sky and animals dying. He remembers people dying but he cannot remember how or why. It was a war."

Ada observed the old man. He had few teeth, he was wearing dark pajama pants. His knuckles were large and his hands were thin.

"Tell him my father was here as a young man."

"I don't know," Vu said.

"Please, I want to tell him this."

Vu obeyed. He spoke to the old man, and then the old man spoke.

Vu translated. "He is sorry."

"What do you mean?"

"He is sorry that your father is dead."

"You told him that."

"I said that he had drowned in the ocean."

Ada sighed. "Did you tell him that he was here as a soldier."

Vu said he had. "I told him and everyone else to go home for lunch."

Ada, Vu, the old men, and the children formed a crowd. The quick brown hand of a child flashed and touched Ada's arm. Vu pushed the child away.

Ada said, "Do they know that my father was here with five other soldiers. Do they know they came here and shot villagers and that my father killed a young boy."

"What are you saying?" Vu had folded his hands in front of his stomach and he was studying Ada.

"That's what happened. I want them to know. Will you tell them?"

"It will serve no purpose. They won't believe me. They are farmers. They don't care about a war that happened thirty years ago. They care about their crops and their next meal."

"Tell them, Vu. Please."

Vu nodded and then he held his hand, palm skyward, and he spoke slowly and quietly. As he spoke he gestured at Ada and then he made a circular motion with his arm and he stopped talking.

The old man looked at the ground. One small child had crouched at Ada's feet.

Vu said, "There."

After some time, Ada spoke. She said, "Did they understand what you were telling them?"

"Yes. I think so."

"Do they remember?"

"Not yet."

"What about the boy my father shot?" She knew that she was speaking too quickly and that she must have sounded desperate but she did not stop. "Does anyone here know about a young boy an American soldier shot?"

"I don't know." Vu tried to take her arm but she shrugged him away.

"My father left a letter. My father left a letter and in it he said what he did here. What he did here during the war." Then she told Vu what the letter had said.

Vu turned to face Ada and his face told her nothing of what he was thinking. She felt that the words she had just spoken were still inside her. Her throat began to ache. She closed her eyes.

Vu led her back to the car, along the dirt path. A dog crossed in front of them, running sideways. The children chattered and called out. Vu spoke to the driver and the car pulled away and the children chased it, their quick hard voices fading. Through the dark glass of the window Ada saw the old man in the doorway. He was squatting now, staring out at something beyond the children and the car and the trees, and finally she began to breathe more easily.

When Vu spoke he said that time climbed upward in layers and that with each consecutive layer the past became buried. He said that an old man like the one here in the village was happy simply to eat his soup every day, sleep in a dry bed, and have regular bowel movements. He said that the old man had no wish to tunnel back through the years. "Your father, on the other hand, needed to go back. As do you, Ada." He paused, and into that silence Ada whispered, "My brother thinks that our father was a coward."

Vu shook his head and said that he did not know what a coward was. He had heard the word used before. On people who tried to escape suffering, on people who refused to act in certain ways, on people who ran from danger. He said that he did not see anything wrong with running from danger. In her father's case, he said, it was different. Killing one's self required strength. It was like running toward danger. Running toward the unknown. It was not easy. "Your father was a good man," he said.

When they got back to Danang, she asked Vu to join her for a meal, but he said he was tired. Speaking English tired him out. In any case, he wanted to go home and drink. She was surprised at this confession and asked him if he was making a joke.

"Not at all," he said. "I am thirsty." Then he said that the following morning, maybe, he would take the train over the pass in the mountains to Hue, where he would visit a friend, and if she wanted she could come with him. He would introduce her to this friend of his, a man he had gone to school with who was also an artist—but not predictable like him, he laughed—and she could visit the famous Citadel there. His voice lifted and then fell away. She thought then of Elaine, and how on the beach she had talked about Charles and the train and the trip they had taken, and how Ada had realized then that they had been intimate.

That night she went to bed early and dreamed she was riding the ferry across to My Khe with her father. They both had bicycles and every time she turned to ask her father a question he would shake his head and shush her, as if she were a baby. They left the ferry and rode up past the swinging tire that hung from the tamarind tree, on up the trail past the metal factory where men with bare torsos worked beneath the welder's arc, swinging their large hammers against the heavy metal. On toward the beach. At one point her father passed her and she called out for him to slow down but he didn't acknowledge her cries. Then he disappeared. She did not reach the beach. She turned back and retraced her route, alone now, down the sloping path toward the ferry. When she boarded, she saw a man who was talking to a large group of people. He was pointing and talking as if describing something in the distance. The man turned to her, and she saw that it was Hoang

Vu. She stood for a while and listened and then moved on, toward
the bow of the ferry, and stood looking out to where the lights of
Danang burned holes into the night.

THEY TOOK THE EARLY AFTERNOON TRAIN AND THE SUN WAS
above them and from her window seat Ada saw the ocean below,
and as the sun hit the water and the waves rolled against the shoreline, she thought of her father sitting on one of these benches beside Elaine Gouds and holding her hand. Ada remembered her
father's hands and the scars on his fingers and she thought of the
tenderness with which he had so often touched her face, even when
she was a grown woman, and of how he used to whisper her name.
She thought of the ocean taking him, or of him giving himself up
to the ocean.

As the train began the slow climb that led to the pass, she
turned to Vu and told him that she had dreamed of him. She described the dream: her father, the men in the factory, the bicycles,
Vu. She touched his hand, and later, she put her head against his
shoulder. His suit jacket was old and worn, and she saw the frayed
cuffs and his thin wrists.

"You are missing someone," he said.

She said that that was probably true. She wanted to touch his
face but did not.

An hour went by. The train continued its climb. Ada slept
briefly and woke with a start as a southbound train passed them. Vu
was smoking, his feet were resting on the seat in front of him. Ada
yawned. The sun fell onto her lap and then disappeared.

Vu said that as she slept her knee had jumped. "From here to
there," he said, indicating the distance.

Ada let her head fall again on his shoulder. She said, "Tell me
something. About yourself. All I know is your name and your age,
and even then I don't know if it's true. And where you live. The
shape of your hands. That I know. But that's all."

Vu looked at his hands as if to verify their size and shape. "You don't want to know more," he said.

"But I do."

He said that he would tell his story but he would dwell only on simple facts. He put out his cigarette. As he spoke he stared out the window and his voice was soft and Ada could feel her hair move as he exhaled. He said, "I grew up in Hanoi. I was a boy and then I was a man. I became a man at eighteen, when I fought in the war. When I came back to Hanoi from the war in 1975, my father was very happy. He gave a party and invited many guests to our small apartment. Some of them I knew, some I did not. My father gave a speech. He rattled on about the glory of victory and the strength of the victors. At the end of his speech he spoke about how fortunate I was. He raised his glass in a toast and people called out. Much was made of my survival. My wife, Ly, was dancing with one of our neighbors, a police officer. Yes, Ada, I was married. I was very young. Too young. In any case, my wife, Ly, had been dancing with this man all night. At one point my father said to me, 'What is that man doing, dancing all evening with Ly?' I looked at my father and said that I was no dancer and it was a good thing that she had somebody. I had been drinking *cung,* and then I switched to whiskey and then someone handed me vodka.

"The following day my wife said that I was a different man than before the war. My father defended me. My wife said that I drank too much. In fact, I was drinking when they had this argument. We continued to live as a husband and wife and she stayed in our house—she made money and brought it home—however, sometimes at night I woke and the hollowness of the house and the unhappiness of my wife made it hard for me to breathe.

"There was a famous historian who lived across from our apartment. His name was Nguyen Khac Vien, and in the mornings before I went out I could see him typing by the window. He had many books on the wall and there was a woman who served him tea and sometimes she stood beside him and talked. She was younger and quite handsome. Children came and went out of his apartment. I was curious about him because he was many things I was not. He was respected, he was an intellectual, he was offering the world something new. He had weight and privilege that had been earned. One day he was not there and my wife said that he had TB and was quite ill. I looked for him, but his chair by the window was empty and I thought that even a man who had studied in Paris and could translate from various languages and who would be given a king's burial, even that kind of man had to die. And then one day he was back, and feeling the time was favorable, I went over to knock on his door. His wife invited me in for tea, and I sat with the famous man. We drank tea and he spoke slowly. He had collected an enormous anthology of Vietnamese literature beginning before A.D. 1000, and as I opened the book and paged respectfully through it I had a brief but important idea: I saw my own life as inconsequential and small."

Vu stopped talking. "I am boring you," he said.

"No, not all." Ada said that she wanted him to go on. She said that she loved the sound of his voice.

"And the story, the essence? That is nothing?" He smiled.

"Of course it is. I meant that your voice makes the story richer. Please."

"As my father indicated earlier in his speech, I survived the war. Of course, we won the war, but even so I felt no joy. I suppose I should have spent time with the men from my brigade, the ones who survived, but I didn't. The few I might have shared an hour with lived in the countryside, but I did not see them. I have not told anyone how I survived, because I myself do not know. My wife said that it had to do with when I was born, the year of the goat, but I knew that Khuc, who was in my brigade, and who had both legs blown off by a land mine and then bled to death, was born in the same year, and so I did not put much faith in my wife's words."

The train had halted at a siding. There were a few small shacks and there were children standing in the shade. Two dogs copulated near a bicycle. They ran in circles while a young boy beat them with a stick. Chickens bathed in the dust. Ada, holding Vu's arm, did not say anything, but she was aware of the movement of his muscles beneath his thin shirt.

When the train finally jolted and began to move again, Vu said, "My mother sold bread. Early in the morning she would ride her bicycle down to the bakery and put bread in her basket and then ride through the street calling, *Ban mi, oy*. It was humiliating for a woman who was well educated to have to work like a peasant. But when she lost her job because of the war, she began to deliver bread.

"My father was the director of a linguistic institute. He came home one day and told me that if I wasn't going to work I should write. When I asked him what I should write about, he said the war. I should write about the war.

"He seemed surprised at my rejection of that idea. He was sitting across from me, drinking tea. He said that I might like to work as a librarian at a teachers' college. I said that I could not be a teacher or a librarian. He said that I wasted money on drink. He had never said this to me before. The pride he used to feel for me was gone. Now all I saw on his face was disgust.

"After that, I drank every day. I began to carry my notebook with me to the café, though I never wrote anything good or important. My father, when he saw me with my notebook, told his friends and neighbors that I was a poet. My wife mentioned this one night. She whispered that my father was very sad because his son was useless. And so now, to save face, he had begun to call me a poet. 'Is it true?' she asked.

"In order to please everyone, I enrolled in biology at the University of Hanoi. I told my father I would do my studies in a political school. This pleased him and he wanted to give another party. My mother convinced him that we should wait until I had graduated.

"At school I was restless and bored. I had a colleague who

wanted to raise chickens by feeding them only jacinth. I thought this was absurd and so I fed poison to the chickens, killing them all. For this farce I was discharged from the school.

"My father called an old friend of his who was a professor of art at a college in Hue and asked if I could work there as a librarian. The friend said that this was not possible; he already had two employees in the library. However, perhaps I would like to be a student. My father presented this proposition to me. I was sitting at home, my writing notebook beside me. There was a blue pencil stuck between the pages. I was twenty-six years old. My wife was pregnant. I agreed.

"The fact was I knew something about drawing, but not much. And so I had much to learn. I moved to Hue by myself and went home once every three months. I still suffered from nightmares. On the nights I was home, my wife shook me awake and asked me who I was talking about. I had been calling out various names, and they were the names of my dead friends. I dreamed about ghosts and dead women. I did not tell my wife about my dreams.

"In the darkness, my wife at my side, I was aware of my father snoring beyond the thin wall, and the rasplike breathing of my grandmother. My wife took my hand and placed it on her belly. She did not speak, but I could tell that she was pleased."

Vu lit a cigarette and closed his eyes. Finally, he said, "I am thirsty. Perhaps Chi will have something good to drink." He sat up straight and put on his shoes. Ada shifted and watched as he tied his laces. She saw the back of his neck, the hollow between the ligaments.

He said, "The story was much too long."

"It wasn't long enough."

"Yes?"

"What happened to your wife?"

Vu laughed. "She married the dancing police officer." He moved his hands and arms in a poor imitation of a dance and said, "There was no baby."

Ada waited for an explanation, but it was not forthcoming. Just that simple fact: no baby.

It was dark when they arrived in Hue. In the taxi, riding from the station to Chi's house, Ada sensed that the driver was going in circles, and that the scenes passing by were ones she had seen not more than a minute earlier. She turned to look at Vu, who was completely calm.

The house was outside of town. It was large and dilapidated, with broken windows and doors falling in and warped wooden floors.

Chi was a big, overweight man. He was wearing silk pajamas and holding a cat in his lap. Chi asked Ada where she was from and how old she was. He turned to Vu and said that she was beautiful. Vu shrugged. There were paintings stacked against the far wall and Ada asked if she could look. Chi lifted a pudgy hand and said, "But of course."

The style was very different from Vu's. Most of the works were abstract with a lot of color, and she found that they did not appeal to her. Vu called out that Chi was famous. His paintings sold for over a thousand dollars each. Chi seemed pleased with this announcement. Ada smiled and pretended to study the work while Vu and Chi huddled closer together and poured glasses of vodka. She heard words that she thought she recognized—*why, yes, no,* and *happy*—and once she heard Vu say her name. He turned to her then and translated. "Chi lives alone. He said we can stay for the night. He said you are welcome to look around the house."

She didn't want to stay for the night. She wanted a hotel room with a private shower. But she nodded at Vu and said, "Okay."

She went upstairs and found rooms that appeared not to have been used in a long time. There was dust everywhere, and in one bedroom two mattresses stood against a closet door. From the window there was a view onto a cement courtyard. There was a large tree and a swing hanging from a thick branch. At the edge of the courtyard sat an abandoned truck, quite large, with its bed raised and rusty. It was ancient and army green. Beside it a jeep with no wheels and in front of the jeep, two misshapen bicycles. She continued her tour of the house and searched for a room that might pass as a place to spend the night. There was one room with a mattress on the floor and a mosquito net folded over a wire that stretched between two walls. The mattress had no sheet, just a wool blanket. She stooped to touch the blanket and then the mattress, which felt damp.

Downstairs again, she went out the back door and into the courtyard. There was a pig in a pen, and a few chickens scratched at the dirt inside a wire enclosure. It had started raining and she was cold and hungry. She went inside and sat down beside Vu, who was gesturing with one hand and talking. She placed a palm on his leg and said, "I need food, I'm hungry."

Vu said something to Chi and Ada heard the word *doi*. She nodded and smiled.

Chi drove them in his old Mercedes to a restaurant on the other side of town. Ada was sorry that she had not changed out of her short skirt. The air-conditioning was on and she wanted to say that she was cold but instead she bit the inside of her cheek and stared out at the wet streets.

At the restaurant she decided to drink. It would loosen her up, and perhaps Chi would like her better if she were more talkative. She drank a hazy-looking liqueur that Chi had recommended. It was harsh and bitter but she drank it bravely and Chi looked at her with admiration.

He said something to Vu. Vu shrugged.

"What did he say?" Ada asked. She knew it had been some reference to her. Perhaps about her body, or what she was wearing, or the fact that she had drunk the liqueur. She was feeling warmer and welcomed the possibility of something.

Vu said it wasn't important. "He talks too much."

"Tell me."

"He said that I am too old for you."

Ada, as if she had been waiting all day for this statement, said, "Only twenty years."

"I am a drunk."

"I can learn to drink."

"I like to drink alone."

"You can. I will be in the next room, and when you call, I will come."

"You are a silly girl."

"I'm happy." Then she said *vui*, and then said it again except with the word *very* preceding it. She smiled. Saw that she could have what she wanted.

Chi was watching them. He was eating a brownish soup with squid and shellfish and using his fingers to pick the shells from his mouth. There was a candle on the table, and each time the rain and wind blew in through the open door, the flame flickered and almost went out. At one point Ada cupped her hand around the flame and felt the heat.

They drank and ate and talked in a mixture of Vietnamese and English. Sometimes, because he said he found it easier than English, Chi spoke French.

"Do you understand?" Vu asked.

Ada said, "A little."

"He's a show-off," Vu said. "And a worse drunk than me."

This was true. As midnight passed and the bottles were opened and emptied, Chi's tongue sped up. He stood at one point and recited something in English, looking from Vu to Ada. "The Substituted Poem," he said, and his eyes widened. His tongue clicked over consonants: "I hope my wife can keep down her rutting. Up north, I've had to put up with this sad dangler, down south, she'd better sit on her yawning clam. I hope it's tight and tortuous still, like a gopher hole." He paused. "And there is more," he said. He closed his eyes. Sat down.

Vu apologized to Ada. "He is not a very good reader of poetry. Nor of women."

SHE FELL ASLEEP BENEATH THE MOSQUITO NET IN THE ROOM with the window that looked out on the courtyard. Chi had given her a kerosene lamp and she felt, for a moment, that she was back on her father's land, in the bunker, waiting for the bombs that would never come. She had brushed her teeth in the kitchen where the water ran weakly from a small spout. She had not asked for a sheet, assuming that there would not be one in any case. She laid two T-shirts on the mattress and covered herself with the wool blanket. Vu's voice rose to her from the main floor. She fell asleep thinking about rats, willing Vu to come to her. When she woke it was quiet and very dark. She heard Vu breathing. He was lying on his back on the floor outside the mosquito net, still in his clothes; he had used his shoes for a pillow. She slipped her hand out of the netting and touched his head and the hair that fell to his shoulders. In the dark, she felt for the buttons on his shirt.

"Is it you?" she asked.

"Yes," he said, and she felt the slight vibration of his chest against the heel of her hand.

"I thought it was some small animal."

"I am some small animal."

She had unbuttoned his shirt. His chest was smooth and hairless.

"I was watching over you," he said. "Like those angels in fairy tales. Not the dark angels who carry you away to the other side, but the other, safer angels." He paused, and she could feel his chest rise and fall. "I thought that if I watched you long enough you would wake up. And that is what happened."

She did not invite him under the netting. The thin gauze between them made her braver, and she touched under his arms and

THE TIME IN BETWEEN 199

felt his throat; it was just as she had imagined. She unbuckled his belt and, with one hand, tugged at his pants. He lifted his hips, and in doing so brushed against her wrist and she moved her hand across him. She came out from under the netting and lay alongside him, trying to touch as much of her flesh to his as she could. His ankles, insteps, the thin legs. He did not move, did not speak. She straddled him in the darkness, and when their mouths met she discovered that he was not a very good kisser. Or that he did not like it. She tasted alcohol.

She placed her hand lightly over his eyes. Felt the movement of his eyelids. "Can you see me?"

He shook his head.

"Touch me, then."

He took a long time to come. Perhaps it was the alcohol, perhaps his age, perhaps fatigue. Vu fell asleep curled against her bum. They were under the mosquito net together. He snored lightly, his left arm twitched. Ada was wet between her legs but she didn't want to fuss with the lamp and look for a bathroom in the dark. She did not fall asleep until the sky began to lighten beyond the dirty window.

When she woke, Vu was gone. She put on a T-shirt and jeans and wandered the second floor in search of a toilet. She found only empty rooms and eventually went downstairs and used the small bathroom off the kitchen. It was a squat toilet, quite dirty. She hugged her knees and stared at the plastic pail in the corner. A cockroach migrated from the pail to the drain. She heard movement in the kitchen. When she came out of the toilet, she saw a young boy who wore only shorts, standing before a single gas burner. He was stirring something in a large pot. He turned toward Ada when she left the bathroom. He said, "Hello, how are you?"

"Good morning," Ada said.

The boy said that his name was Nhat. He was thirteen years old and Chi was his father. He lived with his mother, but he came here every morning to cook his father's breakfast. He waved at the pot. "Would you like some?"

Ada declined. She said that Nhat spoke very good English.

"There are more than two ways to skin a cat," Nhat said. He dipped his head and scooped whatever was in the pot into a bowl.

Ada went upstairs. Her little bag with its meager belongings lay yawning on the floor. She was light-headed and shaky. She sat on the floor and recalled that Vu, just before he came, had grasped the hair at her crown and pulled her head backward and, after, he had kissed her neck and described how it looked in the dim light of the moon. And now, in the brilliant light of day, he had disappeared.

When she arrived back in the kitchen, she asked Nhat if he had seen Vu.

"Hoang Vu is my uncle. He drove away."

"When will he be back?"

Nhat said that he didn't know. "I am sorry," he said. "My father is upstairs."

Ada pretended nonchalance. She ate a banana and sat in the front room looking at the doorway and the light that spilled onto the warped floor. She walked outside into the courtyard. Someone was sweeping leaves in the neighbor's yard. Voices, the yelp of a puppy, cry of a small child.

She bought bread from an old woman passing by the front street on her bicycle and ate it sitting on the porch, looking out across to the welder's shop beyond the trellis of Chi's yard. When Chi finally came downstairs, he said good morning. He was dressed in shorts and a large black T-shirt. His legs were stubby and bruised. He smiled and bowed slightly. "Vu went into town early."

He sat beside her and ate an orange. He said, "Vu is a lucky man. It has always been that way for him. He is full of luck. He survived the war. Then he became a painter and has done very well. People admire him. Now he has you."

"And there will be others after me."

"Perhaps."

Ada said that she didn't believe in luck. She said that whatever happened, happened. This might be called fate or it might be called luck, or it might be fact. She preferred to think of it as fact.

Chi said that might be true some of the time. He rose, breathing heavily, and walked into the kitchen. Ada heard him sharpening a knife. The blade against the whetstone and then the shuffling of his feet as he moved out into the yard. After a few moments a high-pitched squeal of a pig came from the courtyard and it did not abate. She rose and went and looked out into the courtyard. The son, Nhat, had tied the pig's feet and was sitting on its side, as if it were a hassock. Ada stood just inside the doorway and shuddered slightly. She wanted to but did not leave. She did not turn away.

Chi took a plastic pail and held it under the pig's neck. There was a black wire looped around the pig's snout. Nhat pulled on the wire and forced the snout back as Chi pushed the blade of the knife into the animal's throat. Ada heard the tearing of flesh. A thin rope of blood hit Chi's chest. The pig bucked and the boy rode him. The screams were higher now and they filled the courtyard like some ancient and infernal call. Ada wanted to cover her ears but she didn't; she knew that Chi was watching her. The pig sang and with each sucking squeal a fresh rope of blood arced out over the ground. Gradually, the howls became muted and muffled and then, quickly, as if a curtain had fallen across the scene, the pig died. Chi castrated the pig. He held up the testicles for Ada to see, grinned, said, "Very large," and threw them into the bucket of blood. Then he cut off the pig's head with a rusty saw while the boy held the ears. Chi's arms and legs were bloody.

Ada felt dizzy and her breath came in quick gulps. She turned away and walked back into the house and stood in the large front room. She could hear Chi and his son talking. They laughed. She tried to remember what Vu's hands felt like. She imagined a white room with a bed and clean sheets and a window that offered a view of a perfectly clear sky. She went to the toilet and washed her hands and face, and when she was done she smelled her hands. Upstairs in the room she'd slept in she gathered her things and then wrote Vu a note telling him that she was sorry. She told him not to worry, she would get back to Danang on her own. Then she went downstairs and out through the front door and onto the street, and she began to walk.

She knew the direction of the train station, but she did not know how far it was. She walked for about an hour, past roadside cafés and small factories, and then she entered a confusion of cars and bicycles and trucks, and a man on a motorcycle called out, *You,* and then again, *You,* until she turned to him and cried, "I do not know you." He laughed and drove away. She bent her head and carried on, watching her feet as they moved, aware that a window had been flung open onto a view of an alien and foreign place, and then, just as suddenly, it had closed.

The road was straight but at some point she turned left and then right and then left and so on until she halted, breathless, and held her arm out for the next available cyclo. It arrived, at its helm a boy who seemed not to have the strength to pedal her. But he did. Out of the bedlam of the streets and on toward the station, where the ticket master told her that the train to Danang would leave almost immediately.

WHEN SHE GOT BACK TO HER HOTEL IN DANANG, THE DESK CLERK handed her two messages. The first was from Elaine Gouds, who said that she would be at Christy's the following evening around eight and if Ada was available, she should join her. The second message was from Jon. He had called and left his number in Hanoi. She phoned him immediately, but no one picked up, and when the answering machine cut in and she heard a voice with a slight European accent, she hung up.

She tried once more a little later, and again there was no answer, but this time she left a message. She said she wanted to go back home. She wanted him to come back to Danang. "Please," she said, and she hung up. After, she looked at the phone thinking that if for some reason this wasn't the right number, how ridiculous she must have sounded.

Late that night Jon phoned. Ada asked if he had gotten her message. Before she could say anything else he told her that she should visit Hanoi. His voice was light and cheerful. "For a few days at least," he said. "It's done me good. It might do you some good. There's Lenin Park, and the old quarter's great. It's a fascinating city. We can go back to Danang together after." He went on to explain he was staying with someone who worked for the UN. "He's a Dutch man a friend in Vancouver told me about. In case we needed something. Andries. I don't know if he has room in his apartment but maybe I can find you a hotel nearby. How are you doing, Ada?"

She thought of the answers she could give, that she was lonely, that she had just come from Hue and had spent the train trip fighting off a dread that had left her breathless, or that she needed Jon right at that moment, but she said none of this and instead told him she would call him in a few days, and she hung up.

THE SKY AT NOON WAS WHITE AND THEN A FAINT BLUE APPEARED and by late afternoon a pinkness had arrived, washing down to the tops of the trees. She had spent the day aimlessly on the rooftop, and now when she stood to go down to prepare for her meeting with Elaine, her figure cast a long shadow across the rooftop. In her room she poured some scotch and sipped at it as she thought about what she should wear. She chose a dark short skirt and a sleeveless top, and then put on some makeup by the dim light of the bathroom mirror. She wanted Elaine to see her as strong, as someone neither given to nor swayed by petty judgments.

Elaine was alone at a table that overlooked the harbor. She was drinking tea. When she saw Ada she smiled and lifted a hand in greeting, and as soon as Ada sat down, she said, "Look, the other night at Thanh's. I'm sorry." Her long fingers worked at a napkin, smoothed it on her lap, plucked it up again. "Married people do that sometimes. Have their outbursts that should be private but unfortunately aren't."

She seemed tired, her face was more delicate than usual. She touched it now, narrow index finger with a bright red nail. It was her eyes as well. More furtive, but some other quality, as if she expected to see herself reflected in others.

Ada waved a hand as if to dismiss Elaine's concerns and then said that she had had a good time at Thanh's. Jane had been sweet and Sammy was adorable.

"Isn't he?" Elaine said, too brightly. Then she said that she was determined to salvage something from this experience in Vietnam. "I will not run." She called over the waiter and ordered a plate of shrimp. Ada asked for a Coke.

Elaine said that she and Jack knew an American doctor in Hanoi who had lived in Southeast Asia for many years and whose wife had just died in a car accident. A horrible thing. They had two young boys. "And this man is planning on staying in Hanoi," Elaine said. "Most of us might throw up our hands and go home, but he's staying. I admire that. The tenacity, the bravery, even the foolishness." She paused and then said, "I want to be brave like that."

"You are," Ada said. "I look at you and I see bravery."

Ada wasn't sure if this was true, but she knew that Elaine was pleased because she shook her head and smiled.

"You were away," Elaine said.

"I went to Hue," Ada said. "Coming down through the pass on my way back, I kept imagining my father on that same train. I remember you told me that you took that trip with him."

"Yes," Elaine said. Then she said, as if this were a sudden revelation, that after that trip, she had not seen Charles again, though she had tried. "He believed something about me that he wanted to protect me from." She leaned forward to take a cigarette from Ada's pack.

"Here," Ada said, and offered Elaine a light. She saw the small mole on Elaine's jaw. Almost imperceptible. The clean skin, the tiny flaw. Ada felt both empathy and aversion.

Elaine exhaled and said, "Your father was lost to himself. I think I recognized this in him." She turned to gaze out at the harbor and then said softly that she had heard Jon was in Hanoi. Thanh had told her. She smiled slightly and said, "Thanh keeps me informed." She said, "At Thanh's the other day, when I saw Jon's hands, I was amazed. He has Charles's hands. Exactly."

Ada said that Jon wanted her to go to Hanoi but she was thinking she wanted to go home. She said she thought she had been trying to find something that was still out there.

Elaine sat up straighter and said, "Who's the brave one now?" She put out her cigarette, then took a shrimp, slid the plate toward Ada, and said, "Your father told me once that he wanted to go to Hanoi. He didn't say why." Ada was suddenly aware that her father had revealed little to Elaine about himself. They might have talked, might even have been lovers, but Elaine Gouds did not truly know Charles Boatman.

"In his bag there was a ticket to Hanoi," Ada said. "But it had expired." She lifted her shoulders, conscious of the pointlessness of the comment. Elaine called the waiter over and ordered a rum and Coke. "Join me?" she asked Ada and then called out to the waiter, "Make it two."

When their drinks arrived, Elaine again mentioned Hanoi. She said that she knew a family who had returned to Australia for several months. "They have a house in Hanoi. It's in a suburb near the zoo. Sammy loves it. There's a small lake there, the streets are quiet. Before you leave, if you decide to go there and need a place to stay, let me know and I will try to arrange it." She smiled. Lifted her glass and drank, as if cheered by the prospect of someone else's plans.

AT NIGHT, ADA WOKE TO THE BELLOW OF A SHIP FAR OUT AT SEA and the reply of a foghorn. She got up and went to the bathroom. When she wiped herself she saw blood. This relieved her; she had been careless with Vu, giving no consideration to any conse-quences. She put in a tampon and went back to bed. She lay with her eyes open and thought that the following day she would go see Vu and tell him she was returning to Canada.

At noon, she rode her bike over to Thanh Thuy Street. The green gate was locked. She called out. Nothing. She paced the road and then stood in the shade and smoked the last of her White Horse cigarettes. As she was about to leave, Vu's sister came home. She was walking her bike, the basket full of flowers and vegetables. She nodded at Ada. Said, "Hello."

Ada rubbed her cigarette against the sole of her sandal, dropped it onto the road, and stood. "I was waiting for Vu. Of course. Is he still away?" Thien nodded and invited Ada in and they walked back to the kitchen. The dog leaped on Ada and pawed at her chest, and Thien took a knife from the sink and waved the blade at the dog, who scrabbled into the next room. Thien said in broken English that Vu was still in Hue. He would be back soon.

"How soon? Today?"

"I don't know."

Thien looked at Ada, and then the corner of her mouth lifted and Ada thought she must seem foolish and desperate. She said, "I'll go now."

Thien said, "Tomorrow, I am going away with my daughter. Maybe Vu will be here. You can try."

The following morning when she went back to Vu's house, she

found him home. He looked at her as if he had expected this visit. He said that his sister and niece had gone up north for a week or so, to see the family. He served her coffee and bread and sat across from her and watched her eat. He did not mention Hue or the manner of her leaving. She did not say what she had planned to tell him earlier, about wanting to return to Canada.

Later, he climbed the ladder to the small loft above the house. He painted through the morning while Ada moved about the house and then sat in the garden. At lunchtime Vu walked to the street corner to pick up some food. He came back with four bottles of cold beer and pork satay and cucumber-and-mint salad. They ate in the sunshine and talked about everything except themselves. After lunch Vu took Ada up to his loft. She stood with him in the center of the room, surprised by the mess, the empty paint cans, the half-finished canvases, the abandoned drawings. The painting Vu had been working on was on the easel by the window.

She took Vu's hand and looked at him, then leaned in and kissed him on the mouth. He allowed this, and more. She circled him, touching him as if she were a traveler who had stumbled upon some ancient relic. She asked if they should undress completely. "Completely," he said, not as a response, but more as if the word itself interested him. She took off her top and bra and her pants and underwear.

"Do you like what you see?" she asked.

He said that he liked her breasts and the curve of her hip, there, and he was amazed at the amount of her hair. "Here," he said and touched her pubic hair.

She said that she had her period; held up the string of the tampon and said, "See?" He said that for him this was something new; not even Elizabeth, the artist from Chicago, had shown him this. He called it a stopper and Ada said, "Something like that."

They lay together anyway. She was curious about his language and what things were called, and so he taught her and she repeated after him. Later, still naked, she lay down and he took a brush and traced, in Chinese ink, the outline of her body on the floor of the loft.

Over the next days, whenever she went up to talk to him, or to find him, or to make love to him, or simply to watch him, she would see the outline of herself on the floor, and always she would be amazed by her own shape and the emptiness within that shape.

Sometimes they slept in the back room, on a narrow cot, and at night she'd wake and listen to Vu breathing, and above her, in the loft, she occasionally heard a noise, as if a small object were being dragged across the floor.

"Rats," Vu said, when she asked him. He said that he used to have a cat but it had disappeared and now the rats had come.

She said that she hated rats.

One morning she came back from the hotel, where she had gone for a proper night's sleep, and she found him setting a trap in the loft. The trap was the size of a small hamster cage, with a door that swung down from the inside. Vu laid a banana at the back of the cage.

During the night, she woke to a bang and for the rest of the night heard the cage moving across the room. She told Vu, who groaned and said, "Don't worry, we'll drown it in the morning."

Ada got up and sat in the front room. There was a little wine left from the night before, and so she drank that and smoked one of Vu's cigarettes. She knew she could either choose to return home or continue down this strange road. She did not know why she was sleeping with Hoang Vu. Perhaps he was the country, or her father, or simply a notion of the country, or a notion of her father. She knew that she had never loved a man before, and she didn't know if she loved Vu. She knew only what she felt, a happiness in the morning when she heard his feet on the tile, a sense of well-being as she read in the garden while he worked above her, the giddiness of throwing herself at him, the need for sex, though he was slow and not always as interested as she. With other men sex had been hollow, but with Vu, because he was curious about details— the shape of her instep, or the vein leading from her elbow to her wrist—and because he would pause to note particulars with his dark voice, sex was unpredictable.

Vu would disappear. This she knew. One morning she would open her eyes and he would be gone and she would not find him.

She smoked another cigarette and then went back to bed. As she slipped under the mosquito net, he said, "You," and he placed a hand on her hip and she lay an arm over his chest and spread her fingers across his ribs.

In the morning he drowned the rat in the trap. He filled a large bucket with water and dropped the trap into the water. The rat swam very well, chewing at the top of the cage and then diving and returning to push its nose through the holes. When, finally, it stopped moving, Ada noticed that the rat's eyes had turned milky, or the color of dirty clouds.

The next time they caught a rat, Ada asked Vu to take it far away from the house and let it loose. She refused to let him kill any more. She said it was a terrible thing to think of an animal drown- ing. Vu left on his sister's bicycle, and when he returned the cage was empty. He sat across from her and said that her idea of how the world worked was very different from his. "You believe that there is goodness in most things and you believe that all things are equal. The president and the cyclo driver, the beggar and the writer, the rat and the dog. And because you believe this is so, then it must be. But it isn't." He smiled and said that for this reason he was very fond of her.

"And for no other reason?" she asked.

"There are other reasons, yes."

"But my naïveté, this you like."

He did not answer her directly. He said that naïveté was some- times passed off as innocence, or the other way around. Her father too seemed to approach the world in a certain way, though in his case it was neither innocence nor naïveté. "I will tell you this," Vu said. "Your father was disillusioned. I believe that is the word. Or disappointed, maybe. He came to this place and when he arrived he did not know why he had come. He might have thought it was to visit that village you and I went to, or to find people he once knew, or to uncover the same country he had experienced thirty years ago, or to find this, or discover that." Vu paused and moved a hand through the air and let it fall onto his knee.

While he had been speaking Ada had shifted forward, as if worried that Vu's words might slip away and disappear. She said, "But it *was* all those things."

"Yes, yes, absolutely," Vu said. "But suppose that all those things weren't enough."

Ada closed her eyes. When she opened them again, Vu was watching her. He said, "You have a different beauty than I am used to." He reached up and traced one of her eyebrows, and as he did so she pushed against his hand and bit down on the meaty part of his palm. A low moan filled the room. Ada, when she heard it, was surprised to recognize her own voice.

Later that afternoon she told Vu that she was thinking of going up to Hanoi to see her brother for a while and bring him back to Danang. She would take the chance to see Hanoi. She didn't know what to expect. She thought then of her father, of how she believed he had had every intention of going to Hanoi but somehow that intention had gotten misplaced. Vu lit a cigarette and drank from a glass that held a clear liquid which was not, Ada was certain, water. He said that there was nothing complicated in this. "It is simple," he said. "Often things are more simple than we think. Go." And then, as if to soften his tone, he said that if she needed help with something, if she was lost, or even if she wanted company one night, she should call his brother. And he wrote down his name and his work address.

THE TIME IN BETWEEN *211*

Riding her bicycle back to the hotel, she did not know why, but she began to cry. A cyclo driver passed her going the same way. He pulled up beside her and began to pretend to cry, and then he laughed and spat on the road and pulled away. At the hotel entrance, as she was wheeling the bike through the doors, she saw Yen across the street, standing in a doorway, watching. She paused and then turned away and went up to her room and packed her bags, looking out the window at one point to the place where Yen had been standing, but he was gone.

Just down the street from the hotel were the offices of Vietnam Airlines. She walked there and bought herself a ticket for the next day, and then she called Elaine and told her she would be visiting Hanoi and was she certain it would be all right to stay at the house of her friends.

"Yes, yes," Elaine said. "I'll call and tell them to arrange for the housekeeper to go and let you in."

"Are you sure?" Ada asked.

"They would love to have someone there. It's safer. You know?"

Ada left the following afternoon, and when her flight took off it circled Danang and far below she could see the ocean and the white sands of the beach at My Khe.

THE HOUSE WAS LARGE, WITH EVERY AMENITY, AND ON THAT FIRST evening, Ada felt the pull of home and realized that the last weeks had worn her out. The maid had let her in, fixed her a cup of coffee, and explained in slow English how to lock the doors and work the gas stove. Then she had left, and Ada, happy to be alone, explored the house. The living room had leather couches and a big-screen TV. Bunk beds in one room and a large canopied master bed with white linen and a goose down quilt. The art on the walls was modern. The bookshelves were overflowing: South American authors, a tattered version of *Don Quixote*, some mysteries, and there was a copy of *In a Dark Wood* signed by the author. Unlike her father's copy of the book, this one had a dust jacket, and on the back inside flap was a photograph of Dang Tho. He was squatting beside an empty railroad track. He held a cigarette. He appeared to be looking past the camera lens, as if there were something important happening behind the photographer.

In bed later, reading, she turned to the section in the novel where Kiet deserts his company and walks back to Hanoi. As she read, the death of the mother and baby saddened her once again:

the infant's howl, the opening at the mother's throat, the pink bubble. Ada imagined the complexity of her father's response and how he might have seen himself in the story. The war had touched so many lives, even her own now. Here she was, huddled in a chair as small gray moths struck the overhead light, delving into a story that her father had also read, but understanding that even this would not allow her to see how her father saw.

In the middle of the night she woke and called out for Jon. She heard the wind and the beating of something in the eaves of the house and she remembered where she was. She had come up out of a dream in which her mother was an old woman sitting on a chair in a corner of a room and she was calling for Ada to come to her.

It had been years since she had dreamed of her mother. The memory of her fell back on both the slightness and certainty of childhood recollections: the shape of her mother's naked waist as she sat before her mirror putting on perfume, preparing to go out, leaving Ada in charge; the heat of her body beside Ada later, after she had returned, the smoky smell caught in that hollow space where her neck became her shoulder. The scarcity of flowers at her graveside on the day of her funeral.

Ada got out of bed and went to the fridge and poured herself a glass of water. She heard again the beating of something in the eaves, and she saw, beyond the window, quick dark shapes, which in a moment of horrific lucidity she understood were tiny bats. When she went back to bed, in the moments before sleep pulled her in, she was fearful that the bats would find their way into the house and that when she closed her eyes she would dream again of her mother.

SHE SLEPT LATE, AND IT WAS AFTERNOON WHEN SHE LEFT THE house and walked out to a main thoroughfare where she took a taxi to the city's old quarter. She sat on a bench and watched the young boys circle the streets on their Hondas. Once, many years earlier, her father had talked about the hum of bicycles on the Vietnamese streets. A constant whirring, he had said, like the sound of many birds taking off. She did not hear that now. Instead she heard hawkers and the vehicles, the honking of horns. A child laughing. In a café she drank an iced coffee and listened to a British couple argue about the exchange rate on the dong. A legless beggar waited outside the door, holding a tin bowl.

Later, she took a cyclo to Lenin Park. Men and boys begged to shine shoes, lovers stood looking out over the lake, and in the distance very old missiles pointed into a blue sky. Vendors sold small figures made from colored dough, toys shaped out of beer cans, and plastic flags that read, "I love you too much" or "Happy, happy, happy." She walked around the lake and saw, beneath the shadow of a tree, a solitary man cooking a dog on a spit, feeding the fire with a rolled-up straw mat. Boats moved across the lake. A full moon hung swollen in the afternoon sky.

When she returned to the house, she ran a bath and soaked for a long time, looking up through the dusty window of the skylight above her. After, she ate cold cereal from the box and sat in the living room and paged through a photo album. The couple who owned the house had two children, a boy and a girl, and in the photos the whole family appeared bright and earnest.

She had called Jon in the morning, leaving a message on the machine, and when he finally called, waking her, she fumbled for the phone and believed for a moment that she was back in her hotel room in Danang.

"You're sleeping," Jon said.

"No. No." She sat up, the duvet ballooning around her legs.

"Why didn't you tell me you were coming. Where *are* you?"

Ada looked around her room. She said, "I'm in this gorgeous place in a suburb close to the Daewoo Hotel. It's the house of some friends of Elaine Gouds's. She arranged it for me. It's free and I feel spoiled. The whole setting is vulgar." She said that she had come to Hanoi to bring him back with her to Danang.

"We'll talk. Let's meet tomorrow for lunch. Andries will join us for a while. Is that okay?"

She heard, somewhere beyond Jon's voice, the lilting sound of another man's voice.

Jon laughed, not with Ada but with the distant voice. Then he said to Ada, "Tomorrow, okay?" and he gave her the name and address of an Italian restaurant. It was near the area where the embassies and consulates were.

"Okay, Jon."

When Ada arrived at the restaurant, Andries and Jon were there. Andries was a tall balding man who spoke English very well. Ada liked his easiness, his forthrightness, and could see why Jon liked him. Andries talked about Hanoi and literature and various artists he had gotten to know over the years. Then he talked about his work with the UN and about malevolence and the woeful state of the world.

He asked Ada why she was staying so far away from the center of town, and Ada explained about Elaine Gouds and the Australian family. She said that the house was large and too quiet and one night she had seen bats flying past the window.

Andries said that he knew of Jack Gouds. He did not indicate whether he and Jon had spoken of him, rather he said that Jack had some connections to some United Nations workers in Hanoi. "That man has many acquaintances," he said. Then he said that a man like Jack, whom he didn't know other than his type, was possibly the most dangerous kind of man. He believed in doing good, and those who tried to do good, Andries said, were inevitably dangerous, especially in a country like Vietnam. "Jack and his kind see the world as fodder for their beliefs. As if a person were a seedling and all you had to do was stick the seedling into a particular soil, water it, give it a special light, and it will grow into a Christian. A

Buddhist is always a Buddhist, even when converted." He raised his glass and drank.

Ada asked Andries if he had heard of the artist Hoang Vu.

"Yes, of course," Andries said. "For years he lived in the hills with the farmers and did drawings of rural life. Very romantic. However, he is too outspoken and so he's disliked by the authorities. There is a wonderful story about him. Next door to his house in Danang there is a piece of property that was supposed to be used for a factory. Hoang Vu didn't want a factory next to his house, so he sculpted a bust of Ho Chi Minh and placed it in the middle of the land. The digging for the factory couldn't go ahead because no one is allowed to take down anything to do with Ho Chi Minh. Hoang Vu does things like that." Andries paused and then said that Vu was known to like foreign women. "Though that might just be the small gossip of less famous artists. Pure jealousy."

Ada smiled bravely and remembered Hue, and Chi's drunken midnight recitation of the bawdy poem, and the rain driving in through the open doorway and the warmth of the candle as she cupped her hands around the flame. And how later, Vu had lain outside her mosquito net and whispered, "I *am* some small animal." And an angel, too. That was what he had called himself. One of those safer angels.

Andries had taken out his wallet and laid money on the table for the check. He picked up his briefcase and said that he had to get back to the office. He shook Ada's hand and said he hoped they would see each other again.

Ada and Jon left the restaurant and walked through the streets. At one point Ada took Jon's arm and said that she had missed him. She told him that two nights ago she had woken from a dream and called out his name. And then, not waiting for his response, she described the dream. He said that he had very few memories of their mother. In one she was standing at the kitchen counter mixing juice. She was wearing jean shorts and he leaned his head against her bare thigh and she reached down and touched his chin and her hand smelled of lotion. In the other it was dark. He had had a nightmare and had come into the living room to look for her and had found her lying under a man on the couch. "That's what I remember," he said.

"Dad told me once that he loved her terribly," Ada said. "I was maybe twelve or thirteen and I didn't know if he meant that theirs was a terrible love or if he loved her so much that there was nothing to replace it. I didn't ask."

They had come to a small park, where they sat, silent for a time, and Ada felt no discomfort in the quiet. After a while, she said, "We can't put it off forever." Then she said that she felt she was still looking for something, perhaps the thing their father had been looking for. "But maybe that's misguided. You remember the artist, Hoang Vu? He calls me naïve and innocent, though I don't think he means innocent in a complimentary way."

Jon smiled at this and then said that they would fly back to Danang together and they would take care of their father's ashes.

THE NEXT MORNING SHE WOKE EARLY AND MADE HERSELF COFFEE and she stood on the balcony and looked out over the lake. A blond woman pushed a stroller along the path. A little white dog followed. The clouds were gray and low in the sky and the air smelled of rain. The return flight to Danang was the following day and she saw the time before her as both scarce and never-ending. She thought of Vu and how once, in the darkness of his room as they had sat on his thin mattress and talked through the night, he had said that from a certain point onward there was no turning back and that it was important to reach that point.

Midmorning, she walked out to the main street and took a cyclo downtown to the writers' association. She had taken with her the name of Vu's brother and the address. The air was cool and she had only a thin sweater; she hugged herself to keep warm. The night before she had woken and the objects in the room had become shapes of animals and men, and she had stood and gone to the bathroom and then, back in bed, she could not sleep and so she had read and she had thought about her father and for a brief moment she had seen her father and Kiet standing side by side. And then the image had disappeared and she could not retrieve it. It had left her shaking and confused.

Her father was dead.

The writers' association was located in a hollow-sounding building with sparsely furnished rooms, and at first glance Ada was bemused by her foolishness as she imagined a series of strangers pointing her down various dismal corridors into inevitable dead ends. However, she was told, after several inquiries, that Mr. Phan Quoc would be glad to see her. He appeared and welcomed her into his office as if all morning he had expected her visit. He asked her to sit and then poured tea.

Ada said that she was a friend of his brother, Hoang Vu, and that he had given her this address. She moved her gaze around the room as she said "this address."

Quoc smiled and said that she must not misunderstand, but Hoang Vu was using *brother* in a general way. "We are not related. You see? But he is right, we are like brothers." Quoc poured himself tea and asked if she was happy in Vietnam. "Does it please you?"

Ada said it did. Then she said that she was curious about the Vietnamese writer Dang Tho. She thought, if it were possible, that she would like to learn more about him. Quoc nodded and said that he knew Dang Tho and he would be glad to give her information. He waved a hand, happily. He had very white teeth and graying hair. His movements were quick, marionette-like.

Ada saw beyond the window in the room the branches and

leaves of an enormous tamarind tree. A woman in a short blue dress appeared in the doorway. Her hair was long and straight. She dipped her head, entered, smiled, and sat down on the couch.

"Miss Vinh," Quoc said. "She is my assistant." He turned and spoke Vietnamese to her and then turned back to face Ada. The mood in the room changed. Mr. Quoc smiled more and showed his bright teeth. Miss Vinh asked Ada how old she was. Ada told her, and she nodded. Her eyebrows were thin lines, neatly plucked. She asked Ada why she wanted to meet the famous Dang Tho.

"Oh," Ada said. She looked at Quoc and then back at Vinh. "I don't know if I said that. I was only looking for information. My father fought in the Vietnam War and recently he had read Dang Tho's novel and was very moved by it." Ada paused. She was aware of Quoc's eyes. They were more gray than black, and this was disconcerting. She had lost her thought. It had been an important thought, but she had lost it. She took in a quick breath and then said that her father was no longer living.

Quoc said something to Vinh.

"Do you want to go dancing tonight?" Vinh asked. She fell back against the couch and crossed her legs.

Ada looked at Quoc, who smiled hopefully. No one seemed to have heard what she said about her father.

Quoc nodded at Vinh. "Tonight," he said. He spoke to Vinh in Vietnamese.

"About your father. We are sorry," Vinh said.

Ada acknowledged Vinh's comment, and then she said that she would not be able to go dancing that evening. She was sorry.

Quoc did not seem surprised. He leaned forward and said, "I will be honest, it will be very difficult for you to meet Dang Tho. There are formal letters you can write and there are requests for government help, all of this will not help. Unless you write for the *Time* magazine, you will not meet him." Quoc then scribbled something on a piece of paper. Slid it across the desk and said that this was where Dang Tho lived, flat 3-B. "Let me tell you some-thing," he said. "Dang Tho was awarded a prize in 1991 for his novel about the war. Many famous writers have honored him. However, there are many different opinions on the book. My feel-ings are that Dang Tho is perhaps a talented writer but he did not represent the reality of the war. People died but not in the depress-ing way that is shown in the novel. The war was very long and the cost was great. Three million people were killed. There are thirty thousand Vietnamese missing in action. Two million people were wounded. One million women became widows. Millions of moth-ers lost their sons. Five large cities were thoroughly destroyed."

Quoc's forehead looked as if it had been polished. His hands fluttered through the air, grabbed at his knees, fluttered again.

"The sorrow of war depicted in Dang Tho's book is right. Of course, we see that sorrow. However, the writer didn't show the reasons why the sorrow took place. It was Americans who invaded Vietnam. It was not our desire to fight.

"Suffering produces art. And we have suffered a lot. Through the years we have had the influences of France, China, Mongolia, USA. There is a saying, Keep the fire in the kitchen to see if it out-lasts the storms and rain outside. Vietnamese history is full of storms and rain."

Quoc's sentences ran along one after the other and Ada had the thought that she should reach out to trap them, but she didn't know how. Vinh was sitting, legs crossed, smiling and seemingly content with what Quoc had just said. Ada could not imagine Vu sitting down and talking with this brother who was not really a brother.

She stood and said that she did not need anything. She wasn't even sure why she had come. Still, she thanked them for their kind-ness and then said, "Sorry." She said "Thank you" again, and she turned and walked outside. There was the sidewalk beneath her feet and there was the gray sky above her. In a nearby park children played and called out and their cries mingled with the noise of vehicles and hawkers and the solitary ring of a bicycle bell. A cyclo passed by and Ada lifted a hand and called out.

She went to the old city, where the streets were narrow and there were coffee shops and small restaurants, and vendors selling Zippo lighters and watercolor paintings and trinkets. This was where Kiet had come when he returned from the war. He had walked down this street, lived in this building or that, sat by the lake. Ada was conscious of time having passed, that what she was seeing was not what Kiet saw, or even what her father might have seen or found important if he had been here now.

As she sat close to the lake, she thought that Kiet could have been sitting in this same spot. And then his lover, Lien, joins him. She wears a dark and worn coat. A child flies a kite. Lien talks and talks. She talks about an old man whom she will marry. An old man who, because she slept with him, saved her life during the war. From her mouth spill words that slip away, past the kite, and into the air, and they are the words of a woman who has betrayed the man who has come back to her. And they are not unlike the words between another man and woman many years ago. There is the head of the man bent over his glass, low voice, a moaning, and then the woman, gasping lightly, as if she were worried or tired, and Ada remembered the shape of the man in the dark, kissing her and Jon and Del good night, the sharp smell of him. Then he was gone.

Ada sat up and looked about. The light was dull, the air was still cool. There was no accordion music, no child's kite, no thin lover in bare ankles and small black shoes. A few birds swam in the distance. Loneliness invaded her.

She sat for a long time, aware of the breeze that came and went, and aware that nothing is ever as true or as faithful as when it is imagined. She knew that she wanted to look for the place where Dang Tho lived, and so she hired a cyclo driver to take her to Le

Thanh Long. There was some confusion about the address, and Ada was dropped off at the wrong place. She walked up and down the street until she finally found what she thought was the right building. It was painted mustard yellow and was five stories. In the courtyard a grandmother watched over two children. Laundry hung from the French windows. There were parapets and iron railings. At the topmost parapet a woman leaned out, called to someone, and then disappeared. A few people entered the apartment building. One person came out. He was perhaps the age of Dang Tho, but he did not resemble the photo she had seen on the dust jacket. Ada found the directory on the wall by the entrance. There were a few names, though most of the slots were empty. The slot for 3-B was blank. She was aware of her own breathing. When she found apartment 3-B she stood and listened. Silence. She knocked and waited. Knocked again. When the door opened she saw an old woman in a pale blue *ao dai*. Ada said hello. The woman looked past Ada's head.

"Do you speak English?" Ada asked.

The woman waved her hands vigorously.

Ada reached into her bag and pulled out the novel. She held it up and said Dang Tho's name and then she said her own name. "Dang Tho," Ada repeated. She poked a free finger at the novel. "The writer of this book. Does he live here?"

The woman shook her head. Her face was in the shadows. She said, *"Va, va."* Then she spoke quickly in Vietnamese and her hands moved with her words. *"Xin loi,"* she said, and then said it again. Then she stepped backward as if to say good-bye. She glanced into the air and then smiled, said *xin loi* once again, and shut the door. Ada looked at the door and the number on it. She put the book back into her bag, then descended the stairs and went outside.

She wandered through the streets, past vendors selling cigarettes and fresh guava, past an ice-cream shop, and on past a small market where flies rose and fell to the thump of a butcher's cleaver. She walked aimlessly, unaware of the traffic or the men who called out to her. She found herself in a deserted part of town, walking down a narrow lane that led to other narrow lanes. A man stood in a small doorway, holding his hands over his mouth, picking his teeth. His eyes followed Ada as she passed. When he called out to her she ran, turning corners at random until, finally, she stumbled and fell against the wall of a house.

It was dark now and rain had begun to fall. She stood under a ledge that offered little protection and the rain quickly soaked her shirt and jeans. A man in a green raincoat passed by on a bicycle. Ada saw his brown feet in rubber flip-flops. A teenage girl, holding an umbrella, stopped before her and then, without speaking, took her arm, and Ada allowed herself to be pulled down the lane to a small house where she was offered a towel and a plate of milk fruit. She used the towel to dry off her hair and neck and arms. There were small flies crawling on the green fruit. An older woman appeared and leaned forward to serve tea. Ada drank slowly, testing the flavor. The girl did not speak English. She smiled and pointed at herself and said, "Huy," and then picked up the milk fruit and put it into Ada's hand. Ada said no thank you and placed the fruit back on the plate. Music, sharply mournful, came from somewhere at the rear of the house. Ada stood and gestured that she would leave. The girl called out loudly and a young boy appeared, holding a camera, as if he had been waiting for this moment, and at the doorway, before Ada left, he took a photograph of her standing between the mother and the daughter.

THE FOLLOWING MORNING, ADA DRESSED BEFORE DAWN, LOCKED up the house, and took a taxi to the airport, where she and Jon had arranged to meet. He was waiting for her. They took the early flight out of Hanoi and arrived in Danang in time for a late breakfast at their regular spot. Ada was wearing her father's ring on her left thumb and she twisted it now, studying her brother. She told him that the night before, in the grand bed in Hanoi, in the three-story house, she hadn't been able to sleep. There had been strange noises downstairs near the entrance, and she had been afraid to go down to check. The fear, and the way it had found a space some-where near the top of her throat, was how she had felt just before she had looked at their father's body.

"Dad loved us," she said. "I believe we are most alive when we are being thought about by others who love us." She paused. "Do you understand?"

Jon said that it could be true.

She said that she pictured their father as a mirror giving them back a reflection of themselves, and now that he was gone their re-flection had vanished. "And so when Dad died, part of us died too. Or me. Part of me died. I feel that way. You don't have to believe what I'm saying."

Jon stirred his coffee. Lit a cigarette. "Your thoughts," he said. "They go into strange places."

She said that her friend, Hoang Vu, seemed to like it that her mind went into those places. She told Jon that Vu had met their fa-ther and seemed to understand something of what he was feeling. Vu drank too much, but he was a tender man, and his vision for the world was generous. She said that she had stayed at his house for a few nights, after Jon had left for Hanoi.

"He likes you," Jon said. "I'm happy for you." Then he said, "Ada, listen. I'm not going back with you. I've decided. I'll stay on for a bit in Hanoi and take some time to sort things out. You know."

Beside them, a young woman dropped sugar into her coffee and stirred it with a tin spoon. The soft hair on her forearms re-minded Ada of Del. She watched the woman and then turned to Jon. "I want to get flowers. Not too many and not too colorful. A subdued bouquet."

Jon smiled. "Subdued. We will get a subdued bouquet." He paid for their breakfast, and they left.

THE MAN THEY HIRED GUIDED THE BOAT OUT THROUGH THE mouth of the Han River and around the coastline past Monkey Mountain. A cool wind came in off the open water, and the man asked Ada several times if she needed a jacket. She shook her head. When they had reached the bay of My Khe, the driver slowed the engine and puttered in circles. They had gone to the hospital to collect their father's ashes, and Ada sat now holding the cardboard box.

She felt a looseness and then a clarity, as if a lens had been placed before her eyes. She looked at Jon, who nodded, and she tilted the box over the water. The ashes caught in the wind and some came back to rest on her skirt, a light dusting. The driver said something, gesturing with his hand at the box and the water.

"A funeral," Ada called out. She placed the flowers they had bought on the water and they floated away, caught on the swells.

The driver did not understand. He laughed and gave Ada a thumbs-up. Jon pulled a bottle of whiskey and two glasses from his bag. Opened it and poured. He gave a glass to Ada and then offered one to the driver, who waved his hand, then took it. Jon raised the bottle and said, "To our father." Ada felt the spray of the water as the boat hit a wave. Jon refilled the man's glass. "Don't get him drunk," Ada said. "We need to get back." She brushed at her skirt and then looked at her hand, then leaned forward so that her words would not be taken by the wind and asked Jon if he was able now to cry.

He did not answer. He looked at her and then he looked out at the sea and his mouth appeared to move and then he said, "No." He said it softly and at first Ada was not sure if he had spoken at all.

She asked him if he had cried at all since their father's death and he shook his head and said that he had taught himself long ago, when he was young, not to cry.

"Oh, Jon," Ada said.

In the distance, closer to shore, a small round boat appeared and disappeared.

IT WAS ONLY THE NEXT DAY, WHILE SHE WAS SITTING ALONE ON the rooftop of the hotel, that Ada cried. The evening before, she had said good-bye to Jon, and the finality of everything now came to her as a vast emptiness. She was alone, with her face raised to the sun, and at some point she became aware that only several weeks earlier she had been sitting in this same spot and she had not known, at that time, that her father was dead. Now, she knew. And she wept. She wept for her father and for his sadness that she once thought she had understood but could not now, nor ever, comprehend. And she wept for herself and for her loneliness, though at this moment she would not have wished to rid herself of that loneliness, because it came with a certain startling beauty.

In the afternoon she took the bicycle from its storage place on the main floor of the hotel, washed it, and then rode it to Vu's house. When she got there, his sister Thien said that when she had come back to Danang, her brother was gone. She peeked at Ada from under the shadow of a straw hat that had a blue ribbon at the crown, and the blue reminded Ada of Vu's socks.

Ada asked where he had gone.

"Away. I do not know." Thien shrugged. The dog lay in the dust behind her. There was a trellis above the dog and vines grew from the trellis. Someone was running water behind the house. Ada looked beyond Thien toward the back.

Thien lifted her eyebrows and said, "My daughter. She is washing the clothes."

"I want to give Vu his bike," Ada said. She pushed it toward Thien, who stepped backward and said, "He wants you to have it."

"I don't need it," Ada said. "I'm going back to Canada."

Thien considered this, then she said, "Keep the bicycle. We

have others." Then she said that Vu had gone to the town of Quang Ngai and she smiled and shrugged.

Ada asked for an address. Or a phone number. Thien disappeared and came back and said the name of a guesthouse. The careful movement of her hand as she spoke, the shape of her fingers, mirrored Vu's fine bones, and for a moment Ada was unsettled and wanted to reach out to touch Thien's wrist.

"Thank you," Ada said. And then she said good-bye.

ON THE WAY TO QUANG NGAI, HER DRIVER LIFTED A HAND AND pointed at the roadside and spoke for a long time in Vietnamese and then he fell silent. There had been a group of girls in colorful *ao dai*s and a woman holding flowers and a man and a photographer and behind this scene she saw tables and people and food and children throwing bright streamers into the air. And then the view had passed.

It was late when she arrived in Quang Ngai and she knew that she would not look for Vu that evening. Her driver took her to one of the hotels that accepted foreigners and she took a small room on the third floor. Her window looked out over palm trees onto the entrance of a dimly lit café where four men sat at a stone table playing cards. She saw herself as standing at the edge of some great maw and the four men were on the far side, distant and unapproachable. Unable to sleep, she sat on the balcony and waited for the sun to rise. Everything, the stars, the half-moon, the palm trees, seemed placed upon a great and implausible backdrop.

In the morning, using the map the desk clerk had drawn for her, she set out to find Vu. The guesthouse was a string of dark rooms located next to a vast, French-style building in disrepair. An old man sat on a chair holding a heavy book, and she approached him and said Hoang Vu's name. Because the old man seemed not to have understood, she repeated Hoang Vu's name, this time with a different inflection. Still, nothing. She tried again, attempting the lilting tones that she had heard so often in the mouths of others. She found it absurd and disheartening that she could not speak correctly the name of her lover.

Finally, the old man said Hoang Vu's name and he sighed and rose and led Ada down a narrow passageway to a closed door. He stepped back and bowed his head. Ada knocked. There was no answer. She knocked again and waited and looked down the dim walk and then at the old man beside her. She tried the door, it opened, and she stepped inside and called Vu's name. He was not there. The room had a cement floor and a small cot. There was a mirror over a sink and a chair beside a wooden table. An open closet revealed a few articles of clothing. The old man hovered. Ada touched a shirt and pushed her nose against the cloth. Smelled Vu. She closed her eyes. Sat on the cot and through the open door she saw that the old man had disappeared. There was a candle on the table.

She lay back, and after a bit she heard footsteps and she sat up and saw the old man standing in the doorway. Because of the way the light fell behind him she could not see his face. In his hands was a tray that held a teapot and two cups. He poured the tea and held out a cup for her. She took it and said, "Thank you." They drank in silence, and after, the old man poured her more. Again, she drank, the clink of the cups, the splash of the tea, the wordlessness strangely soothing. She left the room and the old man left with her. Ada thanked him and then said the name of her hotel. He lifted a hand from his thigh and waved.

She spent part of the day walking the streets of the town. Once, in a small lane, a man who was squatting at the side of the road rolled a rock at her feet. She ignored him and hurried on. She circled back to the hotel and passed through the lobby and climbed to her room.

That night, Vu came to her. When he knocked, she opened the door and he looked at her and said, "You are sleeping?"

"No, no. I'm reading."

He was holding an unlit cigarette. He said the old man at the guesthouse had told him that a beautiful woman had come for him. Vu smiled. "The old man told me that I would be a fool not to hunt you down."

She hesitated and looked back over her shoulder at the small room and then turned back and asked, "Should we go for a drink or something?"

They went down to the lobby of the hotel and sat on the vinyl couch close to the front window. The night clerk brought them whiskey and glasses. A rooster crowed, the clerk shuffled away on rubber sandals, and Vu poured drinks. He raised his glass and then drank. His suit was rumpled and he looked tired. He said, "I'm here with other artists on a government project." He lit a cigarette for Ada and as he handed it to her their hands touched.

She said, "There are many things I love here. The rooster calling in the courtyard. I love that. Or having tea with that old man today. We didn't say a word, just sat there." Then she told Vu that she and Jon had let their father's ashes go off My Khe two days before. She said that when she had been out in the boat with Jon, and she had looked back at My Khe, she had realized she didn't really know this country. "But," she said, "I have met people here who I will remember for a long time."

Vu did not speak and Ada looked into his eyes as if to divine an answer to a question that had not been asked.

"Come," he said, and he took her hand and led her up to her room, where they made love on the small bed beneath the mosquito net. The balcony door was open and the light from the streetlamp fell like a narrow shaft across their bodies.

At night it rained and the open door banged in the wind and when she got up to shut it she saw the single light from the café across the street. This time there were no men and the light swayed on its string and cast shadows across the empty table. She came back to the bed and sat on the only chair in the room and she watched Vu sleep. When she lay down beside him, he stirred and mumbled something in his own language.

The following day, after breakfast, they took a taxi up to the beach a few miles outside town. Ada swam far out toward the waves that broke against the reef. Vu stood in jeans and shirt at the edge of the water and waited for her. When she returned, walking wet and tired out of the ocean, he said that the sea was dangerous.

They lay in the sand, side by side, and they shared a bottle of water and ate papaya that Vu cut with a knife he had borrowed. Vu fed Ada small pieces and the knife seemed an extension of his hand. The seeds from the papaya were black and they lay in the sand like beautiful and strange pearls.

When they got back to the hotel, they went up to her room and sat for the last time on the balcony and Ada said that, soon, she had to leave. There were things to be done in Danang and then she would be gone forever. "I know," she said, "I am being sentimental. At least that is what you think. But, that is me, that is how I am." She paused and then said she had realized the other day that he knew nothing about her. Not really. He did not know that she was a good cook, and that she could shoot a gun with accuracy, or that she had raised her brother and sister, or that her father's darkness had come to settle in some small way on her own heart. She stopped talking.

After a while, Vu said that he didn't need to know the facts of her childhood or the details of her life. The evidence of the goodness of Ada Boatman was standing before him. "I am not blind," he said. "I can see. And so, to talk too much about Ada would reduce Ada. This is what I think." He smiled. "And it is different than what you think."

She shook her head. She said that life had been real once, and it would be real again. This in between time, the voyage out and back, all of that was a dream. It was like when she had been sick with fever, lying on her bed in the bright room of the hotel, and the world had passed by in clear quick images that, when pieced together, had appeared to mean something but she had not been able to decipher the meaning. She said that there would come a day, back in Canada, when she would be married with children and she would think back to this time. "Perhaps then I will understand."

Vu lit a cigarette. He did not speak.

They drank warm beer and watched the sun set. It went down orange and then red. Beyond the palm trees in the courtyard, down the lane, Ada saw a woman riding a bicycle, her back straight, one arm steady at her side. Vu said that it was important to live without hate and bitterness and fear. "This is possible," he said. In the dusk, a butterfly passed.

Later, he slept on her bed and at some point she went down to the front desk and negotiated the price of a driver and car to take her back to Danang. "As soon as possible," she said.

The desk clerk called up half an hour later to say that the car was ready.

"So soon?" she asked, and then she said that she would be down right away.

She did not wake Vu. She stood in the doorway looking back at him and then she picked up her pack and walked down the wide staircase to the lobby where she collected her passport and paid her bill. It had begun to rain, a light warm shower that raised a smell of barely sprinkled dust. She got in the backseat of the car. As they pulled out onto the street she did not look up toward the third-floor balcony of the room where Vu still slept. The rain fell harder and by the time they reached the main road it was falling so heavily all she could see from her window were the vague shapes of houses and cyclists and a boy herding goats and once, in the doorway of a welder's shop, an arc of light offered a father cradling a baby.

. . .

THE NEXT MORNING IN DANANG, THE BOY FOUND HER SITTING IN a café. She was drinking coffee and eating dry bread, looking out at the rain as it fell.

"Miss Ada," he said.

She looked at him and then looked away.

"You don't want me here?" he asked. He sat, cleared a place on the table, and put his elbows down.

She shook her head, said it was fine.

"I have the perfect tour for you," Yen said. "We'll go up to Hoi An and walk through the museum and then take a boat cruise on the river. You will love it."

She said that she didn't have time. She was going home the following morning.

Yen was surprised. He said that her visa could be extended, she just had to ask the right people.

"And I guess you know the right people?" she teased.

He was hurt. "Of course," he said.

"I have Hoang Vu's bike. He doesn't want it back," she said. "Would you like it?"

"Is this payment for something?" he asked. He took out a crumpled pack of cigarettes. His hands brushed at his shirt and over his head. He said that he could not take payment from her because he had not done anything for her. She had not allowed him.

She was all of a sudden tired. She said that he could do what he wanted. She wasn't going to beg him to take the bike.

"It's okay," he said. "I'll take it." He leaned forward as if to inspect her face and said, "Your heart is broken."

She laughed.

"See. I am right. The artist has broken your heart."

She shook her head. She told him that her personal life was none of his business and that if he persisted in talking about it, he should leave. "Perhaps you should leave anyway," she said. She made a shooing gesture with her hand.

He said, "I would have loved you better than that artist."

She laughed again. Said, "You're fourteen, Yen. What are you talking about?"

"Sixteen," he said. He looked mournful. "You don't take me seriously."

"Of course I don't. Not when you talk nonsense."

He said that he too could draw. In fact, if she liked, he would do her portrait. It was a simple thing that required only a blank piece of paper and some ink. He had learned this from his father. "He is gifted. I have watched him. I have watched many men. And some are better at seduction."

"Oh, Yen. Poor boy. You should be in school."

"Do not pity me," Yen said. He said that he might be only sixteen, or fourteen, but he was able to recognize pity.

Ada said that she did not mean to show pity and she was sorry if she had. She picked up her bag and said she had to go and she didn't know if she would see him again.

"I'll be available," Yen said. He stood and took Ada's hand and shook it. "Good-bye, Miss Ada."

That evening she walked down to a restaurant on the harbor front for a beer. Two old men sat at a corner table playing a game that looked like checkers. She watched them and heard the click of the pieces and an occasional exclamation. She ordered another beer. Earlier she had gone to Thanh's house and said good-bye. He had given her a book of Russian poetry in English translation. Had apologized for the binding but claimed that the words inside would make up for it. He asked her in for a cup of tea, stepping sideways and gesturing at the house, but she said that she was preparing to leave. She had to pack and see to things.

He said that he felt he had failed her.

"No, no," she cried. "You haven't."

He'd taken off his glasses and cleaned them briskly, shaking his head. He said he hated farewells.

After her second beer, she walked back to her hotel and slowly climbed the stairs to her room. Her door was open and she pushed at it and looked inside. The light was on. Yen was standing by the bed. He was holding something and talking. She looked around to see if anyone else was there but he was alone. He was holding her underwear and whispering to himself.

"What are you doing?" she said.

He turned and put the underwear onto the bed. "Hello, Ada," he said as he stepped away from the bed.

She repeated her question and moved toward him. Then she thought again, and moved back, wondering if he was dangerous. She looked around for an object to hold, something to protect herself. There was nothing.

"Don't worry," Yen said. "I am harmless. I came here to talk to you about your bicycle but you were gone and the door was open and so I stepped in and then you came home." He smiled and bowed his head and then looked right at her.

"Get out," she said.

He held up his hands and moved sideways. "You don't understand, Miss Ada. You don't understand my sadness."

Ada was breathless. After, she would think how she had leaped at Yen and she would wonder why. But this is what she did. She took two long steps, and reaching him, she struck his head with an open hand. He ducked and because he ducked and seemed so helpless, she struck him again. This time with her fist and she felt the softness at the side of his face. "Go," she cried. "Go. Go." She beat at him with both hands until he ran from the room. She heard his footsteps and the sound of her own breathing, and then she sat down on the edge of the bed.

Later, after she had checked her bags and clothes and found nothing missing, after she had showered and changed into jeans and a shirt because she was not ready for sleep, she went downstairs to the lobby, past the night clerk, and out into the street. She took the bicycle and walked it down the sloping road toward the ferry. There was little traffic. At one point she called Yen's name and then realized how foolish this was. She stopped at the ferry landing and looked out past the dark gates to the boats. No one was there. Again, she called Yen's name.

For an hour she walked the streets. Once, she passed three boys and she said Yen's name but they did not look at her and she saw that Yen was not one of them. She went to the Chess Hotel and knocked on the service door. No one came, and so she left the bicycle and pushed the door open and entered. There was a dim light on at the end of the hallway. She called Yen's name. He was not there. She called for Yen's uncle Minh and when he did not come she turned and went back outside and stood in the darkness. She recalled Yen saying that his sister worked the street near the Empire Hotel. She walked there, still wheeling the bicycle. There were two women standing on the sidewalk, one wore yellow, the other black. Ada approached and said her name. She said that she knew a boy called Yen and the boy was her friend. Did they know the boy? The women looked at Ada. They talked together and then one repeated Yen's name.

"Yes," Ada said. "Are you his sister?"

The woman laughed. "Sister?" She shook her head. "No sister."

"He has no sister?"

She shook her head. "No sister."

Ada said that they didn't understand. Yen was a small boy, about fourteen, and she wanted to give him the bicycle. She moved it toward the woman in black, who stepped back and said, "No."

She crisscrossed the streets in the rain calling his name. After a while, she stopped calling out and at some point she found herself back down by the ferry landing. She leaned the bicycle up against the blue shuttered door of the ticket booth. Then she stood, look-ing out at the boats anchored throughout the harbor. The first time she had come here it had been raining as well. Back then she had carried an umbrella and the wind had been warm. It had been early evening, just after dusk, and the lights of the approaching ferry had appeared as many small beacons to carry a traveler home.

ACKNOWLEDGMENTS

While living in Vietnam, I encountered the generosity and kindness of complete strangers, strangers who then became genuine friends. Thank you to Tran Cau and Hoang Dang, who, through their conversations and late night company, guided me deeper into the heart of their country. Thank you as well to Vinh Quyen, Nguyen Van Muoi, and Professor Hoang Ngoc Hien. And thank you to Kathryn Munnell, who turned a small light onto the life of the historian Nguyen Khac Vien, and who opened her home to my family.

Bao Ninh's novel *The Sorrow of War* had a significant influence on the writing of my own novel, as did, to a smaller measure, *The General Retires* by Nguyen Huy Thiep.

Thanks to Denise Bukowski, who pushed me to write this story.

Finally, a special thanks to Ellen Seligman, Stephanie Higgs, and Daniel Menaker.

ABOUT THE AUTHOR

DAVID BERGEN is the author of three highly acclaimed
novels: *A Year of Lesser* (1996), a *New York Times* No-
table Book and winner of the McNally Robinson Book
of the Year Award; *See the Child* (1999); and, most recently, *The Case of Lena S.* (2002), winner of the Carol
Shields Winnipeg Book Award and a finalist for the
Governor General's Award for Fiction, the McNally
Robinson Book of the Year Award, and the Margaret
Laurence Award for Fiction. He is also the author of a
collection of short fiction, *Sitting Opposite My Brother*
(1993), which was a finalist for the Manitoba Book of
the Year. Bergen won the Canadian Broadcasting Cor-
poration's Literary Prize for Fiction in 2000. He lived
and taught in Southeast Asia for three and a half years,
and currently lives with his wife and four children in
Winnipeg.

ABOUT THE TYPE

This book is set in Fournier, a typeface named for Pierre Simon Fournier, the youngest son of a French printing family. He started out engraving woodblocks and large capitals, then moved on to fonts of type. In 1736 he began his own foundry and made several important contributions in the field of type design; he is said to have cut 147 alphabets of his own creation. Fournier is probably best remembered as the designer of St. Augustine Ordinaire, a face that served as the model for Monotype's Fournier, which was released in 1925.